LONE PRINCE

AN ACCIDENTAL PREGNANCY ROMANCE

LILIAN MONROE

Cover photo by Wander Aguilar
Cover design by Mayhem Cover Creations
Editing by Lawrence Editing

journey seems to have hit a dead end at the last stop on a long train line.

I rub my hands over my arms, sucking in a breath of air. No matter how long I stare at the train station entrance, Grandma isn't walking through it.

Not exactly the welcome party I thought I'd get. I'm Nord's new lead architect on the redesign of the Summer Palace. I've spent the past year working on this project, dedicating every resource at my own architecture firm to it, and this is my first site visit to put the finishing touches on my design. I wasn't expecting a red carpet, but they could have at least sent a taxi.

Sighing, I do another lap of the room.

Still no Grandma.

I should have stayed in Farcliff. My architecture practice is well-respected and multi-award-winning. It's steady, comfortable work, and there's lots of it. I mostly design houses for the Farcliff elite—of which there are many. My office building also has central heating, a fact that I never quite appreciated as much as I do now.

But I became an architect to create beautiful, important buildings, and I couldn't turn this project down. How many architects get to work on a royal palace in a foreign kingdom? How many architects get to make a name for themselves so early in their career?

The wind bangs against the door, mocking me. My teeth rattle. Does this rickety old station not have any insulation?

The few passengers that disembarked with me at the station have long since disappeared, tucking their chins in their chests and braving the bitter weather outside. I watched them leave, one by one, waiting for my grandmother to toddle through the door. I kept a thin thread of hope alive, picturing her rosy cheeks and happy smile.

As my shoulders drop two hours later, I finally resign myself to the fact that she's not coming.

It's out of character for her. Something isn't right.

Trying to stifle the panic that threatens to well up inside me, I hug my favorite red peacoat tighter around my body. It won't be enough to keep out the cold, but it's all I have.

Balmy Farcliff, remember? They don't sell arctic-proof jackets down there. Plus, I was told the weather wasn't that cold this time of year up here. Google told me a peacoat would be fine.

Um, yeah. *Wrong.*

It's not even October. I can only imagine how much worse it'll get once the real winter hits.

Dragging my small suitcase over to the ticket office window, I bite my lip. A steel roller door has been padlocked over the opening and I haven't seen anyone come in or out of the office behind it.

Still, I knock. I've done it a dozen times already, but maybe someone's in there. Maybe they were asleep. Or busy. Or deaf.

Who am I kidding? It's hopeless, but I do it anyway.

Surprise surprise, no one answers.

A few steps down a dingy hallway, I find a door marked 'Office'. I pound my fist on it as panic rears higher inside me.

Nothing.

I'm alone.

Sucking in a breath, I squeeze my eyes shut.

Stay calm, Rowan. There's an explanation for this. Maybe she forgot I was arriving today?

I shake my head. I spoke to her this morning. Grandma wouldn't forget. She has a better memory than I do, and she's been managing the Summer Palace for over thirty years. Her mind is sharp. She would've sent someone to get me if she couldn't make it to the station herself.

Something is *wrong*. I can feel it in my bones—although that might just be the cold making my skeleton tremble.

Walking back out to the main station lobby, I take a deep breath. The place looks like it's about two hundred years old. Thick, stained glass windows are set high in the walls, and crumbling mortar is sandwiched between discolored bricks. The tiled floor has a worn-out strip through the center of the lobby, where passengers have walked from the front door to the platform.

And most importantly, there's not another soul in here.

Just me and my inadequate jacket.

I could sleep in the train station and wait for the staff to arrive tomorrow morning. That's probably the safest thing to do, isn't it? Wait here, where there's shelter?

Maybe Grandma just got delayed. Maybe she's on her way, but the storm outside held her up.

I should stay.

But what if she's just outside? There could be a taxi waiting for me, or a royal vehicle ready to take me to the palace. Or maybe someone outside will be able to help. One of the locals. They could point me in the direction of the palace. Give me a ride. Call a taxi for me. *Anything.*

A cold draft snakes around my legs, and I curse myself for wearing a dress. My tights may be thick, but they're no match for the cold. I thought I'd be in a warm train, then a warm car, then a warm castle. This is my first time in Nord since I was an infant, and my only chance to make a good first impression. Dress to impress, they say.

Ha.

Dress to freeze to death, more likely.

If I stay in the lobby, will I even survive the night? I lift my chin and exhale, watching my breath dissipate in a white puff before me.

It's frigid in here.

I need to find some help.

Glancing at my phone once more, I lift it up above my head to try to get a signal. Nothing. I open the messaging app to try to sneak a message through to my grandmother, but it bounces back as soon as I hit *send*.

When I click out of the message screen, I see the very last message I received while I was on the train. My ex-boyfriend of six months sent me a nasty slew of insults at three o'clock in the morning last night. Drunk, probably.

Gerry: Don't expect me to be waiting here when you get back, Rowan. Enjoy Nord. It's as cold as your fucking heart.

I read the message for the thousandth time, my fingers squeezing my phone so tight my nail beds turn white. My eyes prickle. For the first time since I left Farcliff, I want to cry.

Gerry and I were supposed to get married—but then he told me he wanted me to stay at home once we were husband and wife. He told me he expected me to leave my career behind to care for our future children. He expected me to be a housewife.

Don't get me wrong, there's nothing wrong with being a housewife. My mother was a single mother who worked hard and also happened to be a damn good homemaker. She was an angel, and she died with no one but me by her side.

She took care of me like it was her sole purpose in life, and sometimes I wonder if she would've been better off without me. After all, I wasn't anything but a burden to her, from the time I was born to the time she died. She could have moved on if not for me. Maybe even lived longer instead of working herself to death for my sake.

When she died, I vowed I'd never again be a burden to anyone. I promised myself I'd be able to stand on my own two feet and support myself.

My work is my life. I started my architecture firm when I was twenty-seven years old, and I've spent the last six years working my ass off to make a name for myself. I'm supposed to give that up for Gerry, or some other guy who wants to be the hero who supports me?

Please.

I don't want to do laundry for four hours a day while I wait for my husband to come home. I don't want to feel like he needs to take care of me—that I'm relying on him for my survival.

No, I want to sit behind a desk and make my designs come to life. I want to win every architecture award there is to win and leave a legacy when I go.

Independence, in every sense of the word. That's what I want. Not that I want to die alone or anything—but I don't want to feel like I'm dead weight being dragged around by my future partner.

So when Grandma told me about the redesign of the Summer Palace in Nord, I applied. I didn't tell Gerry, but why would I? It's my company. My name on the wall. My initials on the company letterhead.

It wasn't until I got the official contract of employment that I told him about the offer.

Gerry didn't take it well. He gave me an ultimatum—told me it was the job, or him.

Didn't think I'd choose the job. Did he ever really know me?

That was a year ago, and we struggled along for another six months before calling it quits. I still get the occasional drunk dial, just to remind me that I'm a terrible excuse for a woman.

As I glance around the deserted train station and hug my jacket closer to my body, I'm starting to miss the warmth of his arms. It was comfortable, at least. Maybe this was a mistake. Maybe Gerry was right, and it's better to stay home and have a gaggle of children.

Steeling myself against the weather, I head for the lobby doors. Against a gust of wind, I push open the heavy, metal door and step outside.

It's worse than I expected.

Cold air slaps me across the face. My eyes water. It hurts to breathe, like a million icy daggers stabbing my lungs. I duck my head against the wind, sucking in a breath as I flip my collar up to try to protect my face from the cold.

It doesn't help. The wind is vicious.

My heart hammers. I take another step, dragging my suitcase out of the train station and finally lifting my eyes to look at the scene in front of me.

If it weren't so cold, it would be beautiful.

A thick blanket of snow covers everything, from individual tree branches to tall, gothic-inspired streetlights. The roads have been cleared, but the harsh wind carries gusts of snow and ice across the black asphalt. They look like thin sheets of white crystals whipping across the pavement.

Straight ahead, at the end of a long, black road, is the Summer Palace.

Against the white backdrop, it looks huge, dark, and imposing. I've seen pictures of it, of course. I've studied the two tall towers that frame the castle on either side and seen details of the arched doors that lead to the entrance hall.

But even from this distance, I can tell the palace is bigger and gloomier than I'd anticipated. I shiver.

At least I don't need directions.

Down a street to my right, a car turns a corner and moves out of view, the sound of the engine muffled by the wind and snow.

Then, a louder noise.

The lobby door shuts with a bang, carried by a particularly strong gust of wind. A latch clicks, and my panic cranks higher.

"No!" I stumble to the door, yanking. My fingers feel like wood. They're not working properly. I claw at the door handle, my fingers sticking to the cold, frosty metal. I peel them away, wincing. If I grab that handle too hard, I'll lose a layer of skin.

My heart jumps to my throat. Wrapping my hand in my scarf, I grab the door again. It won't budge. I pull and pull and pull, trying to pull the door open as tears fall from my eyes and threaten to freeze on my cheeks.

I'm locked out.

No, no, no!

Leaning my forehead on the door, I stifle a sob.

I'm going to die here. I'll freeze to death two miles from the castle.

Where the hell is Grandma?

This was supposed to be the greatest project in my architecture career. It was supposed to catapult me to international recognition. My crowning glory.

Now?

I might die before I make it to the front gate.

Unzipping my suitcase, I reach my stiff, cold fingers inside and dig around for my second hat and scarf. My fingers feel the knitted material of my warmest sweater, curling around it and yanking.

I pull the clothing out of my suitcase and huddle beside

the building to use whatever shelter it'll provide against the wind.

Which is not much, by the way. The wind feels like a claw that reaches through my jacket and scrapes sharp nails across my skin.

Then, with a deep breath, I strip my favorite (useless) red peacoat off, and throw my sweater on over my dress. The wind slaps my skin. I inhale sharply. It hurts to breathe. The air is too cold. It attacks every exposed inch of me, invading my lungs and showing me just how fragile my life really is.

My jacket goes back on, followed by the scarf and hat, then a second scarf and a pair of gloves.

It's slightly better. Still cold, but better.

Sighing, I try the door one last time. Just in case.

Nope. Didn't magically unlock itself.

This is a type of cold I've never felt before. It's an attack. Like the weather is on the offensive, and I'm caught in a battle I wasn't prepared to fight.

My gloves take the worst bite of the wind away as I drag my suitcase down the half-dozen steps and onto the snow-covered sidewalk. I shove my chin into my double scarves, keeping my eyes on the little patch of ground in front of me.

My brand-new, fancy, leather ankle boots slip on the hard-packed snow and ice. I pause, legs shaking like a baby deer, lifting my eyes to stare at the long, dark, bleak road in front of me.

I know how far it is. I've seen the topographical maps and studied the drawings of the area already.

Just over two miles. In Farcliff, it would take me, what, thirty minutes? I wouldn't blink at having to walk that distance.

But now? With the wind finding every weakness in my

jacket, with nothing but a pair of tights on my legs, with unlined boots on my feet?

Two miles seem like the end of the earth, and my destination doesn't look very friendly.

Glancing down the road where the car disappeared, I shudder. The nearest town is twenty miles in the opposite direction. There's a grocery store beside the train station that looks dark and definitely locked, and there are a handful of homesteads between here and the nearest town. There's no guarantee I'll meet someone along the way, so shouldn't I choose the closest option?

My eyes follow the long, straight road that leads to the Summer Palace. It looks...cold.

The alternative to walking those two miles to the castle is standing still, which is a death sentence. I have no choice.

Tucking my chin in my chest, I start the long walk to the Summer Palace, hoping I won't freeze to death before I get there.

2

ROWAN

ONE FOOT in front of the other. Step, by step, by step.

The soles of my feet are cold, as if the earth is reaching up through the rubber and freezing my skin. There's a little strip of exposed skin between my jacket and my glove. It stings.

Wind knocks me sideways, and I stumble off the road. My roller bag tumbles over, and I fall onto my hands and knees. Sucking a breath in through my scarf, I drag myself up. The castle is still so far away. Still so black and imposing. The landscape barren and desolate.

Scrambling to right my bag, it feels like my limbs weigh twice as much as they usually do. I brace myself against another angry gust of wind. It feels like the weather is screaming at me. Howling in my ears.

You don't belong here.

A chorus of gods laughs at me from above, watching me crawl along the surface of the earth like a lonely little insect, slowly freezing her little ass off.

I keep going. If I stop, I die. If I turn back, I might find someone to bring me to the castle or give me shelter—or I might die.

As long as I keep going, I can make it to the castle. Two miles. I'll find Grandma, who will wrap me in a hug and hold me tight. She'll smell like cinnamon and cherries, and it'll feel like home. There'll be a fire to thaw my frozen flesh, and a mug of something warm.

Grandma will tell me why she didn't pick me up. She'll show me to my room, where there'll be a huge, plush bed.

A *warm* bed. With lots of blankets. Maybe even a bath.

Everything will be warm, and soft, and nice.

I just need to take one more step. And then another. And another.

When did my bag get so heavy? I try to pull it loose from the snow and rocks that drag along the base of it. My lungs scream. My shoulders hurt.

Somehow, I'm sweating. How can I be cold and sweaty at the same time?

I blink, the crusty, frozen mass of eyelashes brushing my cheeks. My fingers are numb. My thoughts are slow.

I start counting my steps, just to prove to myself that my brain still works. When I get halfway between three and four hundred, I lose count, so I restart.

One, two, three, four, five...

My chin stays buried in my chest. My shoulders hunched. My eyes glued to that little strip of ground directly in front of my feet.

When my shoulders stop aching, it's a relief. When I start to feel a bit warmer, I think it might be because I'm moving. A tiny, faraway voice in my mind tells me it's a bad sign. It tries to scream at me, to warn me.

I *should* be cold. I *should* feel the bite of the wind.

This new warmth, snaking through my body? It should scream danger. The sleepiness that makes my eyelids droop should ring some sort of alarm bell in my mind.

But that little voice is so quiet. The alarm bell sounds more like a lullaby.

Warmth feels *good*.

I can do this. I blink my eyes open, dragging them up to look at the castle.

It's so far away.

Wind whips past me, making my eyes water. I stand still for a moment, squeezing them shut. Icy tentacles pierce my red jacket, my sweater, my dress. I feel naked.

Maybe I should take a break. Just a little breather. That snowbank on the side of the road looks soft. I could just curl up and...

No.

Raking a painful breath through my lungs, I bring my brows together. Must get to the castle. Must keep walking.

Step, by step, by step.

My toes are so cold they sting. The leather of my boots is frozen stiff, and every step makes the material dig into the top of my foot. It hurts so much. Everything hurts.

Maybe I should just stop. I feel warm now. I could strip off one of these scarves. Pushing the material down past my chin, I gulp down a breath of air. It doesn't taste so cold anymore.

I frown and try to focus on the castle. I must be Alice and this is Wonderland, because it's not getting any nearer. Perspective and distance are all messed up. The farther I walk, the farther the castle is. It still looks dark and dangerous and so, so far away.

Keep walking, a voice screams. *Don't stop.*

My grip on the suitcase handle is weak, but I drag it as best I can. I bury my chin in my chest and walk. On, and on, and on.

When I see the gate looming up ahead, I stumble forward

and fall. It almost feels like I'm watching it happen to someone else. An out-of-body experience. Everything is so hazy. So slow.

But at least it's not cold. The warmth is back, and it feels *good*, even as I fall to the ground.

I catch myself on my hands and knees and snow slides into my glove. Slowly, almost curiously, I tug my glove off and watch the white powder fall out.

My hand doesn't feel cold. It almost doesn't feel like my hand at all. I turn it around, staring at my palm as if it belongs to someone else. It's almost as white as the snow on the ground. My fingertips are a pretty shade of purple. Huh. Wow.

I can't think straight. It's so very hard to stand up again.

A gust of wind blows snow across my face, partially obscuring the tall, wrought-iron gate and the fence that seems to go on for miles. The palace is so far beyond the gate, it feels like I've made no progress at all. I lean against my suitcase, resting my eyes for just a moment.

I just need a second. I'm so, so tired.

Then, a creak. A distinctly unnatural sound in this otherwise silent landscape. It doesn't sound like the wind. It's almost like some animal, letting out a howl in the fading light. The screech gets louder, grinding against my ears as I struggle to open my eyes.

Movement.

Something black.

The gate.

When did it get so hard to breathe? I try to stand up, holding on to my suitcase for support, but another gust of wind knocks me back, and I fall on the hard, frozen asphalt.

Everything goes dark.

3

WOLFE

I LOOK up from my laptop when Eyvar, my driver and personal bodyguard, makes a low noise. It's a cross between a huff and a grunt, but it speaks volumes. The big Icelandic man looks like Thor himself, with a big beard and ice-blue eyes. His hands are so big they nearly cover the top half of the steering wheel and his shoulders bulge out beyond the width of the seat.

He doesn't usually speak. It's one of the reasons I hired him.

Even a soft grunt from Eyvar means something's wrong, and as soon as I glance up from the screen, I know what the problem is.

A woman in a red jacket collapses on the road just ahead of our vehicle. She lands on her back and doesn't move as the car inches forward, her black suitcase making a slow nose-dive into the ditch.

Eyvar slows the car. He wouldn't normally make an unscheduled stop without my instruction, but we both know what it means for someone to collapse outside in these temperatures.

This is the worst storm I've seen in all my life. It's not even October, but it might as well be the depths of winter, it's that cold.

The woman has minutes to live if we don't do anything. Anger flashes through my chest, hot and bright. What kind of idiot goes walking in these temperatures? By the look of her clothes, she forgot she was only a few miles from crossing into the arctic.

Did she not see the storm? Thought it was a good day for a stroll? Has no sense of self-preservation?

Fucking southerners. I can tell just by the look of her unconscious form that she's not from Nord. Stupid, stupid southerner. They don't understand this place. They don't understand the danger. The weakness of the human body. Just how vulnerable we are.

She doesn't belong here. I know it already.

Eyvar pulls the parking brake and opens his door. A bitter blast of wind slams it closed behind him, and I button my jacket all the way up. My driver crouches over the woman, putting his huge palms to her face and neck, checking for a pulse. I exit the back seat of the car, standing by the open door.

Fuck, it's cold out. I should have stayed in Stirling, the capital city, instead of coming all the way to the Summer Palace—but then I'd have to deal with the yearly memorials for my dead fiancée. Coming here was supposed to be my escape, and I'm greeted with yet another woman collapsing at my feet.

My heart aches.

Eyvar glances up at me, pale eyes somber. With a grunt, he scoops the woman up and starts marching toward the car. Even that mountain of a man has to brace himself against the wind, the woman limp in his arms. A strand of red hair falls free from her hat, whipping against her lily-white face.

Between her hat and her scarf, I see delicate features. A pink mouth. Eyes closed, with frost clinging to the lashes. Her skin so frozen it's almost transparent. She looks like some sort of ethereal ice goddess.

What the hell is she doing walking to the Summer Palace in this weather?

A protective instinct flares inside my chest. I nod to the back seat. "In here," I say.

"I can put her up front," Eyvar says. The back seat is reserved for me.

I shake my head. "Lay her down there. I'll try to wake her up. Grab her bag."

Eyvar grunts, his eyes lingering on mine. He doesn't approve. I don't give a shit.

Why don't I give a shit?

I'm not some Good Samaritan out to save some moron who decided to take a walk along the Arctic Circle. Does she have a death wish? As far as I'm concerned, this woman deserves to freeze. Where was she headed, anyway? The castle? With a fucking roller suitcase?

After Eyvar puts her in the car, I slip into the back seat and lift her head onto my thighs. Her skin feels like ice, but there are soft breaths passing through her lips. I close the door again, thanking everything that's holy for heated seats.

Unwinding the woman's scarf from her head, I toss it aside. It's half-frozen-stiff and half-soaked with melted snow. She's wearing a second scarf underneath, soaked in sweat. Her hat is the same. If she's hypothermic, those garments will only make it worse.

She needs to get warm and dry. Fast.

Eyvar hauls her suitcase over, slams the trunk, and gets in the front seat. My bodyguard glances at me in the rearview mirror. I jerk my head at the gate. "To the security lodge. It's closer, and it'll be easier to warm up a small room. We don't have much time."

"You know her?" His eyes narrow, flicking to the woman in my lap.

I bristle. I don't like his tone. Maybe my employees are getting a little too comfortable with me. No matter how close we are, Eyvar still works for me. I'm his liege. He should act accordingly.

"Drive, Eyvar." I don't owe him a fucking answer. I don't owe anyone anything.

There's a hole in my heart and poison leeching into my soul. When Abby died, she took part of me with her—and it was just like this. Head in my lap, eyes closed, the Reaper stealing her away from me in a few short breaths.

I belong here, alone in the frozen north. Surrounded by cold and death. The lord of a castle made of ice, with no one to answer to but the elements. This is my home.

But my hand moves to the woman's cheek, and I feel the silkiness of her skin. She doesn't belong here. She's too soft. Too fragile.

And unlike Abby, this woman is still alive.

Eyvar sets his jaw and puts the car in gear. He cranks the heat up as high as it'll go, and I unzip the top of the woman's jacket. The skin on her chest is so cold, she might as well have been walking naked out here.

My eyes drift down her body, imagining just that. I bite down on the inside of my cheek to dispel the thought. The last fucking thing I need to do is think about this woman naked. As soon as she's awake and alert enough to speak, she has a lot to answer for. She'll be getting on the first train back to whatever place she's from, with strict instructions to never return.

If she has a death wish, it won't be fulfilled here. I won't have another soul on my conscience.

Eyvar parks the car by the security lodge. I jerk my head toward it. "Unlock the door and crank the heat. Start a fire, too."

Eyvar's teeth grind. He doesn't like me being near an uncleared person. It's a security risk, and he knows my head is a mess right now. Isn't that the whole reason I'm at the Summer Palace? Keep me safe from the media and the masses and myself? Stay tucked away on my own, where no one can see me break down?

My tone of voice leaves no room for argument, though, and Eyvar is too well-trained to protest. He heaves his massive body out of the car and unlocks the lodge as I get out of the car and carry the woman to the building.

She's light, as if I'm just holding a bundle of clothes. Her legs are covered in nothing more than a pair of thick tights, which is about three layers less than she needs out here.

Is this her first time in Nord? What kind of lunatic would start walking along the road to the palace in a peacoat and a fucking dress?

Anger winds its way through my core, setting everything aflame. But the woman's eyelids flutter, and she mumbles against my neck. Her soft breath washes over my skin, easing the bite of the wind.

I don't hate having her in my arms. As I march toward the lodge, she melts against my chest. She smells sweet, like candy. It feels good to hold her.

Too good.

I shouldn't enjoy it. I shouldn't want to protect her. To save her.

It's just the gremlins of my fucked-up past, poking their ugly heads out ahead of the fourth anniversary of Abby's death. Fate is sending this woman to me, unconscious and near death, to remind me of everything I've already lost.

Well, don't worry, Fate. I remember. Every fucking day, and I know I'll never forget.

When I kick the door closed behind me, the heat is already blasting in the lodge, and Eyvar is stoking a roaring fire. I jerk my head to the closet. "Blankets."

Eyvar complies without a word. That's better.

I lay the woman on a long sofa, dragging it closer to the fire. She whimpers, trying and failing to open her eyes.

"*Gran...Grandm...*" she whispers.

"What's that?" I say, cupping her cheek. "What's your name? Who are you?"

Her eyelids flutter, but her gaze is hazy. They close once again. My heart clenches. My bodyguard takes off her boots and jacket, then spreads two thick blankets over her, moving quickly and efficiently. She's limp as we tuck her in, her eyes staying closed as her breath grows shallow.

"Radio the palace and get the doctor." I tuck the edge of the blanket around her and touch her cheek again. I need her to be okay. I need her to live. It feels almost desperate, a sense of doom looming just beyond my consciousness. This woman can't die. Not here. Not with me.

Not again.

Eyvar moves to the desk by the door. He presses a few buttons to turn on the radio, then grunts in frustration. I glance over to see him frowning. "Dead battery. Must have been left unplugged. Maybe a power outage."

"Drive, then," I say. "Get the doctor. And quick, Eyvar. She needs medical attention."

"Your Highness, I can't leave you here with—"

"You'll do what I say, Eyvar." I level him with a glare. "This woman will die."

"Your Highness, your safety—"

"This woman isn't going to magically wake up and try to stab me, Eyvar. She's ice-cold and hypothermic. Go."

Eyvar glances at the woman and finally lets out a long sigh. He turns his back to me and slips out the door without another word.

Turning my attention to the woman, I lay the back of my hand against her chest.

Frigid.

Sighing, I drag her closer to the fire and heap another blanket on top of her. I take a seat in an armchair, letting out a long breath.

For a few moments, I tent my hands under my chin and stare at the flames. Orange and yellow, they dance as logs crackle. The smell of wood smoke fills the lodge.

It would be pleasant if my mouth didn't taste so bitter. I don't want to be here. I shouldn't need to be here. I should be in the capital beside my three brothers and sister, where I belong. I should be standing tall, protecting them like any good brother would do. My sister, the Queen, is the eldest, but I'm the oldest man in the family. I've always been there to look out for them.

But I'm weak. Every year, October eighteenth rolls around, and the kingdom mourns. This year, I just couldn't take it. I couldn't stay at the balcony of the Stirling Castle and watch the thousands of candles flickering at Abby's yearly vigil outside. I couldn't stand the songs and dedications. The video compilations set to sad, mournful music.

The inevitable resurgence of those videos and photos of her last moments in my arms.

The memories of everything the media didn't know—that

none of us knew at the time. Abby's autopsy doubled my grief all over again.

I was supposed to read through my public statement for the press and send back comments, but when I glance at the mystery woman's immobile body, the last thing I want to do is official royal business. Moving to her bag, I unzip the front pocket to see if she has any identification. I open it up wider, and a lacy black thong tumbles to the floor. Picking it up with the edge of my finger, I arch an eyebrow.

Who did she think she was going to wear *that* for? Did she know I was coming to the Summer Palace? Is she here to try to seduce me?

I scoff.

You can try, baby girl.

In the soft light of the fire, her hair looks like glowing copper. A smattering of freckles covers her cheeks and forehead, barely visible on her pale skin. Her lips are a dull pink color, tinged with blue, and firelight dances over her skin.

I rummage through her things until I find a wallet. Bingo.

Rowan Reed.

I frown. Reed? That's the name of the palace manager who just had an accident. Earlier today, she fell on the ice and broke a hip. Had to be airlifted out of here before the storm came in.

Taking another step closer to the hypothermic woman, I lean over her face. Could she be related? Is she here to take Mrs. Reed's place? I tuck a strand of hair behind her ear, heart clenching at the softness of her skin.

Do I see a hint of the old woman in the shape of the nose? Or am I making connections that don't exist? Whoever she is, she's gorgeous.

And almost dead. I touch her forehead with the back of my hand, happy to find her skin isn't quite so cold. But when

I reach down further, I feel the snow melting on the neckline of her dress. Her clothes are wet with sweat and moisture, and just as cold as her skin.

"Fuck," I whisper under my breath, flipping the blanket back. Her dress is soaked through and clinging to her body. Still fucking freezing.

The radio crackles by the door.

"Your Highness? Come in, Your Highness."

I walk to the desk, seeing one new yellow bar on the device's battery indicator. I grab the handheld radio and press the button on the side.

"Yeah?"

"You need assistance at the security lodge, sir?" I recognize Doctor Williams' pinched, nasally voice.

"Hypothermic woman," I respond. "Found her outside the gates. Her clothes feel wet to the touch and she's not warming up."

"I'm gathering my things. We should be there in ten minutes."

Damn these huge palace grounds and the leagues that separate the security outbuildings from the main castle. It's great for privacy—not so good in an emergency. I glance at the woman, noticing her limp hand hanging off the edge of the sofa. She hasn't as much as stirred since we got here.

"I'm not sure we have ten minutes," I answer. "Her clothes are wet."

"Undress her, Your Highness," Doctor Williams says. *"Take all the wet clothes off and cover her with blankets. Don't submerge her in warm water or heat her up too fast, but we need to bring her body temperature up."*

"Got it. Over." I leave the radio on charge and move to the sofa. Tearing the blankets off, I stare for a moment. She lets out a soft moan, her smooth brow furrowing ever so slightly.

Moving slowly, I remove her sweater then tug the zipper on the side of her dress.

"Easy," I say, as if I were speaking to a nervous animal. I pause, hesitating. Her eyes are still closed. Body limp. It feels wrong to undress her like this, to take this scrap of fabric off her body and see what's hiding underneath.

I shake my head. This is necessary. Her life is on the line.

Gingerly, I lift the hem of her dress, averting my eyes as I slowly, gently pull the garment up. When I get to her stomach, my eyes drift over her skin. There's a dark freckle near her belly button, and I have the urge to run my tongue over it.

I squeeze my eyes shut. What the hell is wrong with me?

With a shallow breath, I pull one arm free, then the other. Lifting her torso off the sofa, I tug the dress over her head and toss it aside. It lands on the floor with a wet *thunk*.

Rowan's body falls against mine and damn, she's cold. Not warming up at all.

My eyes drift down over her skin-colored bra, not wanting to touch her too much. I put my hand on her thigh, feeling a line where dry meets wet on her thighs. Her jacket must have covered the dry part.

"Rowan" I say softly, touching her shoulder. "Can you hear me?"

I pause. Nothing.

Covering her torso with a blanket, I squeeze my eyes shut. I should really take her bra off. It's soaked too, and she needs to get warm. Fuck. I haven't been with a woman in four years, and I didn't think the first naked woman I'd see would be unconscious.

Reaching under the blanket, I wrap my arms around Rowan's body and unclip her bra. I pull it free, keeping the blanket over her body.

Sighing, I pinch my lips and tug off her tights. Inch by

inch, ice-cold white skin is revealed. My eyes linger on the scrap of underwear around her hips, then I look away. I touch the edge of it—dry enough to leave on.

I'm not some fucking creep. I'm just trying to help this stupid woman who apparently doesn't understand that being in the arctic means it gets cold. Why would she *walk*? Why didn't she call anyone? Grab a taxi?

When I drag her tights down to her feet and pull them free, I fold the blanket down over her legs and lay the tights across the arm of a chair. She can keep the underwear on. I've done enough.

My heart is beating too fast, and I look away from the woman with a scowl.

She's an inconvenience, is what she is. A potential security risk. Nothing more.

4

———

ROWAN

WARMTH TINGLES over my skin as I blink my eyes open. A face looms in front of mine, an older man with a thick, white mustache.

"Miss Reed," he says, his voice pinched, yet friendly. "You're awake." I try to sit up, when the man puts his hand on my shoulder. "My name is Doctor Williams. You were found on the road leading to the Summer Palace with severe hypothermia. You were brought here. We've given you warm intravenous fluids and warmed your body temperature up. Please rest."

I lie back on the sofa, suddenly keenly aware that I'm not wearing any clothing. My fingers brush against my thighs as my heart leaps in my chest, and I feel the edge of my underwear around my hips. But when my hand drifts higher...

Oh, shit.

I'm not wearing a bra. My breath catches as discomfort races through me.

At least I have undies on. I'm not *completely* naked.

Blinking, I look from the doctor to the roaring fire. Dr.

Williams shoves a side table closer, where a steaming mug of tea sits waiting. I nod in thanks.

Then, movement.

My eyes are drawn to the edge of the room and I notice him for the first time. I suck in a breath, eyes widening.

I've seen those amber eyes in photos before. The soft curls of black hair. The sharp jaw and dark brow.

The Prince.

"I...I..." I stammer, then stop. Why is Prince Wolfe here? And why is he staring at me like he wants to sink his teeth into my neck and rip it to shreds?

And I'm *nearly freaking naked.*

I've never seen anger like that before. He might as well be a predator, stalking his prey in the dead of night. He watches me, analyzing every movement with those fiery eyes the color of honey.

His hands are interlaced under his chin, elbows resting on his knees. Even seated, I can tell he's tall. Powerful. It's the way his limbs fold on each other, all graceful muscle and coiled power. The width of him almost obscures the armchair he's sitting in, as if the furniture in here is just a bit too small to hold him.

He stares at me, unmoving.

Is he the one who found me? *Has he seen me naked?* Oh my goodness. Oh God. No. I take a breath, trying to sit up. The doctor makes a noise and puts his hand on my shoulder again.

"Rest, Miss Reed."

"I'm fine," I croak, eyes drawn to the Prince once more.

He shifts in the chair, leaning back. He props his head in his hand, keeping his eyes on me. I crawl up on the sofa, keeping my arms clamped over my chest to hold the blanket against my skin. I wish I had a shirt on.

The fire crackles. The doctor rummages somewhere behind me. Wind howls outside, banging against the shutters.

But none of it matters.

The Prince is *here*.

And he's angry.

Why does that make my insides feel warm? Why are my thighs clenching at the way his eyes sweep over me?

"Do you know where you are?" he says slowly, his voice rippling across the distance between us. It's warm, with harsh edges that make every nerve in my body bristle with warning.

This man is dangerous.

I nod. "At the Summer Palace in Nord."

He stares, his eyes dropping to my bare shoulders. I try not to squirm. When his eyes drift up my neck, pausing on my lips, a new kind of heat curls lazily through my core. I drop my chin, reaching for the mug of tea on the side table.

"Why were you outside in a peacoat this close to the Arctic Circle?"

"It's all I have," I admit. "I thought..." I frown, stealing a glance at him over my mug of tea.

Big mistake.

His eyes drill holes through me. They make fire burn hotter in my core and steal the words right out of my mouth. As he lounges back in the chair, his long limbs extending toward me, I have the urge to crawl to him. To curl up on his lap and purr against his chest, just to feel the power that lies within.

Blinking, I look down again. "My grandmother was supposed to pick me up. There was no one else. I had no cell phone reception. All the taxis were gone. I had no choice."

When the Prince doesn't answer, I look up. His lips are pinched, but it doesn't take away from their fullness. They'd feel good to kiss. I just know they would. A shadow of hair covers the bottom half of his face, as if he's the kind of man who never quite looks clean-shaven. Stubble grows within an hour of a razor touching his skin.

The Prince parts his lips. "Mrs. Reed is your grandmother."

It doesn't sound like a question, but I nod anyway. His eyes are still on me, tracing the lines of my face and dropping down to my body again. He watches me take a sip of tea, catching every movement I make. I hate the way he stares, but I don't want him to stop. He scares me, like a deep, primal trill in my brain telling me to run away.

"Are you here to replace her?" he asks, his words slow. He blinks slowly, then arches a brow. As if the idea of me being here is laughable.

I frown. "No. Why would I be replacing her? Where is she?"

Suddenly, her absence sends panic shooting down my spine. I glance around the lodge, seeing only the Prince, the doctor, and a huge, bearded beast of a man standing by the door.

No Grandma. No smell of cinnamon and cherries.

No safety.

Three strange men. And me, mostly naked. Weak. Exposed. I suck in a breath, gripping the mug to stop my hands from trembling.

"You haven't heard?" For the first time, the Prince's voice holds a hint of surprise. I meet his eye, seeing a twitch in his eyebrow. His eyes flash, golden-brown gemstones looking predatory and warm all at once.

"Heard what?" I reply. "Your Highness," I add as an afterthought. Am I supposed to curtsy? I'm not wearing any clothes.

He tilts his head, interest sparking across his face. "Your grandmother had a slip on the ice. She's been transferred to the hospital in Stirling."

"What? When? I spoke to her this morning." I sit up, the blanket slipping. I catch it, but not before the Prince's eyes flick down. I blush, warmth creeping up my neck as I claw the blanket back up my chest. I want clothing. I need dignity. Some scrap of power in this deeply unbalanced situation.

The Prince glances at the clock on the wall. "About six hours ago."

"I was on the train. Flew into Stirling then took a train right away. I didn't check my phone because reception was spotty and I was working..."

"You're here to visit her, then? Where are your papers? I wasn't able to find any security clearances or authorizations in your things."

"You went through my things?" Heat spears my chest. My cheeks flush.

The Prince looks amused. "Among other things." His eyes drift down the blankets covering my body, and my blush deepens.

He didn't. He's not... Did the Prince of Nord undress me?

Squeezing my eyes shut, I try to stop my heart from racing right out of my chest. No. No, no, no. No way. This wasn't supposed to happen. This isn't reality. It's a dream. A nightmare. I'm dead. This is what death feels like. I pinch the inside of my arm, trying to wake myself up. I fell asleep on the train, and this is all some sort of hallucination.

I did *not* walk to the Summer Palace, get so cold I became severely hypothermic, and then have to be undressed by the Prince of freaking Nord. No way. Nun-uh. And Grandma isn't in the hospital, and I'm not here all on my own. This isn't happening.

My eyes snap open again, and I do my best to square my shoulders. "I'm here to work, Your Highness. I was engaged by the royal family to redesign the Summer Palace. This is my first site visit, where I intend to take photos of important features that will be retained, and go through the palace archives for original building drawings and survey information. I need them to finalize my design before approval by the Crown. Construction starts next summer."

By some miracle, my voice doesn't tremble. My heart, on the other hand, is thumping so hard I think my ribs might crack.

The Prince arches a brow. I hate that I amuse him. I hate that he looks at me like I'm some little plaything sent for his entertainment. I hate that I'm not wearing any clothes and that my body still feels cold, despite the warmth of the fire and the heat in my core.

My hands tremble, and I force myself to meet his gaze. "Is my grandmother okay?"

He dips his chin, and relief washes over me. "She'll be fine. She broke her hip, but she's stable. No need for surgery, but she'll have a long recovery, considering her age. They tell me she probably won't be back to the palace until spring."

I let out a long breath. "Okay. Can I talk to her?"

"The cell tower is down. We have no reception, and the short-wave radio doesn't reach that far south. There's a satellite phone at the palace, but I doubt the hospital will let you speak to her until visiting hours tomorrow." The Prince unfolds his long body to stand up. He towers over me, his golden eyes still glued to my face. "Once you're recovered, you'll report to me at the palace. The staff will bring some adequate clothing for you to wear." He takes a step, then pauses beside the sofa. Leaning down, a cruel smirk crosses over his lips. "You're not in Farcliff anymore, princess. Welcome to Nord."

I inhale sharply and taste his scent. Woodsy. Strong. Like whiskey and fire. It makes my head spin, and I can't manage to make my tongue work well enough to answer.

Instead, I just dip my chin and listen to his footsteps as he walks out. The door opens, sending a cold jet of air blasting through the lodge. When I glance over my shoulder, both he and the huge man by the door are gone.

The doctor gives me a tight smile. "Don't mind him. He's just... Well, never mind. He's a complicated man and October is always difficult. Not used to being this far north when the weather is this bad."

I sip my tea in silence for a while as the doctor takes my vitals. Glancing at the older man, I tilt my head. "Do you like it here?"

The doctor nods, shifting his gaze to my IV bag. "There's a certain kind of magic in the isolation up here. I don't mind it. Your grandmother likes it."

My throat feels tight as the reality of my situation closes in on me. "Will she be okay?"

"She's strong. She'll be fine," Doctor Williams replies, shifting his kind eyes to mine. "She was lucky to get out when she did, so we should all be grateful for small mercies. This is going to be a big storm. We'll be shut in for at least a week. Maybe longer."

"A week?" My eyes widen.

"It's safer that way. Even here, at the security lodge, we can get cut off from the main castle in whiteout conditions." He glances out the window. "As soon as you're strong enough to move, we'll have to head back. Soon would be preferable. Your IV fluids should be done in ten minutes, then we'll head back."

I knew what I was getting into when I agreed to this job. Grandma warned me about the cold. She warned me that people get cabin fever if they don't adapt to the loneliness and isolation. Told me to plan for a short visit, so the harshness of the arctic wouldn't have time to get to me.

But nothing could have prepared me for this.

Wrapping the blankets around my body, and ignoring the doctor's protests, I wheel my IV pole to the window and glance out. Even through thick, double-glazed panes, the cold bites through the glass. I watch wind whip little tornadoes of snow and frost over the desolate landscape, as if every ice crystal is dancing in some complicated choreography.

The palace sits between two huge mountain ridges, their tops obscured by the clouds. This looks like another planet. I took a train to Nord and landed on Mars.

I think of Gerry, and the way he'd throw a blanket over my legs when I spent hours reading on the sofa. Was that really so bad? Did I really feel stifled, or was I just a spoiled little girl who thought she wanted to have it all?

The black castle looms in the distance, its windows yawning yellow with light. I shiver, but not from the cold. The windows are the same color as the Prince's eyes. Pale amber, like his namesake.

Wolfe.

I wonder if he's a predator, too. If he sees me as prey. If my time at the castle will be one long hunt, and this was all just a terrible, terrible mistake.

But then I remember the way his eyes drifted to my lips. How his gaze sent warmth spiraling through my core when he let me know he'd undressed me. How for the first time in a long time, I feel alive.

Maybe it's the after-effects of a near-death experience. It's what happens when someone is severely hypothermic and comes back to life. You start imagining things that aren't there. You imagine heat that doesn't exist. You get confused and your mind plays tricks on you.

That's what's happening. My body is responding to delusions.

I turn away from the window, slumping back down on the sofa. The doctor places a bundle of warm clothes on the seat next to me. "Put those on. As soon as you're strong enough, we'll move you to the castle. The staff has prepared your room."

I stare at the clothes, then shift my gaze to the window. Excitement pierces my gut, and I know it's not from the near-death experience.

This is real. The Prince is here.

And I'm stuck at the palace whether I like it or not.

5

———

WOLFE

ON MY COMPUTER screen is yet another speech identical to every other royal statement I've ever given or heard. I give it a cursory glance, approving it with zero comments. When I close my laptop, I lean back in my chair and glance out the window.

The doctor's car is making its way from the security lodge to the main castle. I lean closer, watching the vehicle approach.

She's in there. Rowan Reed. Probably sitting in the back seat, her perky little ass being warmed by heated leather seats. Maybe she's wrapping her arms around her torso, staring out the window at the white expanse that surrounds us.

The woman who almost died. The red-haired beauty who looks like she's not quite human. Part fairy, part elf, and one hundred percent delicious. I want to eat her.

I grunt, turning away from the window.

The last thing I should be doing is thinking of her. I'll stay in my wing of the castle and let her do her design work. I'll hole myself up in here and wait for October to pass. I might even stay the winter—being here on my own doesn't sound so bad.

Wasn't that the plan? Hide away here, far from misplaced sympathy and pity-filled stares? Lick the wounds that never heal, or at the very least, grit my teeth and make it through this month.

My eyes drift to the wall, where a photo of Abby and me hangs. I frown, tightness squeezing my chest.

I'd never met anyone like her. An angel with golden hair and a bright smile. Able to pull me out of my darkest depths and show me the beauty of life. The woman I was supposed to cherish and protect.

The woman I failed.

Bitterness overwhelms me. Resentment tastes like ash. Pushing my chair back, I stand and walk to the wall. I stand in front of the photo, staring at the image of my own face. A huge smile stretches across my lips, and my arm is slung around her slim waist. I don't even know that person. Abby's hand rests on my chest, and she tilts her head back, a coquettish smile gracing her red lips.

She always knew how to take a good photo—but then again, it's hard to take a bad one when you're beautiful. The media adored her, and she gave them smiles and waves and pictures they could sell newspapers with.

Nord's darling. Our princess. My future wife.

We'd been back from our first official trip abroad when that photo was taken. I'd just asked her to marry me. Life was bright and hopeful and good.

Gingerly, I unhook the photo from the wall, staring at our smiling faces. My thumbs brush the glass of the picture frame, pressing hard enough to feel the cool smoothness of the material beneath my fingertips.

I guess I'm not getting away from these memories, even at the Summer Palace.

My thumbs press harder, the pads of my fingers leaving imprints on the glass. Anger swells inside me as I stare at Abby's smiling face, her soft, blond curls falling down to her waist. I stare at the hand resting on my chest. At the glittering ring that always caught the light just so. My eyes drift down to her flat stomach, which still hid the secret that her death would reveal.

I failed her. When the time came for me to act, I froze, and she was gone.

Dropping my shoulders, I toss the picture, frame and all, into a drawer and slam it closed. I stalk out of the room without looking back.

My feet take me across the palace to the south wing. I pass oil paintings of my ancestors and intricate sculptures that Mother and Father commissioned when they were newlyweds. Before they had the four of us kids. Before they, too, died—at least I was too young to really remember much. The sting of that particular grief doesn't send me to the edge of the arctic for months at a time.

I walk by huge windows that, in the summertime, reveal vast meadows of wildflowers and swaying grasses. Now, all I see is white snow and a dark, starless sky.

Pausing at one of the windows in a formal sitting room, I run my fingers through my thick, black hair. The snow is beautiful, in its own way. It muffles the world, as if giving you permission to be sleepy and warm and safe inside. Its harshness appeals to the primal parts of me. The bite of the cold reminds me of my own heart. The whip of the wind across the barren landscape reminds me what it feels like to be alone. The isolation is comforting.

There are no reporters here, following me everywhere to catch a glimpse of my misery.

Turning away from the window, I continue walking through the castle. I thought I'd hate it here this winter. I didn't like the idea of being hemmed in here for weeks, but it was better than the assault of Abby's memorials.

This palace is meant to be enjoyed in summertime, when the arctic is lit by the sun nearly twenty-four hours a day. When the meadows are teeming with life, and caribou bound across the landscape.

Now, it's dead and cold and sleepy, and I like it. It feels like home.

Throwing on a thick jacket, boots, and all the warm accessories I need to brave the cold, I make my way through the big brown doors to the kennels. It's cooler in here, but still sheltered from the worst of the elements. The warm smell of dogs greets me, followed by a few soft whinnies and cold snouts pressed against kennel gates.

Harvey, the kennel master, looks up from his crouch at the far end of the kennels. His eyebrows jump. "Your Highness." He straightens up, giving me a low bow.

"Harvey." I nod. "How are they?" I move to a kennel in the corner, opening the gate for the big husky with eyes like crushed ice.

"Daisy had her litter. They're all healthy. AJ's asthma is still bothering him, but the vet said he'd be okay if we take it easy on him this winter." Harvey glances at the huge husky exiting the kennel beside me. "Ah. And Chief missed you."

The beast lets out a low huff, nuzzling my leg. I reach over to scratch the back of his head, sighing. The tension between my shoulder blades finally eases, and I kneel down to rub my cheek against Chief's fur.

"Hey, buddy," I whisper, turning my head as he licks my

face with his rough, pink tongue. I chuckle, scrubbing his neck. "I missed you too."

When I stand up, Chief stays by my side. The warmth of his body radiates through my pant leg and sends a calming pulse through me. I forget about the picture in the office and the cold loneliness clinging to my spirit. I forget about why I'm here, and how life would have been different if I hadn't failed Abby when she needed me most.

I'm just here with my dog, and I finally feel like I'm home.

Harvey gives me a pinched smile. "He's been antsy since you left last time. Hard to tame."

"Look at him, as gentle as a baby." I give Chief another scratch.

Harvey snorts. "With you, he is. Damn near chewed my fingers off when I fed him ten minutes late last Wednesday. Snapped at AJ, too. I think he can sense the weakness."

"That's why we like each other. Come on, boy," I say, knowing Chief will follow me. I nod to Harvey. "He'll sleep in my chambers tonight."

"Of course, Your Highness." Harvey bows, and I walk back through the kennel doors into the warmth of the palace.

Chief's claws click on the stone floor as he pads ahead of me. I strip my jacket and boots off, laying them on a bench left out for that purpose. My dog glances back at me, his big head dipping down ever so slightly before turning back toward the hallway.

I frown, following.

"Slow down, Chief," I say, but the dog ignores me. He walks through the empty hallways, pausing every few seconds to let me catch up. A smile teases at my lips. This dog has a mind of his own, and he doesn't care that I'm a prince. We understand each other on a primal level.

So, I follow him.

What else am I going to do? Wallow in my own misery and think of my failures? Look at old pictures of things that will never happen? Wonder if Rowan's sweet blue eyes are nothing but another lie, an opportunity for me to fail her, too?

Chief pauses at the base of the main staircase, then gives a low bark. He climbs the stairs two at a time, stopping again at the top to let me catch up. I grin. He leads me all the way down the long hallway to the north wing and pauses outside a guestroom door. Finally, I frown.

"What do you want in there, boy?"

He whinnies, scraping his paw over the door. I scratch his head, burying my fingers in his thick fur. It feels good to have Chief by my side again. He stays at the Summer Palace year-round with his brothers and sisters, but whenever I come here, we're inseparable.

Except right now, when I push the guest bedroom door open. Chief rushes through the opening as soon as it's wide enough for him, then leaps onto the bed. With a huff, he drops down and nuzzles beside a sleeping form.

"Chief!" My voice is a hoarse whisper caught halfway through my throat.

That sleeping form has long, coppery hair and a soft, pink mouth. Rowan is fast asleep, covered by two extra blankets with a fire just dying down in the hearth. My dog stretches out so he's lying along the length of Rowan's body, his snout resting against her neck.

"Chief," I hiss again, snapping my fingers for him to come back to me.

He lets out a snort in response, his eyes closed. My shoulders drop. He's not leaving. With one hand on the doorknob, I stare at the two of them. Something twinges in my chest at the sight of Rowan next to the dog who usually never leaves my side, and I let out a frustrated sigh.

Chief's tail flicks, teasing me.

"Fine. Stay there. Just don't expect any treats when you wake up."

Chief lifts his head, blinking his eyes open to look at me over his shoulder. After a second, he turns back to Rowan and promptly falls asleep.

I pinch my lips together as heat spears my chest. Am I... am I jealous of Rowan right now?

...or am I jealous of the dog?

I back away silently, leaving the door ajar in case Chief changes his mind and comes to sleep on his spot in front of my fireplace later tonight.

He doesn't.

6

———

ROWAN

I WAKE up to something wet nudged against my cheek. Then I feel the slow rise and fall of breath beside me, and I smell the unmistakable scent of dog.

Opening my eyes, I freeze.

It's a wolf. Holy shit, there's a wolf in my bed. What kind of godforsaken place is this that wolves roam the hallways? My heart takes off, and the beast opens its eyes. Pale blue, with a dark rim around the edge.

A husky.

My heartbeat doesn't slow, but the panic inside me ebbs away ever so slightly. The dog lets out a huff, his tongue sliding out to lick the edge of my ear. I flinch at the wetness, huffing out a laugh.

"Hey, puppy," I say to the dog that most definitely isn't a puppy anymore. But all dogs are puppies, aren't they?

The dog makes a low noise, nudging my face with his cold, wet nose. Slowly, tentatively, I lift my arm from beneath the mass of blankets and reach for the husky's head. I stroke his fur, letting a soft smile tug at my lips.

"Good boy," I whisper, giving him a long scratch that

43

earns me a rumble from the dog's chest. "At least, I think you're a boy." I grin. "This is a nice surprise. Maybe this place isn't so bad, after all."

"I see you've met my dog," a voice says from the doorway. I pause my scratches when I see the Prince of Nord leaning against my doorway. How did he get there without me even noticing?

Sitting up, I glance under the covers to make sure I'm still wearing clothing. Flannel pajamas. Phew.

My eyes crawl back up to the Prince's, and it takes all my self-control not to gape. His crisp, white shirt has the top button open, giving me a glimpse of the muscular chest beneath it. His arms are crossed, all bulging biceps and broad hands.

Even from all the way across the room, he exudes power. Masculinity. Heat wraps around my core, reminding me that I'm a woman.

I shouldn't be thinking this. He's royalty. I'm not. I broke up with my boyfriend because I was determined to make it on my own—the last thing I should be doing is fantasizing about someone else.

Or maybe that's the best thing to do?

I'm not going to be here long, anyway. What would it hurt to indulge in a few innocent thoughts?

I clear my throat. "Good morning, Your Highness." I dip my chin. "I'm sorry. I just woke up and he was here."

"Chief came straight here last night," he replies, clicking his tongue at the dog. Chief stands up from my side and hops off the bed, padding on the plush carpet toward the Prince.

I miss the weight of the dog's body next to mine, but I force a smile. "Oh. He came to me? Why?"

"Fuck if I know," Prince Wolfe spits, shooting me a glare.

I wince.

He rests a hand on the dog's head, and he looks like a wild, tribal king showing me who's in charge. I'm so very keenly aware that I'm in bed. That he's only a few steps away. That there's heat licking the inside of my stomach in a way I haven't felt in a long time.

The Prince's eyes sweep over me once more. He tilts his head. "Are you going to do any work today, or are you just going to lie in bed all morning?"

Heat turns to anger, flaring bright in my chest. *Rude.*

"I was hypothermic less than twenty-four hours ago," I snap, then immediately blush. He's royalty, after all. But fuck if I'll let *anyone* speak to me that way. I had enough of that from my ex, and I left him behind in Farcliff. No one gets to talk to me like anything less than an equal.

"You were. I hope you learned the importance of appropriate clothing. I don't exactly make a habit of saving damsels in distress." His amber eyes flash, a deep well of contempt flowing just for me.

How wonderful.

"I learned that I could count on you to undress me when I'm unconscious," I spit, meaning the words to sound like an insult—but the Prince's lips curl into a smirk, and I draw in a sharp breath.

He chuckles gently, still stroking his dog between the ears. "Is that a request for more of my services? I'd be happy to undress you while you're awake, if you prefer."

"Don't make me barf."

Lie.

My body heats up at the thought of the Prince's hands on me. Are they as rough as he is, I wonder? Or are his palms smooth and soft? Would he grip me tight and cage me in, showing me just how wild he can be?

The Prince stares at me like he can read my mind. "Don't kid yourself, princess. I see the way you look at me."

"Oh, good. You really are arrogant and rude. I was worried for a second. I thought that might have been an act last night."

Prince Wolfe tilts his head, a playful light shining in his eyes. "You know nothing about me, do you?"

"I know you enjoy being an ass." *Ahh, shut up, Rowan!* This guy is literal royalty, and I'm running my mouth. Am I drunk? Can I blame this on hypothermia?

"I'm not an ass," the Prince says, pushing himself off the doorway. His eyes grow hard. "I'm much worse than that. Now get dressed and get out of bed. The office is ready for you. I have some issues to discuss with you regarding your preliminary designs for the palace."

"You've looked at my designs?" My brows tug together. Then, for the first time, I notice the dark smudges under his eyes. The drawn skin. The deep tiredness that seems stitched into his very being. Did he stay up all night looking through my work?

Instead of answering, the Prince clicks his tongue for Chief to leave the room.

"Wait!" I call out. The Prince pauses, glancing over his shoulder. I motion to my phone on the nightstand. "There's no reception on my phone. I'd like to call my grandmother."

"The cellular network is down on account of the storm. You can use the satellite phone once we've talked over the design issues," he says, his voice hard.

Ice freezes my veins as my jaw hardens. How *dare* he. I grit my teeth. "You're going to use my grandmother as a bargaining chip for your stupid design ideas? I need to speak to her. *Now.*"

He arches an eyebrow. I cross my arms. Tension heightens

between us, and I do my best to look tough. My lips pinch together, but it's less out of anger and more to stop my bottom lip from trembling.

The Prince stares at me for a moment, then walks away.

My heart beats erratically. I feel flushed and cold and confused.

Why is he here? This wasn't supposed to happen. It was supposed to be me and Grandma for a few weeks. She said she'd take me up the mountain in a snowmobile. I'd do some research and finalize my design, then head back home.

No Prince. No royalty. No drama.

Looking at the open door, I sigh. Of course he wouldn't close it behind him. That would be far too considerate. Big Bad Prince Wolfe doesn't close doors when he leaves rooms. He probably has an army of minions scurrying behind him to clean up after His Royal Jerkness. He probably expects me to kiss the ground he walks on.

Screw. That.

I refuse to curtsy for that asshole. Sure, he saved my life. He brought me in when I could have died, exposed to the elements—but he's made me feel like absolute garbage ever since. Mocked my choice of clothing, when everyone says they've never seen a storm like this so early in the year. And I haven't been able to speak to my grandmother, who was a huge reason I came up here in the first place. Yet he expects me to jump out of bed and discuss the design of the castle?

Who cares about the design of this stupid place! Even the best architect couldn't save this gothic, dark, gloomy hellhole without the use of a very big bulldozer.

Sliding out of bed, I stomp across the room and slam the door. Letting out a long breath, I drop my chin to my chest. My body feels weak, and I'm worried for Grandma. The last thing I want to deal with is a moody prince who thinks he owns the world.

Padding to the bathroom adjoining my room, I inhale sharply. Floor-to-ceiling marble. Soft, white towels. Gleaming chrome finishes with a rain shower bigger than my head. There are luxury soaps and shampoos and conditioners, and even a brand-new electric toothbrush for me to use.

I strip off my pajamas and with them, my thoughts of the Prince. I wash all my bitterness away and tilt my head toward the stream of water, thinking of my grandmother. Everyone says she's safe and she'll recover. They say she had a fall, but she's resting at the hospital with the best doctors in the kingdom. Still, I worry.

When I get out of the shower, I'll find the satellite phone the Prince was talking about and I'll call her. Her voice will soothe me, and she'll tell me what I should do. I'll make sure she's okay, and then I'll book the first available plane or helicopter or bus or train—whatever mode of transportation will get me out of here quickest.

Without Grandma here, I have no reason to stay. I'll spend the next couple of days doing my research, then I'm leaving as soon as the storm lets up.

Away from this northern wasteland, and away from the Prince.

Turning the taps off, I let out a sigh. As soon as I open the shower door, my skin starts prickling with goose bumps in the cool air, and I rush to wrap myself in a giant towel. Mm... fluffy. When I open the door to the bedroom, my eyebrows jump. Someone's been here to make the bed and bring a tray full of breakfast. Croissants, steaming-hot coffee, fresh fruit, eggs—the works.

Maybe I shouldn't leave right away. I grin, attacking a croissant as my eye catches another bundle near the door. A big, black phone that almost looks like a walkie-talkie rests on the floor near the door. Beside it, a card with nothing but a phone number on it and one letter. *W.*

Wolfe?

My heart thuds against my ribs. Did the Prince send this? Found the number for my grandmother's hospital room and everything?

I shake my head.

He has minions. One of his minions did it. Not him.

Still, he listened to my protests and heard me when I said I wanted to talk to Grandma. That counts for something, right? Is this the same man who demanded I get out of bed and do some work? The same man who resents the fact that he had to help me yesterday? The same man who isn't even supposed to be here?

I bite my lip, doing my best to ignore the fluttering in my belly.

Fine, I'll admit it. He's gorgeous. He's all broad and strong and manly. When he talked about undressing me, wetness leaked out of me like I was a hormonal teenager lusting after her first crush.

But he's an asshole. I don't care if he saved my life. I don't care if he does something nice, because he's infuriating and rude and arrogant and—

Ugh.

It would be so much easier if my body would cooperate. Stop seeing him as a big, powerful man with intoxicating eyes. Stop imagining what he'd look like naked. Stop getting wet and hot and twisted up inside over a man who will never be mine.

Never, ever, ever.

Shaking the thought of the Prince away, I dial the number on the card. My grandmother answers on the fourth ring, her soft voice immediately making my anger evaporate.

"Hey, Grandma," I say, sitting on the edge of the bed.

"Rowan, honey." Grandma sighs. "They told me you had to walk from the station. I'm so sorry, baby. I had everything organized and then I had to go and slip on the ice and break my hip. I'm getting old."

"I want to see you."

"I'm fine, Rowan," Grandma replies. I can hear the smile in her voice, but she sounds tired. "I'll be up and walking in no time."

"What did the doctor say? Was it a bad break?"

"Don't you worry about me. The royal family made sure I have the best doctors here, and they said they don't need to operate. I just need some rest. As a bonus, I get to avoid that big storm. I'm lucky."

"I'd hardly call a broken hip luck."

Grandma chuckles. "You just square away the design and get the pictures and details you needed from the palace. They told me the Prince arrived at the same time as you."

"Yeah," I answer, biting my lip. "He's...Is he always such a..."

Grandma sighs, filling in the blanks when my voice trails off. "He was a very happy baby, but things changed when he got older. You know the King and Queen died when they were young, and the Prince felt like he had to take care of his siblings. His sister's older, but he was always the protective one. Then there was everything with his fiancée..."

"What happened?" I frown, raking through my mind for memories. I remember reading something about his fiancée dying a few years ago, but I mostly go out of my way to avoid news of Nord. Reminds me too much of my mother and the ancestry I've never felt a part of.

Grandma makes a soft noise. "The Prince has a protective spirit. He'll warm up to you."

I scoff.

Grandma pretends not to notice. "The Summer Palace still tends to loosen him up. Don't you worry about him. His bark is worse than his bite."

"As soon as I'm done here, I'll come straight to see you."

"Okay, honey," Grandma says. "I love you. Be good."

When I hang up the call, I stare at the phone for a few moments. Grandma's okay. She sounds strong. She might not be beside me, but maybe at her age, it's better to spend the winter somewhere south of here. This could be for the best.

But my plan still stands. As soon as I've had this meeting with the Prince and I've gotten the pictures and details I need, I'm gone. When the storm lets up, I'll be on the first train out of here.

7

WOLFE

ROWAN WALKS into the office looking like a red-haired goddess. My stomach clenches, but I hide it behind a scowl. It isn't fair for someone to be that pretty. Even the way she walks is delicate. Entrancing. She closes the door gently, staring up at me through long lashes.

She doesn't curtsy, choosing instead to jut her chin out at me.

Damn, it's hard not to smile.

"Thank you for bringing the satellite phone to my room."

I nod. "Did you speak to Mrs. Reed?"

"I did." Her eyes shine, deep blue and full of life. She doesn't look down at the ground when she faces me. Looks me straight in the face.

I jerk my head to the wall, where a screen has been set up. "Walk me through your design. I have comments."

"Would it kill you to say please?"

"Probably." I grin.

She rolls her eyes, stomping toward the desk. I love the way her cheeks get pink when she's angry. How she tries to look mad, all clenched fists and gritted teeth.

It's cute.

I could have fun torturing her. Show her just how little she understands about this place. Let her know that I rule this particular corner of the kingdom, no matter who commissioned her to do this redesign. Then, I'll send her home and enjoy the sight of her ass as she walks away.

Choosing an armchair beside the desk, I sit back and lift my eyes to the screen. I wave a hand. "You may begin."

"Gee, thanks." She huffs, and my smile widens. Her glare cuts to me. "Are you always like this?"

"Like what?"

The redness on her cheeks deepens and spreads. Would she blush if I kissed her? Touched her? Would she scream my name if I made her come? Would she hate me even more if I made her feel good?

Rowan doesn't answer my question. The keyboard clacks as she types, and I see a 3D image of the proposed palace design on the screen. Rowan stands, taking a deep breath. She moves to the screen and turns to face me.

"The new design will retain the historic features of the palace while taking advantage of twenty-first century technology. We could create the first true eco-palace in one of the harshest environments on earth."

I tilt my head, watching the way her breath catches when she meets my eye. She feels it too, the energy between us. Rowan squares her shoulders and walks back to the computer, flicking to another image.

"Every aspect of the new castle will be designed to trap heat in winter and keep the palace temperate in summer. I believe the Summer Palace can be utilized year-round, not only during the short summer months. With tripled-glazed eco-glass and cutting edge insulation materials, we can make this a truly iconic destination."

"A destination for who?"

Rowan stares at me, opening and closing her mouth. "I, uh...for you. And your family."

"This palace was the birthplace of the nation," I say, staring at the gleaming new design on the screen. "It means a lot to the citizens of Nord."

"I understand."

"Do you?" I arch an eyebrow. Turning back to the screen, I frown. "You got rid of the turrets." I nod to the edges of the image, where the two tall turrets that frame the palace have been replaced with round glasshouses.

Rowan nods. "Those two faces receive the most sun in winter months. We can capture it and use the concrete floor as a heat sink. It'll be more thermally efficient."

"Those turrets were the scene of epic battles in Nord in the eighteenth century. They're important."

I like watching Rowan squirm. What I'd like even more is to watch her squirm underneath me as an orgasm rips through her body. Her face could be just like it is now, with eyes flashing and lips parted.

I blink the image away. Not now. I can't think of that. I *shouldn't* think of that.

No matter how pretty she looks when she's angry, I can tell she doesn't get it. Nord. Me. This palace. She doesn't understand where she is. She doesn't know Nord's history.

She's the wrong person to redesign it.

It doesn't matter that her grandmother has lived here her whole life. It doesn't matter that Nordish blood flows in Rowan's veins. She's an outsider.

But damn, she looks good standing in front of me. Rowan tucks a strand of hair behind her ear, taking a deep breath. "I didn't know about those battles."

"What do you know about this place?"

Her cheeks turn pink, and I like the fire burning in her eyes. A little too much, maybe. My body seems to be forgetting that she doesn't belong here and that her design is all wrong.

Clearing my throat, I stand up and walk to the corner of the room to fix myself a cup of coffee at the kitchenette. I'm half-hard, and I need to get a grip.

She's not here for my amusement, and I'm not here to fuck the first available woman who walks through the door. I shouldn't be thinking about her at all. It shouldn't turn me on to see her mad, and I definitely shouldn't be imagining her in a multitude of compromising positions.

Most of all, I shouldn't feel this burning heat in my chest when I look at her fancy palace design that happens to be totally wrong. Why does it frustrate me so much that she doesn't see how little she understands about this place?

I want her to get it. I want her to redesign this place in a way that honors our past. That takes us to the future without erasing our history.

I want her to understand *me*.

Frowning, I shake my head. I don't give a shit if she gets me or not. She's not here to be with me.

I'm damaged. I'm a ticking time bomb. A black hole, who can't help but suck in all the light and life around me into my void. Isn't that what happened to Abby? Through my status as a prince, I lifted her up to fame, then watched her slip through my fingers.

Someone like Rowan? Soft and graceful, delicate and fragile?

She doesn't belong here. It's obvious from her clothes and her designs and her attitude.

But when I turn around to see her sitting down in the desk chair behind the computer, I can't help but enjoy the anger shooting from her eyes. She looks good when she's mad.

Rowan lifts her eyes to mine. "Can you elaborate? Tell me what would be more appropriate?" She tilts her head. "*Your Highness.*" She says my title like an insult, and I can't quite hide my grin. I stir some sugar into my coffee, listening to the soft clink of the spoon against my mug.

"The glass houses on either end. They look great in a field of grass and flowers like that image you've rendered, but what about the winter? What about right now?"

"Well, that's the beauty of them. It's new technology that is thermally—"

"Step away from the eco-aspects for a moment. The turrets *mean* something to the people of Nord. There are school tours that take children through them and teach them of the battles that occurred there. Destroying them would erase that. It's not right."

Rowan chews on the inside of her lip. Her freckles look brighter than they did when I found her in the snow, and I catch myself studying each individual one. I shift my gaze back to the screen, taking a sip. "Show me more. What's going on inside the palace in this design?"

Rowan takes a deep breath. "Well, one of the reasons for my site visit was to get a feel for the current state of the castle. I want to retain as many original features as possible. For example, the flooring—"

"I hate the floors. And they aren't original, by the way. They were replaced when I was a kid."

Her lips snap shut. I'm starting to love that glare.

Rowan folds her hand in her lap, taking a deep, cleansing breath. Her chest rises and falls, my eyes lingering on the swell of her breasts. My body feels tight and hot and a little too big for this room. I haven't felt this on edge in years, but I can't quite stop myself from staring. From wanting more.

Is it because she's an outsider that I want her so much? Because she seems familiar and exotic, all at once?

It's the beast inside me waking up. Opening its eyes and seeing its next meal.

I bet Rowan Reed tastes as sweet as she looks.

Rowan gulps, her graceful throat clenching and releasing. I follow every micro movement of her body, studying her as if she were the most curious creature I've ever seen.

She's not afraid of me, for one. The Wolfe of Nord. The man who lost everything, whose heart died with his fiancée.

I know what the papers say about me. They say I've turned cold. That Abby's death broke me.

And Rowan *should* be scared.

But she doesn't tremble before me—except when she trembles from rage. I love how she doesn't try to hide her emotions. She wears them like a badge of honor all over her face and body, letting me see just what an effect I have on her.

And she doesn't curtsy for me. Doesn't bow her head in deference. Doesn't use my title, except to mock me.

I should have her arrested, or at the very least sent away.

But I'm a man, and I'm weak—and she amuses me.

"Highness," she says, keeping most of the bite out of her tone this time. "With all due respect, you are not the one who commissioned me for this project. Her Majesty the Queen—"

"My sister will listen to what I say. She trusts my judgement, and she loves this palace for what it represents in Nord. Have you shown her this design?"

Rowan sucks in a breath, glaring at me. "I was given a brief, proposed a concept, and initial approvals were granted."

"Well, they're un-granted."

Her lips mash together. "What would you prefer for the interior? The brief I received was to retain as many of the original features as possible. If that has changed, I'll have to revisit my entire design."

"Stone floors are cold in winter," I say. "And they're not original."

"We can install under-floor heating. Why do you want to get rid of the floors if you want to keep everything else?" Rowan tilts her head, daring me to engage. "Even if they aren't original, aren't they part of the history of the place? Showing the palace's evolution?"

Touché.

I grin. She huffs.

I wouldn't be such an ass if she didn't make it so much fun.

Waving my hand at the screen, I take my seat again. We go through the preliminary design from start to finish, and by the end, I don't know what to think. She's designed a castle that might be at home in California, or on an island in the Caribbean. It's all about capturing light and having a jewel in the valley, and not about honoring the history of this kingdom.

This is Nord. We're dancing on the edge of the arctic. She doesn't seem to understand the elements. The harshness of the landscape. How tenuous our relationship with life is without the strong, thick walls around us.

Typical southerner. No wonder she almost died of hypothermia on her first day here. I'm surprised she has Nordish ancestry at all.

Rowan lets out a sigh, glancing my way. "Once I get pictures and details from around the castle and get some of the original survey plans from the archives in the library, I'll be able to implement the changes you've asked for."

I nod, unsure if the archives will do anything to make her see this place for what it is. "Maybe you should spend some time here. Try to understand Nord. Come back in summer and see the difference in the landscape, spend some time with the locals. Hear their stories. You'd learn more from that than any book."

"I'll start with the archives," Rowan answers with an edge in her voice. A ding sounds from her pocket, and Rowan's eyebrows jump. She pulls out her phone. "Reception is back."

"It'll be spotty for the next few days," I say. "You can use the satellite phone whenever you need."

Rowan glances at me, surprised. As if she expects me to be cruel.

Hell, maybe she's right. I'm not exactly kind.

She gives me a soft smile, dipping her chin to her chest. Heat rips right through my chest at the sight of it, and I feel like I don't deserve her smiles. I don't deserve her softness. Her deference. I've treated Rowan like a silly little girl since she got here, shot down her work, and tried my best to ignore the fact that she makes my body burn up.

Yet here she is, smiling at me. Grateful that I'm letting her use a phone. Showing me a chink in her armor I know I'll only want to exploit.

She should keep her guard up around me. It would be better for both of us.

___

8

ROWAN

THE PRINCE HAS A NICE ASS. Yes, I stare at it as he leaves the room. Yes, it feels wrong.

I refuse to feel bad about it.

Letting out a long sigh, I stare at the screen on the wall.

He hated my design. Had comments about every single aspect of it, asking me to make a million little changes and a few thousand major ones. I'll basically have to go back to the drawing board, even though I've spent the better part of a year coming up with this design.

Biting my lip, I glance at my phone.

Gerry: I'm sorry about those texts. I was drinking last night. Call me? I miss you.

My heart sinks. I shouldn't ignore him, but the last thing I want to do is call Gerry and listen to his excuses about his behavior. We've been broken up for six months, and I know he's been seeing other women. He was very clear when we broke up—my job, or him. I couldn't have both.

I don't want to give in to the temptation of calling him. Of sinking into old habits and settling for what's comfortable. Now that I'm far away from him, I wonder what we really had. Was it just complacency? Comfort? The ease of a long relationship? The promise of stability even if we couldn't have true love?

He was someone to throw a blanket over my legs when I was cold, but did he ever really make me feel warm?

Gerry doesn't make my heart thump. He doesn't make my cheeks burn. He doesn't fill my dreams with images of his strong body on top of mine.

No, there's another man who does that now.

I stare at the open doorway before squeezing my eyes shut.

Wrong. Bad. Stop it now, Rowan.

See? Another door the Prince didn't bother closing. Spoiled, bratty royal. No-good jerk who doesn't understand common decency. He's no better than Gerry, and I'm better off on my own.

Focus on work. On my architecture firm. On the projects that will be my legacy. Take care of *myself*. Rely on no one else. Be a burden to no man or woman or parent. Independence.

So why is my stomach clenching at the thought of the Prince?

Ignoring Gerry's message, I open up a browser window. I type in the Prince's name and let my finger hover over the 'search' button.

Do I really want to read up on him? I vaguely remember him being in the news a few years ago. His fiancée died, or something, but I was neck-deep in my fledgling business, and my resentfulness toward Nord was at an all-time high.

The place that didn't want me, or my mother. The land that chewed her up and spat her out.

Yet, here I am. Back for my own round of rejections.

My mouth is dry. My heart thumps uncomfortably. I

finally press my thumb on the search button, but the browser goes blank. A gust of wind bangs against the windows, and the reception fizzles out.

Leaning back in my chair, I drop my chin in my chest.

I need to get out of here. The Prince has gotten under my skin, and he's distracting me from what's truly important—work. The project. Architecture. Designing beautiful buildings that will stand the test of time. Having a stable income that will ensure I'm never a burden to anyone, ever.

"Excuse me? Miss Reed?" A woman stands at the door dressed in a palace uniform. She has chocolate-colored hair styled in a low bun and wide, brown eyes.

I sit up. "Yes?"

"I'm Vikki. Doctor Williams asked me to come check on you." She slips inside the door, giving me a kind smile.

"I'm okay. Just doing some work."

Her eyes move to the screen. A smile spreads across her lips. "Is this the new design? It's gorgeous."

"The Prince doesn't seem to think so," I reply, failing to keep the bitterness from my voice.

Vikki laughs. "He's like that. It takes a while to get on his good side, but once you do, he's very loyal. He'd go to war for the people he loves."

"The only one he's loyal to is his dog." I snort, shaking my head. "I basically have to start over from scratch. I was only here to get a few photos and details from the archives, and now I probably have six months of work to redo."

Vikki crosses her arms, still staring at the screen. She spins around to look at me, a hopeful smile on her face. "I can show you around if you want. I've lived here since I was a little girl. I know every corner of this palace."

I straighten up. "You'd do that? You don't have to work?"

"Showing you around is the perfect excuse not to do it."
Vikki winks. "Come on. What would you like to see first?"

I bite my lip. "The library, I think. I'd like to look at the archives."

Vikki jerks her head to the door. "It's just down the hall."

As we start walking, Vikki tells me about every king and queen with portraits hanging on the walls. She tells me when each rug was bought, and who designed the dozens of chandeliers that throw the whole palace into a soft, glowing light.

We get to a tall, hardwood door with intricate inset panels, and Vikki gives me a bright smile. "I love this room." She pushes the door open, and I gasp.

Gorgeous.

Floor-to-ceiling books. Plush sofas. Massive windows. I walk over to the window, staring out at the white countryside.

"It's gorgeous in summertime," Vikki says, standing beside me. We look out at the white expanse. "Teeming with life."

"It's beautiful now, too." My voice is soft.

"Wild and unforgiving. Makes me appreciate being inside these walls and not out there." She smiles. "Have you seen the visitor's cottage?" She points across the barren snow-covered meadow to a tiny lodge in the distance. "It used to be the main residence before the palace was built. If you want to see true heritage and history, that's the place to do it. They say the old kings used to hold court there. The ceiling is still stained black from soot above the old hearth. Every time I go there, I get chills."

My eyes widen. "No one told me about that. It wasn't in the brief. I love old buildings."

Vikki's face breaks into a smile. "I'll take you, but we might have to wait for the storm to pass. They say it'll only get worse. We've had a bit of respite today, but it'll be whiteout conditions within a couple of hours out there. Be the same for the next week or so. It's not safe to go that far."

Vikki laughs when I pout. She jerks her head to a door at the far end of the room. "Come on. I'll show you the archives instead."

She leads me through the door and into an intimate, dim space. It smells like old books, and I immediately feel at home. One wall is covered in bookshelves, while the other has a row of filing cabinets. Vikki points to an old, clunky computer on the desk to our right.

"The password is *password123*. You can log in and view the digitized archives or search for what you need."

"That doesn't sound like a very secure password." I grin.

Vikki laughs. "The last person who was in here was a historian from Cambridge University about fifteen years ago. We're not hiding anything. Nobody really cares about this place outside of Nord." She gives my arm a quick squeeze. "I'd better get back to work. If you're not in the dining room by seven, I'll have them send your dinner here."

"Thank you." I give my new friend a soft smile, glad to have found someone who seems nice, for once. She hasn't once made me feel like an unwelcome outsider with silly ideas about the palace redesign. Vikki walks out of the archive room, and I do a slow turn, inhaling deeply.

Then, I get to work. The archives are a treasure trove of information that I could have used for my preliminary designs. I look through old plans and read about the history of the place, from its first construction a few hundred years ago to the various restorations that have happened since.

Before I know it, my back aches and it's dark out. A knock sounds on the door, followed by a butler with a tray laden full of food. I thank him and inhale my dinner, turning once again to the old book I'd been reading.

Books are a time warp. I don't know how much time passes when I jerk upright at the sound of a deep, masculine voice. "They told me I would find you here." The Prince looks at me through hooded eyes. He stretches his arms over his head as he leans against the doorway.

My eyes drift down to a little strip of exposed skin at his hips. Yum.

Then, the Prince reaches for my dinner tray, grabbing an untouched bread roll and tearing a piece off. "Have you found what you're looking for?"

"More." I can't help smiling. I know I should keep my distance. I know he's dangerous. Spoiled. Royal. But this room fills me with a deep well of excitement. I have *ideas*. A thousand of them, springing up from somewhere deep. Instead of the glass turrets, I want to restore the old wings that extended in a big U-shape and recreate the original courtyard that existed here a century ago.

But when I open my mouth to tell the Prince, I see his hard eyes. His sharp, angular face. His mistrust. The words die on my lips. I gulp, watching him swallow the last of my dinner roll. "I was going to eat that."

The Prince grins. "Oops." He crosses the room in four long steps, sitting down in a plush armchair that faces me. With his head propped in his hand, he looks at me just like he did in the security lodge when I first woke up.

Like he wants to eat me and kill me and fuck me, and he's just trying to decide which one to choose.

My heart hammers and I do my best to swallow past the mass in my throat. "Can I help you with something?"

"I've organized for the plane to take you to Stirling to see your grandmother as soon as it's safe to fly," he says without preamble. "It might be a couple of days, though. Maybe a week or so. They don't know how long the storm will last."

I gape at him. Jaw on the floor. Catching flies, my mouth is so wide. "You...You did?"

"Is it so surprising that I'd do something nice for you?" His brow arches.

"Um, yes." I frown, leaning back in my chair. I cross my arms. "What's the catch?"

"No catch. You're right. Your grandmother's health isn't a bargaining chip, and I apologize for implying it was before."

I stare at him for a beat. "You apologize? As in, you're sorry?"

"Yes." He dips his chin, eyes still on mine.

"I was right, and you were wrong. That's what you're saying?"

"Careful," he growls, still grinning. "But yes. You were right. I was wrong."

"Did you bump your head? This doesn't sound like you."

The Prince chuckles. It's a warm sound that sends little thrills rushing down my spine. *More.* I want him to laugh all the time. I want him to smile wide and show me he's really human.

But his chuckle fades, and the Prince shakes his head. "You really have no desire to show deference, do you?"

"Is that what you're into? Chicks who *show deference*?" I wiggle my eyebrows when I repeat his words. I'm not even sure what the innuendo means, but the Prince's eyes flash. Heat whips around my core, blazing all the way down through my thighs. My cheeks warm, but I force myself not to look away.

His jaw tenses, but it's the only evidence that he's anything but relaxed. Staring at his fingernails, he shrugs. "I happen to like women who can hold their own."

Eyes flick to me. His meaning is clear.

He likes women like me.

My brain blares on high alert.

No. No, no, no. Danger. Wild, savage beast ahead. Run. Fast. Now.

My body, on the other hand, is currently melting into a sopping wet puddle, enjoying every lick of the Prince's gaze as it travels up and down my body.

He pushes himself off the armchair, taking slow, measured steps toward me. I inhale, fighting to stay alert as his scent floods my nostrils.

God, he smells good. Like *really* good. Good enough that anytime he's near, every sense tunes in to him. Every cell in my body sings with pure delight, wanting to melt into his arms and inhale him forever.

He puts both hands on the arms of my swivel chair, caging me in. His face hovers in front of mine and for a long, long moment, I think he might kiss me.

Those lips on mine. His hot mouth tasting me. Taking me. Owning me.

Yes, I want that. I want it so, so bad. I didn't even know what *want* felt like until I could feel his hot breath on my neck.

The Prince's lips drift over my cheek, close enough that I can feel the soft curve of them. It sends fire tumbling through my veins and I squeeze my thighs together. Everything is needy. Everything wants him.

Then, a whisper. "If you were planning on wearing those lacy black panties for anyone, just make sure it's for me."

He pulls away, a cocky smirk tugging his lips.

My face is on fire. "You looked through my underwear?"

"I happened upon them while I was looking for your identification," the Prince responds, touching his finger to my cheek. His thumb drifts over my chin as he tilts my head up to look at him.

Why does he have to be so big? So strong? So freaking beautiful?

"Good night, Rowan." The Prince says my name in a way that makes everything too sensitive. My clothing prickles against my skin. My underwear rubs every sensitive part of me. A stray piece of hair tickles my neck.

Again. I want it again. *Say my name, please. Whisper it like it means something to you.*

I blink my eyes closed, taking a moment to contain myself.

The Prince drops my chin and walks out without looking back.

9

WOLFE

Chief whines when I bring him to my chambers, but I can't let him go to Rowan's room. Not again.

"Either we both sleep next to her, or neither of us does," I say. My dog tilts his head, then makes a slow circle on the rug in front of the fireplace and plops himself down. I let out a long breath, lifting my eyes to the ceiling. This is bad. I actually meant that. I don't want anyone sleeping next to Rowan —not even my fucking dog.

A knock on the door snaps me out of my mind and I open it to see Eyvar on the other side. He nods. "Sir."

"Everything okay?"

"The girl checks out. Architect. Got the job through official channels and planned this visit with Mrs. Reed."

I open the door wider for Eyvar to step in. Taking a seat on a chair, I motion for him to sit. He stays standing, clasping his hands behind his back.

My bodyguard widens his stance, his big boulder shoulders flexing. "She's made a reputation for herself as an architect. Started her own firm when she was only twenty-seven.

Won multiple awards. Not surprised she got this contract. Has a nice house, a boyfriend—"

"Boyfriend?" I straighten up. Rowan didn't mention a boyfriend.

Eyvar dips his chin. "Gerry Sanders. Been dating him for at least two years, according to our intelligence reports, although he's been seen with other women in the past few months, and it looks like they may have split."

"She didn't tell me she had a boyfriend." My tone is curt. I stare at Chief, who sleeps on the rug, unbothered by this new information.

Eyvar grunts. "I think you should be careful around her."

"Why?"

"This time of year is always...difficult." He clears his throat, staring at a spot on the floor.

Yes, it is. I'm reminded of the most painful moment of my life. When everything changed, and my future didn't seem so bright. When I realized that I'm not a hero. Not some great protector. I'm just a weak man who can't even cry for help when his fiancée collapses in his arms.

Maybe Eyvar's right. My attraction to Rowan is only a distraction from my true feelings. I let out a long sigh, nodding at my bodyguard. "Thanks, Eyvar. Get some rest."

He nods, handing me a file that he put together on Rowan. Then, Eyvar backs out of the room and closes the door behind him. For a large man, Eyvar moves as softly as a cat. I don't hear a single footstep on the hard stone floor as he makes his way back down the hall.

I read the file six times, front to back. I inhale every scrap of information he was able to find on Rowan, but by the time I'm done, I don't know how I feel. Jealous? Intrigued?

Rowan Reed's mother was from Nord. Father is unknown. Moved to Farcliff when she was a baby. This is her first time in Nord that we know of. Has had strong ties with her grandmother, but Mrs. Reed always went down to Farcliff to visit Rowan, and not the other way around.

Tossing the file aside, I climb into bed. For the next few hours, sleep doesn't come. I lie in bed, twisting and turning, and finally push myself to my feet and let out a breath. I give up. Putting on a sweater to guard against the chill, I slip some shoes on and head for the door. Chief sleeps soundly, so I leave the door ajar and walk away. Passing through the lower levels of the palace, I listen to the silence. Everyone's sleeping.

Well, everyone except me.

I like the solitude of the Summer Palace, especially in winter. Is that some sort of sick symbolism? I don't enjoy things the way they're meant to be enjoyed. I prefer the opposite. When the wildflowers are months away from blooming. When the bears are hibernating, and the caribou have migrated to warmer ranges. When the wind howls and the snow blankets the world.

When everything's dead, just like my heart.

My feet carry me to the library. Embers are dying in the fireplace, and the room is starting to cool down. The door to the archives is closed, and I wonder what time Rowan went to bed. Is she sleeping soundly right now? Dreaming of glass houses and turrets and new designs? Maybe even dreaming of me?

Or, is she like me—awake. Troubled. Wondering who to trust.

I step farther into the library, making my way to the comfortable sofas in the deepest part of the room. My eyebrows jump.

Rowan didn't go to bed at all. She's curled up in a little

ball on the sofa, with books strewn across the floor and a thick blanket piled over her sleeping form.

Her lips are parted, eyes closed, breath steady. She looks innocent and angelic, her pale skin against the dark fabric of the sofa. Long hair like spun copper strands splayed out around her head in a halo.

My heart hasn't clenched like this in years. Truth be told, I haven't even *felt* my heart beating since Abby died. I've been living in a dream. But now...something inside me is waking up. Everything is coming into sharp focus—mostly Rowan.

When I take a step toward her, she stirs. Her eyes flutter open and a frown pulls her brows together. Blinking two or three times, she looks at me. "What are you doing here?" Her voice is muffled and sleepy. It tugs at something deep in my chest.

"Came looking for you," I answer truthfully.

She tucks her legs in closer to her body, and I sit down where her feet used to be. The residual heat of her body still warms the cushions, and I lean back, staring at the black sky outside.

"You have a boyfriend," I say.

"Had," she answers, straightening up and combing her delicate fingers through her long hair. "Past tense."

"You broke up?"

"Why do you care?"

"Humor me."

Rowan stares at me for a long moment, then lets out a breath. "He told me it was him or the job. The company I've spent more than half a decade building." With a bitter snort, she shakes her head. "And, well, I'm here, aren't I? But judging by your comments, maybe I shouldn't have chosen work, after all."

"You've been with him for a while," I say. "You gave up that relationship for one contract?"

Rowan's eyes narrow. "You seem to know a lot about me and my relationships."

"Plural?" My eyebrow arches.

Rowan huffs, and I hide a smile. She pushes her hair over her shoulder and stares out the window. The storm is hitting us hard now, throwing its weight against the palace walls. Snow climbs up the bottom of the windows as the wind pushes it against the building.

Finally, Rowan glances at me. "Yes, I chose the contract. I'm an architect, Your Highness. This is my dream. How could I pass up an opportunity to design a royal residence?" She snorts. "Even if it is in the middle of nowhere."

"You don't like it up here."

"Can you blame me?" Rowan sweeps her hand toward the window. The storm rages in response. "This place is about as hospitable as the bottom of the ocean."

"How can you think to redesign this castle if you don't understand the landscape?" There's an edge to my voice. Why do I care? Why do I want her to see the beauty of this place? Why do I want her to like it here?

Rowan swings her eyes to meet mine. She drops her gaze, letting out a long breath. "I'm sorry. You're right. I spent the evening reading about Nord and the history of the Summer Palace. I had no idea about any of it before I started working on the design." She bites her lip. "I should have done more research. Grandma told me stories and I knew the broad strokes of the history, but there's so much I didn't realize."

"My ancestors united dozens of small villages and tribes that lived in this area," I say. "I think what my sister meant, when she said she wanted to retain the historic details of this castle, is that she wants to honor all the people who have come together to create Nord. There's been...unrest in Nord lately. My sister needs unity."

Rowan doesn't understand that. She doesn't understand that changing this palace into a *destination*, as she called it earlier, won't honor the fractured relationships and century-long resentments that have festered within certain groups. She doesn't see this palace as a symbol of the kingdom's harmony.

But as Rowan reaches for a book, flipping to a bookmark, her smile makes me still. She shows me an image of the visitor's cottage how it was when it was first built. A true palace, where court was held and relationships were formed. Nord was born in that cottage, centuries ago.

"I'd like to restore the visitor's cottage, too. I was thinking we could commission artwork from every tribe and village that came together there. We could engage local artists. Celebrate the history of each individual community." Her eyes lift to mine, deep blue hitting me like a lightning bolt to the chest.

Maybe she's not clueless.

I nod. "You're learning."

Rowan gives me a soft smile. "I should have come up here as soon as I got the contract."

"Yes." I hold her gaze. "You should have."

"I'm sorry," she says softly, sucking her bottom lip between her teeth. I stifle a groan. She blinks, taking a deep breath. "I understand your comments about my design. I'm starting over from scratch."

I rest my hand on top of the blanket, feeling her ankle beneath it. Why does it feel so comfortable being here beside her? Why does my heart beat easier when she's near?

Eyvar says I shouldn't get too close to her, but here, in the silence of the night, it's easy to forget his words.

Rowan looks away from me, her cheeks turning pink. "I heard about your fiancée. I'm sorry."

"So am I."

Her gaze finds mine as silence stretches between us. In the darkness of the library, it feels intimate. More intimate than I've felt in a long time.

"Is that why you're here? To get away?"

I stare at the howling storm outside before answering. "The memorials and vigils remind me of everything I lost. October has always been difficult." As I turn my head to look at Rowan, though, my words feel empty. The sting of my emotions has lessened, and my loss doesn't seem so painful anymore.

"I'm sorry," she says again.

"It's not your fault."

"I shouldn't have brought it up."

"It's not a secret." I shrug. My gaze drifts back to watch the storm, but every other sense is tuned into Rowan's frequency. She shifts on the couch, letting out a long sigh. When I swing my gaze to meet hers, though, I see no pity in her eyes. Empathy, yes. Understanding.

But no pity.

It's...refreshing. A lump forms in my throat and I glance away. Pushing myself up to my feet, I glance down at Rowan, who's still curled on the couch. "You should go to your room. It gets cold in here without a fire burning."

Then I walk away, feeling Rowan's wide-eyed stare on my back.

10

ROWAN

I DRAG myself up to my own bed, head reeling from my conversation with the Prince. He's been doing research about me—he knew I had a boyfriend. Did he seem relieved when I said we broke up, or is that just my twisted imagination?

Distrust and dislike come off him in waves, yet he still ends up seeking me out. He was right about one thing, though. My design was all wrong. After just one day reading through old stories of Nord and seeing the way the storm battered the palace, I know my original ideas don't work.

Now that I'm here, I understand the importance of this redesign. Not only for my career. Not for the royal family. For the whole kingdom. Updating this palace needs to represent the kingdom as a whole.

So how did *I* get the job?

I let out a breath, wishing Grandma were here. She'd make me feel at home. She'd remind me I have Nordish blood in my veins, and I belong to this place as much as anyone else. She'd tell me about my mother's childhood, and how she came to work at the palace.

But she's up in a hospital bed, and I'm here, alone.

Needing to navigate my complicated relationship with the Prince and figure out where I went wrong with my design.

Tomorrow. I'll deal with it tomorrow.

But I hear the creak of my hinges and sit up in bed to see a big, furry creature padding toward the bed. Letting out a sigh, I smile. "Hey, Chief."

The dog hops up on the bed and curls up next to me. Finally, I can sleep.

I DON'T SEE the Prince for over a week. The storm rages around us, but I stay warm and fed inside. I spend a lot of time in the archives, inhaling every scrap of information about the palace and the royal family. In the evenings, I return the library, half-hoping the Prince will be there waiting for me.

He isn't.

Disappointment tastes bitter, but I try to push it down. Vikki keeps me company, finding me when her day of work is done and telling me about all the gossip about the castle.

One evening, we sit curled in one of the smaller living rooms, watching a big fire burn in the hearth. "I haven't seen the Prince in days," I say.

Vikki glances at me, sipping a warm mug of tea. "He keeps to himself."

"Will he stay here all winter?"

"I doubt it," Vikki says. "He'll probably to go back to Stirling before the weather gets really bad."

"Oh," I answer, hope flaming in my gut. Why does that excite me? Is it because I've been thinking of staying in Stirling with Grandma until she's healed?

"It makes me sad when he's here," Vikki says, glancing at me. "He's so different now."

"How so?"

"Colder. Doesn't laugh anymore."

"I can't imagine him being very jolly before."

Vikki chuckles, throwing me a glance. "You'd be surprised. When"—she drops her voice, glancing over her shoulder—"when his fiancée was alive, he was really happy. Always had a smile on his face. Wouldn't leave her side."

My shoulders drop as my chest squeezes. I've judged the Prince so harshly. Thought of him as a spoiled, arrogant ass—but what if he's just hurting?

Pinching my lips together, I push my sympathy down. We've all been through shit. We've all lost people we loved and had our lives change as a result. I know I have. Just because the Prince has been through something similar doesn't give him the right to be rude.

But I think of those moments I had alone with him, and I wonder who the Prince really is. Why doesn't he trust me? Why did he seek me out, then leave me alone for over a week? He's hot and cold. Trusting and suspicious. Rude and kind. He's one big contradiction, and I just want to figure him out.

Vikki sits up. "I have an early start tomorrow. They say the storm should clear overnight, so we might get out of this place come morning. Maybe we can go see the visitor's cottage in the afternoon."

"Sounds nice." I smile. "Good night."

Vikki takes my empty mug as well as her own down to the kitchens, and I stay by the fire until the embers glow red and the night is black outside. Then, I peel myself off the couch and make my way upstairs.

If the storm clears, that means I can leave. I can go see Grandma. I have enough information to put together an updated design.

But do I want to go without seeing the Prince at least one more time?

My NEW ITERATION of the palace renovation is coming along nicely, but my eyes are turning square. I've been looking at my screen too much. When I glance out the office window at the clear blue sky outside, I save my work and turn off the computer. I need to get out of here. I've been at the palace two weeks now, all of which have been spent holed up inside waiting for the storm to clear.

Reading my mind, Vikki pokes her head in the office. "Just finished the lunch service. You ready to go see the visitor's cottage?"

I smile. "Thought you'd never ask."

"Come on. I'll show you."

"I, uh." I clear my throat. "I don't have appropriate clothing for that weather." I bite my lip, remembering my unfortunate arrival at the palace. I've been warm and safe inside, but no matter how blue the sky is, I know it's freezing out there.

Vikki's smile beams. "We brought some up to your room earlier. I'll help you get dressed, and then we'll head to the kennels to take the dogs."

"The dogs?"

Vikki laughs, as if my question delights her. "Yeah, the dogs. You've never been dog sledding?"

My eyes widen. "No. We can't take the dogs... Can we?"

"It's either that or a snowmobile, but Mrs. Reed told me I wasn't allowed to take the snowmobiles out anymore. I crashed one last winter and almost killed myself." Vikki laughs again, a melodic sound that lights up her whole face.

As if crashing a snowmobile is funny. As if almost dying is something to laugh at.

But that's Vikki. Completely in her element. At home.

Unlike me. I wish it didn't bother me that I'm such an outsider. I should just treat this as a working holiday. A chance to see a foreign land...

...but my heart clenches, and I know I feel some sort of connection to this place. Deep down, I know I belong here, but I'm still a foreigner. It's hard to reconcile those feelings.

I shoot Vikki a sideways glance. "I almost died when I got here and I'm not quite as jolly about it as you are."

"You'll learn," Vikki replies, hooking her arm into mine. She leads me through a back staircase up to my room, opening the door and leading me to the closet. "Coats, pants, boots. Your grandmother made sure we had it all ready for you." Vikki bites her lip. "I'm sorry about your arrival, Rowan. I don't know if I ever said it. We all feel really terrible about leaving you at the station. It was just with everything with Mrs. Reed and the Prince arriving..."

"I get it." I nod. "No hard feelings. At least I got to meet the Prince." I roll my eyes, and Vikki giggles. She hands me the bright red jacket. It's big and puffy with a fur trim around the hood, and it looks *warm*. Much better than my favorite peacoat.

It's...appropriate. Like it belongs in Nord.

I squeeze the puffy jacket and smile. "My grandmother picked this."

"How did you know?"

"The color. She knows I love red. I've had red jackets since I was a little kid. My first rain jacket was red with matching red boots." I smile, running my fingers over the fur trim. My grandmother might not be here, but her influence is everywhere. I miss her. She'd know how to handle the Prince, and she'd make sure I felt comfortable in the castle. She'd remind everyone that I'm her granddaughter, and I'm a child of Nord—even though I feel like a stranger here.

Vikki helps me get dressed for the cold, handing me a thick hat and gloves before leading me back downstairs. We stop off at the staff quarters to grab her things, and then make our way to the kennels.

Vikki pushes the door open. "Har-vey!" she calls out in a sing-song voice. "Can we take the dogs out? Rowan wants to see the visitor's cottage, and I am *sick* of being inside." She stops dead in her tracks, dropping into a quick curtsy. I bump into her, causing her to stumble. She catches herself, yelping, her face so red it's nearly glowing.

At the other end of the kennels, standing tall with Chief at his feet, is the Prince of Nord himself, looking at home among the dogs. Feral and beastly and every bit a monarch in this wild, unforgiving place.

I square my shoulders. "Your Highness." I give him a quick nod. I'm not sure where we stand. Last I spoke to him, he seemed to be warming up to me. I thought we were making progress.

Then he ignored me for the better part of two weeks.

The Prince smirks, eyes flashing. Ah, so he's back to being arrogant. Lovely. He combs his fingers through his hair, letting his eyes drift down my body and back up again. "Miss Reed." He looks at Vikki, then gives her a wave of dismissal. "I'm taking the dogs out. I'll take Miss Reed to the visitor's cottage."

"That's okay," I say, shaking my head. "We can go later."

Vikki's eyes widen as she gives me a loaded stare. I guess people don't usually talk back to the big bad Wolfe.

The Prince's lips pinch. "I insist."

"Of course, Your Highness." Vikki curtsies and shuffles out the door.

"Vikki," I hiss, staring after her. She arches her brows and shrugs as if to say sorry, but doesn't slow her exit. Traitor.

I lift my eyes to the Prince's, who's still wearing that insolent smirk. He jerks his chin at my new clothing. "I see you've learned from past mistakes."

"Are you disappointed you won't get to undress me this time?"

"Never say never." His eyes flash and heat rips through my core. Damn him and his amber eyes. Damn his sexy smirk. Damn his broad body that looks like it would feel a bit too good pressed on top of mine.

And most of all, damn my own body for betraying me. This man is hot and cold. He tortures me with his presence, then teases me with his absence. He's here to hide away from tough memories and using me as a punching bag for his emotional immaturity.

A coward, and an arrogant one at that. Winning combination.

I definitely shouldn't be feeling hot and bothered by him. My nipples shouldn't be tightening to stiff peaks beneath the multitude of layers I'm wearing. My underwear shouldn't be clinging to the space between my legs, already damp with arousal.

Wrong, wrong, wrong.

I pinch my lips together, taking a step forward. Chief lifts his head, trotting over to nuzzle against me. I kneel down, scratching the fur behind his ears. "At least you'll be coming with us, Chief. I like *your* company."

The dog huffs, nudging my legs with his snout. I glance up to see the Prince staring at the two of us, half-insulted, half-amused.

I stand, nodding. "Well, what are you waiting for? Let's go."

"You didn't get much etiquette training, did you?" His grin widens.

"I think respect is earned, *Your Highness*." I spit the words.

"You might as well call me Wolfe if you're going to say my title like an insult every time."

"That would imply a level of amiability between us, and I don't like to lie." I give him a saccharine smile. "*Your Highness*."

11

WOLFE

WHEN WE STEP OUTSIDE, the dogs are excited. Rowan looks terrified.

I grin. "Don't worry, Miss Reed. You're in safe hands."

"What, yours?" She arches a brow. "Remind me again why I should trust you?"

"I've already saved your life once, haven't I?"

"So you keep reminding me." Her pink lips press together, the cold air making her nose redden. She hikes her shoulders up, stuffing her hands in her pockets. "It's colder than it looks out here."

"It'll only get worse."

"Just another reason for me to get out of Nord as soon as possible," she says under her breath.

I glance at Rowan as something twinges in my chest. She wants to leave? I shake my head and walk toward the sled. Of course she wants to leave. She probably wants to go see her grandmother and get back to somewhere more temperate for the winter.

Why does that make my chest constrict?

I don't want her here. I'm not looking for another woman

to save—that worked fairly horrendously the first time. Not only did I fail to save Abby, I had to watch her die in my arms —and then have videos of the moment played over and over and over again, every year, just to remind myself how useless I was when Abby really needed me.

Why would I want another woman in my life? Especially one as ill-equipped for this place as Rowan.

As Harvey straps up the dogs and checks the gear on the sled, I walk to the front of the pack. Chief sits patiently, his head thrown back as the proud leader. He's always been the one to listen to my commands, and the one that other dogs follow most obediently. The natural alpha.

Chief chose Rowan to sleep with. Lifting my gaze to the sled, I watch as Harvey explains to her how mushing works. He points out the basket of the sled, the front portion that she'll occupy, and where I'll stand behind her. Rowan glances up at me, her face immediately schooling itself to hide her fear.

My lips tug. It's hard not to enjoy her company, all attitude and false toughness.

If I hadn't grown up around dogs, I suppose I'd be nervous too. I walk back toward Rowan and Harvey, jerking my head to the basket. "Hop in."

Rowan takes a deep breath and takes her seat. I nod to Harvey and stand behind her, my legs resting against her back. My hand drifts over her shoulder, squeezing gently. She leans back ever so slightly, and…I like it. That tiny movement that tells me she's comfortable being here. With me.

I stiffen. That's not why she's here. She's here for work, and I'm here to ride out the worst month of the year. I'm here to get away from all the memories I can't erase. I'm here to stay away from women like Rowan, who make me want to save them when I should be pushing them away.

I grab the driving bow, the handle I'll be holding during the ride, and put an inch of space between me and Rowan. She feels the distance and doesn't lean back.

Good.

"*Hike!*" I shout the command, and the dogs start moving. Rowan lets out a sigh, sitting up in the sled to watch the landscape pass us by. I relax, trying to forget that she's here. It's just me and the dogs, and the landscape I've always loved.

But how can I forget that Rowan's here? How can I ignore the warmth of her body so close to my legs? How can I stop myself from glancing at her copper hair, the profile of her face, her soft lips?

"This is incredible," Rowan says, turning her head to smile at me. She looks fucking beautiful in the bright winter sunshine. With pink cheeks and a little red nose from the cold, and her freckles dusted across her face, I'm pretty sure she's part goddess.

"Wait until we really get going." I grin. Her hand grips the edge of the sled, a smile tugging at her lips.

I shouldn't be enjoying spending time with her. I should be keeping my distance. I shouldn't be thinking about protecting her from the cold, or the storm, or hypothermia, or any other threats that might exist up here.

"*Haw!*" I call out, and the dogs turn left. We cross the snow-covered meadow as we make our way toward the visitor's cottage, cold air whipping around us. The dogs run like a dream. Like they've missed this as much as I have. I lead them past the cottage and onto the trail that leads up to the nearest ridge. Rowan doesn't protest. Her head spins around to take in the sights as she takes deep breaths of the clean, fresh air. There's just something about cold, snowy air that tastes better.

When we pass through some snow-covered pine trees

and travel up the wide trail, I slow the dogs down and sink the sled's snow hook into the ground as an anchor. I hop off the sled, extending a hand to Rowan.

"Come on."

"Where are you taking me?"

"If you want to redesign this palace, you need to understand how it sits on this land. You need to understand the arctic. The snow. Everything."

Plus, I want to see her face when she has the world at her feet.

Rowan smiles, pulling herself up and taking my hand. Even with gloves on, it feels right to have her beside me.

No. Stop.

She's nobody. I'm lonely. Abby's memory still stings, and I'm just looking for comfort, that's all. I have an addiction to saving damsels in distress. Rowan came into my life nearly dead, and it hit me right in my weakness, at a time where I was most vulnerable. It's my dumb brain making connections that aren't there.

Right?

Rowan takes a step onto the trail and promptly slips into a tree well—the softer snow at the base of a tree. She yelps and I lunge for her, catching her arm as she falls.

Rowan laughs, accepting my help to climb out from the soft snow. When she stands in front of me, I don't let go. My hands find the bottom hem of her jacket, skating across the clothes she's wearing underneath.

Clear, blue eyes stare up at me, her hands resting on my jacket. "Your Highness," she says softly, and this time, it doesn't sound like an insult. She blinks, her tongue darting out to lick her bottom lip.

I want to kiss her. Desperately. I want to taste those pink lips and feel the warmth of her core. I want to see how her body splits open when she comes, pleasure written all over her face.

It's because I'm weak. Because no matter what, I can't resist a woman who needs my help. Who doesn't know how the world works up here, and who needs a protector. I pull away, jerking my chin past her shoulder. "This way." I stalk ahead, ignoring the thumping of my heart and the heat that wraps around my spine.

Then...*thunk.*

Something hits me in the center of the back. I pause, frowning, and turn to see Rowan leaning over to ball up another handful of snow.

She giggles, winding back to throw a snowball at me. It flies wide to the right, missing my head. Rowan stands tall, staring me down. "Are you just going to stand there, or are you going to defend yourself?"

"Rowan, are you challenging me to a snowball fight?" I don't miss the sharp intake of breath when I say her name. If only she knew how good it tasted on my tongue and how badly I want to growl it softly in her ear.

Instead of answering, Rowan leans over and gathers up another handful of snow. I stand there, letting her throw it at me, arching an eyebrow. It hits my shoulder and explodes in a puff of white.

When I don't move, Rowan's shoulders drop. "You're no fun."

Before she can react, I grab a handful of snow and throw it at her, hitting her square in the neck. She squeals, brushing the snow off as it falls down the back of her jacket. I rush her, circling my arms around her waist and hauling her over my shoulder. Rowan giggles, thumping her gloved fists on my back. I laugh, almost surprised that the sound is coming from me.

I can't help it. She makes me want to laugh. Smile. Have a snowball fight for the first time in decades.

I carry Rowan toward the lookout, tossing her into a big snowbank and watching her sink down, arms and legs sticking up in the air.

She pushes her hat back from her forehead and blows a strand of hair away from her face, grinning. "Fine. You win."

"Of course I win." I smirk. "What did you think was going to happen?"

She extends a hand toward me and I yank her upright, spinning her around to look at the landscape that extends below us. My arms rest on her shoulders and she leans back against me, letting out a long sigh. "Wow."

"Now, do you understand?" I say softly. "You need to appreciate this place if you're going to redesign it properly."

"I hate to say this," Rowan says, turning to glance at me over her shoulder, "but you might actually be right in this one particular situation."

My lips tease into a grin. "You're too sassy for your own good. Have you forgotten that I'm a prince?"

"How could I forget when you keep reminding me every four freaking seconds?" She nudges her shoulder against me. "Check your ego and maybe you'll get more respect from me."

Rowan steps away from me and looks back, arching a brow.

Heat winds through my core, and I know I'm in trouble.

Rowan doesn't need to be saved. Doesn't need to be protected. She's not some damsel in distress who needs me to swoop in and be her champion. Rowan is stronger than that —and it makes me want her even more.

12

ROWAN

DOG SLEDDING IS something I never knew was missing from my life. It's exhilarating and peaceful. It's quiet, fast, and makes me feel an odd sort of power. There's nothing but the soft clinking of the harnesses and guidelines, the breathing of the dogs, the scraping of the sled along the white snow.

There's no motor. No smell of gasoline. No artificial warmth and comfortable leather seats. Just me, the Prince, the dogs, and the quiet natural beauty that surrounds us.

I can't believe I thought this place was harsh and unforgiving. When I first arrived at the train station, I hated Nord. I hated the cold. I hated the fact that I was alone and afraid. I hated that no matter what my heritage says, I'm not from here.

Now?

I see past the cold to the beauty beyond. Every minute that passes, I watch as the Prince relaxes, unwinds, and shows me more of himself.

As we ride toward the visitor's cottage, I glance back at him and see him smiling. Truly smiling. Not a mocking smirk, or a triumphant grin. Just a soft tug of his lips as he watches the dogs run ahead of us.

My heart squeezes—shit. That's bad. This isn't some heady desire winding its way through my core. This is more.

Last week, I thought he was the biggest asshole to ever walk this earth, and now I think I might *like* him? Unacceptable. Wrong on so many levels.

The only way this can end is in disaster.

He's royalty, for one. People open doors for him wherever he goes, moving up and down so much to bow and curtsy they probably get seasick. He's lived in luxury since he was born.

And me?

Mom struggled with three jobs and died in poverty, saddled with debt with a brave smile on her face. I watched her work herself to the bone, slowly being worn down by life's constant assault. Putting me first all the time and protesting when I tried to sacrifice for her, for once. No one curtsied for her. No one bowed for me or called me *Your Highness*. I had to work from the time I was fourteen until now. I'm under no illusion as to how difficult life really is.

The Prince and I come from different worlds. Even if we did have some connection, it would never work.

My head is a mess.

I'm not here for him. I'm here for work.

Work is what I do best. It's my anchor in a stormy world. It's the only thing that gave me purpose after my mother died. Work is the only thing that gave me the opportunity to have true independence. To stand on my own and know I'm a burden to no one. It's everything to me.

So why do I feel like it doesn't even matter right now?

We arrive at the visitor's cottage and the Prince tosses me a set of keys.

"I need to take care of the dogs. You go inside." The Prince goes around the side of the building, where I see another door leading to kennels.

I turn away from him and head for the door. When I step inside and out of the cold, I pull my gloves off and let out a long breath. My gaze travels up to the ceiling to see the soot stains from centuries ago. I take in the old room, a big, rectangular hall with a small dais at the other end. Probably where a throne once sat.

History is woven into these walls. I can feel it. The old stones have witnessed centuries. Kings and queens and normal people who lived in this land long before us. And...I didn't even know this place *existed*. My original design didn't take it into account at all, but I can't ignore it now. This place needs to be preserved. Restored. Celebrated for what it is.

This is the birthplace of Nord, and it's as important to the history of this kingdom as the Summer Palace.

I take off my jacket and throw it over a hook on the wall, then pull my hat off and comb my fingers through my hair.

The door opens behind me and a cold blast of air follows. The Prince stomps his feet, blowing a breath into his hands. He brushes past me and moves to the big fireplace on the side wall, starting a blaze within moments.

Maybe not a coddled, arrogant prince, after all. Why do I find it sexy that he knows how to start a fire?

The firelight casts shadows and light across his angular features, and I find myself walking toward him. He's crouched near the fireplace, and when I approach, he turns his head to look at me. My hand drifts over his strong jaw, his stubble prickling at my fingertips.

The Prince lets out a low groan, closing his eyes as he tilts his head toward me. "Rowan," he says softly, and oh, I want him to keep saying my name like that. His voice is gruff and raspy, and it makes every part of me tingle in anticipation. He says my name like it tastes good on his tongue. Like he wants to taste more of me. When the Prince stands, I don't step back. His hands drift up my sides, brushing the fabric of my sweater.

"You have such beautiful eyes," I whisper, immediately blushing. "I've never seen any that color before."

"As soon as I opened my eyes, my mother knew she would call me Wolfe. Or so the story goes," he says, a sad smile ghosting over his lips. Those beautiful lips. Full. Soft. So perfectly kissable.

We're so alone here. Isolated. Nothing but the fire to keep us company. Would it be so very wrong to kiss the Prince? To feels those lips on mine and enjoy the touch of his broad, strong hands? Would I regret it tomorrow if I enjoyed his eyes drinking me in? *All* of me?

As the fire crackles beside us, it doesn't feel wrong. It feels like the only right thing that has ever happened. Every hour I've spent building up my architecture firm has led me right here, to this moment. I tilt my head toward him, parting my lips. Asking for a kiss. Wanting him to take it. To take *me*.

But the Prince drops his chin and backs away, letting his hands fall away from my sides.

Disappointment crashes into me, closely followed by embarrassment. Silly girl. Of course the Prince doesn't want to kiss me. Who am I, anyway? A young architect who naively thought she designed a beautiful palace when she didn't understand the first thing about this kingdom. Why would he want to kiss me?

Wind rattles against the door, and the Prince walks to a window. His brow furrows. "Storm's coming in."

"Another one? Should we go back?"

He shakes his head. "It's too late. The storms come in quick over the mountains, and it could be here within minutes. We could get lost and not make it back. It's not worth the risk. We'll wait it out."

"Here?" I ask. "Alone?" I wish my voice didn't tremble so much.

The Prince swings those amber eyes toward me, tugging his jacket's zipper down. "Is that a problem?"

"I..." I clear my throat. "No. Of course not."

Instead of answering, the Prince turns his back to me and tosses his jacket on a hook. I watch him strip off his scarf and hat, kick off his shoes, and readjust his other layers of clothing with a sort of sick fascination. He unbuttons his next layer, folding the sweater neatly and laying it on a bench by the door.

What if he...didn't stop? Just kept undressing until we were alone here, naked, cut off from the world?

Blinking, I turn away.

What. Is. Wrong. With. Me.

I need to get a grip. Walking to the opposite end of the cottage, I start studying the walls. The artwork. The rugs. The intricate tile work on the dais, and the way the floor is brighter in a patch in the center where a throne once sat.

I look anywhere but at the Prince.

When I finally gather my courage and look back, he's sitting in front of the fire, watching the flames. Lost in his own thoughts.

Definitely not lusting after me, so I can get that little fantasy right out of my head.

Taking a deep breath, I walk back to him and take a seat on the opposite armchair. He lifts his gaze to me, darkness dancing in his eyes. My chest constricts.

"Storm sounds bad," I say. *Good choice, Rowan. The weather. Stick to that topic. Definitely don't mention how much you want to lick his chest.*

The Prince grunts. He leans back, his long limbs stretching toward the fireplace as he lounges in his chair. My eyes snag on every inch of exposed skin. A little strip at his ankle. A tiny triangle at his waist. His rolled-up sleeves revealing muscular forearms.

I turn to stare at the fire. It's safer.

"You can look, you know. I don't mind." The Prince flashes a grin at me, and my whole head bursts into flame.

I gulp. "Are you always this insufferable?"

"Now, now, Rowan, play nice. We're stuck in here together." The Prince's eyes glimmer. My core ignites. Damn him and his stupid, sexy eyes, reminding me of how isolated we are in this little cottage.

"Your Highness—"

"Call me Wolfe," he says, holding my gaze. "Please. At least for tonight."

My breath catches. What else will we do, just for tonight?

I turn back to the fire, sucking in a deep breath. It does nothing to calm me. "Wolfe," I start, liking the way his name sounds. The Prince lets out a low breath. I don't have the courage to look at him. Instead, I stare at the fire. "You were right about my design. It wasn't right for this place. It didn't reflect the history or the people who have come before."

When I find the nerve to glance at the Prince, a smile tugs at the corner of his lips. For once, it's not mocking. He dips his chin. "I'm glad to hear it."

"I wanted to say thank you." I pause. "For letting me know I was on the wrong track."

"Anytime, darling." His grin turns wolfish, and I grimace.

"Do you always have to be such an arrogant asshole?"

"Tends to spice things up a bit, no?"

"Tends to make you look like a jerk," I reply, rolling my eyes. "There are better ways to spice things up."

"Enlighten me." His voice drops, sending a thrill coursing through my veins. A flush creeps up my neck, but I refuse to meet his gaze. I stare at the dancing flames, ignoring the innuendo.

The Prince gets up, and I steal a glance his way. He moves to a small bar by the wall, fixing two glasses of dark alcohol. He stalks toward me, handing me one of the crystal tumblers.

"Scotch," he explains.

I wrap my fingers around the cool glass and nod in thanks, then return to stare at the fire.

The Prince takes his seat, then shifts in his chair. "Rowan," he says in a low growl. "Look at me."

Damn him and his irresistible commands. I drag my eyes to meet his, ready for the assault of his gaze—but instead of hard, mocking eyes, I see softness.

"October has been the hardest month of each of the past four years. I know I'm not always a nice person," he starts, his mouth staying open for a moment as if he's going to speak. I stare at him, seeing a crack in his hard exterior. His shoulders round and for a moment, his face is open. He's thinking about his fiancée. I know it, and damn it, I'm jealous of a dead woman.

I'm a freaking *mess*.

Letting out a sigh, I shake my head. "I'm sorry."

"For what?" Hardness returns to his gaze, but I try to ignore it. He lifts the glass to his lips, taking a sip.

I shake my head. "About your fiancée. For everything you lost. I'm sorry you have to relive it every year."

He sucks in a long breath, raking his eyes down my body

and back up again. "This October hasn't been so bad." He shifts in his seat and for just a moment, I see him as a real person. A man who's been hurt. Who thinks he's failed.

Turning to stare at the fire, we listen to it crackle for a few moments. Then the Prince speaks. "We were going to an event together," he says. "There was a crush of reporters and paparazzi outside the venue, as usual. They went everywhere Abby went. She was everything they wanted in a new princess, and the media was relentless. So, she decided to get out and walk into the crowd to greet some young fans who had come to see her. I had no choice but to agree." His eyes get a faraway look in them as he sips his drink, then continues. "She collapsed. Right there on the sidewalk beside me. I've seen the videos and photos of those moments, but I don't actually remember any of it." The Prince's face contorts. "I just sat there, cradling her body. I didn't do CPR. Didn't do anything. I just held her as she died. I froze."

"Wolfe..." I whisper, afraid to talk.

"She had a fatal arrhythmia. Her heart just...malfunctioned. They say there's nothing anyone could have done, but..." He shrugs, then finishes his drink in one gulp. "Sometimes I think that's a lie. There had to be *something* I could have done, you know?" I watch him stand up to pour himself another drink, then turn around and tilt his head. "What about you?"

I glance at him, questioning. My throat is tight as I try to swallow, feeling the weight of his grief on my shoulders.

He jerks his chin at me. "Have you ever lost someone you loved?"

Usually, I'd shut this conversation down. I'd ignore any mention of death and grief, and I'd steer the conversation toward safer topics. Work. The weather. Architecture. Right now, though, my shoulders relax, and I find myself dipping my chin down. "My mother," I reply. The Prince's gaze meets mine, and all of a sudden, I want to tell him everything.

13

———

WOLFE

I CAME to the Summer Palace to get away from the people I can't protect. I came here to stop playing the hero when all I ever do is fail. I wanted to run away from the images of those moments, when my true weakness was on full display for the kingdom to witness.

But Rowan dropped into my lap, and all I want to do is shelter her from the storm that rages outside. As I watch her fidget in her seat, my heart thumps. I love the faint blush that stains her cheeks, and the way her eyes flash when she looks at me.

She knows pain. I can see it in the tension in her jaw and the way her eyes tighten when she mentions her mother.

"What happened?" I ask, needing her to tell me. Needing some sort of connection that goes deeper than fealty.

She leans back in the armchair, letting out a long breath. "My mother brought me to Farcliff when I was a baby, and you can probably imagine how difficult it was for a single mother with an infant child to get by." She glances at me, tilting her head. "Well, maybe you can't."

"I'm not so out of touch I don't know how hard life can be, Rowan."

"Have you ever gone to sleep instead of eating because you had no food?"

I stare at her, not answering.

Rowan sighs, glancing at the fire again. "I didn't mean to snap. It's just..." She waves a hand at the cottage. "Even somewhere as nice as this, we didn't have it. Mom worked three jobs. Did everything she could to make sure I had a good life. She took no time for herself and I'm pretty sure she never even went on a date after my father."

"Who was he?" I ask. "Your dad."

"Fuck knows," Rowan spits. "The only thing I know for sure is he didn't want me." She smiles bitterly, shaking her head. "From what I can gather, my mom was the other woman. He had a whole other family that was more important to him than we were. Mom didn't know about it until she went down to Farcliff and found him, living with his perfect wife and perfect kids. I was a couple months old."

We're silent for a while. The bitterness in Rowan's voice hits me right in the middle of the chest. Yes, I enjoy making her angry. I enjoy seeing her cheeks turn pink when I frustrate her. But this is different. She understands what it means to suffer for a long time. Years. Decades.

Finally, I speak. "How'd she die?"

Rowan swings her eyes to me. "My mom?"

I nod.

"Cancer." Rowan pinches her lips together. "She was a smoker. Had a lump in her neck. I finally convinced her to go get it checked out after three fucking years. When they opened her up to remove it, she was just...riddled with it. The cancer had spread everywhere. She died within six weeks of the operation."

I exhale slowly. "I'm sorry."

"Me too." Rowan lets out a bitter snort. "I still feel like it's my fault, you know? She worked to pay for me, for my architecture degree, for everything we had. She ignored her own health to take care of me when no one else would."

"Scotch and isolation," I reply.

She swings her eyes to me. "What?"

"That's how I dealt with grief." I lift my glass. "Still do. You?"

"Work," she replies, pinching her lips into a smile. "I was twenty-three when she died. The day after the funeral, I went to work. Threw myself into it as if nothing else existed. Started my own business four years later. I blinked, and five more years had passed. I was sitting in my own office with my name on the door and a wall full of awards behind me, reading the email that awarded me the contract to redesign the Summer Palace. That was a year ago, and it happened to be the anniversary of her death."

There's a heaviness in my chest. Rowan stares into the fire, tension rippling through her body. And I get it. I feel her pain the same way I feel my own. I understand the feeling of being in a tailspin, of latching onto anything that will make you feel any kind of normal.

Rowan glances at me, letting out a dry snort. "I've never spoken of this to anyone."

"Not even your boyfriend?"

"Ex-boyfriend," she corrects. "And no. Our relationship...I don't think I ever really let him in."

"You broke up with him when you took on this project," I say, remembering the file of information on her.

"He gave me an ultimatum, and I chose," she replies, shrugging.

"Why wouldn't he want you to come here?"

Rowan chuckles, shaking her head. "He would've preferred if I stayed at home and popped out a couple of kids for him."

My brows twitch. I nod, doing my best to keep my face steady. "Ah. You don't want kids."

"I don't *not* want kids," Rowan says. "I just...I want other things, too. I want to come here and see the Summer Palace in person. I want to have my name attached to it. I want to be a leader in my field."

"You want the glory."

Rowan sucks in a breath. "I don't want to die alone in a shitty little apartment with cancer spreading through every organ because I didn't have the time or opportunity to actually take care of myself. I don't want someone else to be saddled with the responsibility of feeding me and clothing me and making sure I have what I need."

"I'm not sure being alone is the best way to accomplish that." I arch an eyebrow, sipping my drink.

Rowan stares at me and finally huffs out a laugh. "And I'm not sure running away every October is the best way to honor your fiancée's memory."

"It's survival."

"Exactly," she replies, staring into my eyes. The air grows thick around us, and on some primal level, we understand each other. Being alone here, with her, as the storm batters the walls of the cottage, I wonder if she's here for a reason. If she was sent here by some higher power.

"Why did you take this project?" I ask in a low voice.

"How could I refuse it?" She blinks, then lets out a sigh. "Maybe I just wanted to get away."

"From your ex?"

"From my *life*." Rowan's eyes blaze, and something stirs in my core.

How many times have I wanted to get away from my life? From my grief? From everything that makes me a prince?

Rowan gulps. Her eyes shift back to the fire, and we sit in silence for a while. Nordish blood flows in her veins, but I still don't feel like she belongs to this place. She says she understands why her design was wrong—but does she truly get it? It won't fulfill her ambitions as an architect if she tries to bend this landscape to her will.

The landscape doesn't care. The arctic bends to no one.

Just look at her first few hours here. Near death.

"I want to do something more with my life than just be someone's wife," Rowan says softly. "Gerry was fine. He'll be a good partner to a woman one day, but it's not me. I need something...more. I need to see the world. Explore my career. Put my ideas on paper and see them come to life. I need to do something so that when I die, I don't feel like I've wasted my life or been a burden to the people I'm supposed to help."

"What if you never find what you're looking for?"

Rowan blinks, then shrugs. "Then I guess I'm destined to wander until I die."

I've never met anyone like Rowan before. She's giving up safety. Security. A stable relationship. For what? To explore the unknown? To carve her own path?

Abby wasn't like that. She had very few ambitions of her own and was content to follow me wherever I went. I thought it was because I'm a prince, and she had no noble blood, but when I stare at Rowan, I know I'm wrong. Abby didn't have the fire, the will for life that Rowan has. She didn't have the ambition or the independence to be on her own.

Rowan leans forward, resting her elbows on her knees as she stretches the graceful column of her neck from side to side. Her eyes have their own fire burning, and she's propelled through life by some force I don't understand. She doesn't need a protector. She doesn't need me—or any man—to save her from the dangers outside.

Well—unless she decides to go for a walk in sub-zero temperatures with nothing but a thin jacket on.

There's a deep well of strength in her that sparks something inside me. It makes me pause. Pushing myself up to stand, I jerk my head toward the bar trolley. "Another drink?"

Rowan nods. "Yes, please." She stands with me and meets me at the trolley, extending her glass toward me.

When I top up Rowan's drink, her eyes flick up to mine. Warmth wraps around my chest and snakes lower through my stomach. This girl will be the end of me.

She's not afraid of me. Not intimidated. She looks me straight in the eye—and I like it. She's the first person to treat me like a man and not a prince. The first person to listen to me talk about Abby and *understand* the pain, not just pity me for it.

I take a sip of my drink as I watch her over the rim of my glass.

Rowan meets my gaze and sticks out her tongue. "Do I have something on my face?" she asks, popping a brow.

"What?"

"Didn't anyone ever tell you it's rude to stare?" Pause. "*Your Highness.*"

"Can you blame me?" I say, my voice dropping lower than I intended.

Rowan blinks, biting her lip. Damn. I put my glass down and stand up, extending a hand toward her. She stares at it suspiciously, letting her gaze crawl back up to mine.

"What are you doing?"

"Take my hand, Rowan."

"Why?"

"I want to show you something."

"What is it?"

"Take my hand and find out."

"You haven't exactly proven yourself trustworthy so far, Your Highness."

I try to hide my grin. "Rowan, call me Wolfe. If you call me Highness one more time, I'll—"

"What?" She arches a brow. Cheeky girl. "What are you going to do?"

Lifting my outstretched hand to her shoulder and letting my fingers curl around the nape of her neck, I brush my thumb over her cheek. "I'll make you regret it," I growl.

Rowan's breath trembles through parted lips as she blinks in rapid succession. Then, as if in a trance, she puts her tumbler down and takes a step toward me.

"Okay. What do you want to show me?"

I erase the distance between us, letting my chest brush against hers. There it is—her soft, hesitant breath. Yielding to me. Rowan lifts her eyes up to mine, staring at me through thick lashes. I let my fingers drift down the side of her body, resting them on her hip.

"Do you get nervous when I'm close to you?" I ask, my voice barely above a whisper.

"No," Rowan says, her voice quivering ever so slightly.

"Liar." My fingers slide around to her back, pulling her body tight to mine. "I can feel your pulse hammering."

"Doesn't mean I'm nervous."

"What are you then?"

A blush stains Rowan's cheeks as she struggles to swallow. Closing her eyes, she shakes her head. "Nothing. I'm just... It's nothing." Rowan's palm lifts up to press against my chest, and she flicks her eyes up to mine. "Your heart is hammering, too."

"You make *me* nervous." I grin.

"Bullshit." Her fingers slide higher, teasing the edge of my neck.

My eyes drop to her lips, tracing every full curve as I imagine how she would taste. We're frozen against each other. I can feel her pulse thumping. I can see the desire blooming across her face. Her pupils dilating. Lips dropping open.

She wants this as badly as I do. We're alone here. No servants. No staff. No media.

Just Rowan and me.

Would it be so bad to act on a few impure desires? To finally taste those lips and see if she's still insolent when I'm inside her?

"Your Highness," Rowan whispers.

My grip on her waist tightens, pulling her close. "What did I say about using my title?" I roll my hips against her, loving the way she gasps when she feels my hardness.

Yes, I'm hard as rock.

Yes, it's for her.

Yes, I'm struggling to think of even one reason why we shouldn't do this.

"We shouldn't do this," Rowan whispers, teasing my jaw with her fingertips.

"Do what?" I lean down, letting my lips hover just an inch from hers.

Rowan smiles, shaking her head. She's so sweet when she's like this. Pliable. When her tongue isn't sharp and her smiles are easy. I want more. "Kiss, Wolfe. We shouldn't kiss."

I nearly groan when she says my name. I thought I enjoyed the sass of her using my title. I thought I liked that she spat it at me like an insult.

My name sounds so much better.

"Why not, princess?"

"I'm not a princess."

"And you didn't answer the question."

"Because we'd regret it." Her thumb brushes my chin, just under the curve of my lip.

"I wouldn't." I growl, closing my eyes. How can her touch feel so good?

"I would." Her voice is so soft, I barely catch it. Pulling away, I look into her ocean-blue eyes. She gives me a sad smile, shaking her head.

I frown, thinking about the past two weeks. Has there been a day, an hour, where I haven't thought of Rowan? Has there been a night I haven't snuck into the library to see if I'd find her sleeping? Has there been any other woman on my mind, or any question about what I want to do to her?

"Why would you regret it?"

"You're a prince."

"I'm a man."

"I'm afraid."

"Of me?" I frown.

Rowan smiles, her fingers still teasing my jaw. My neck. Toying with the edges of my hair. She shakes her head. "Of how quickly I'll fall for you."

"You think I'm an asshole."

"I make a lot of bad decisions."

"So why not make one more?"

Rowan pulls away, shaking her head. "You're dangerous, Wolfe."

I drop my hand from her waist and grin, catching her hand. "Come on. I'll show you something you'll like."

14

ROWAN

I can't blame the Scotch whisky for what's going on in my body—this goes much deeper than a shot and a half of alcohol. I'm burning up. I follow the Prince out of the main room and through a doorway, stealing glances at his broad frame. Every step he takes reminds me of the power inside him. Every movement, so controlled and restrained, makes me want to melt into his arms.

...but I said no.

I pushed him away and told him I didn't want to take it any further.

That's the right thing to do...right? Sleeping with him would be fun tonight, maybe, but I'd regret it tomorrow. This is work, after all. He's royalty.

I'm only a contractor here to do a job. I'll be gone as soon as the storm clears.

So why does this taste a lot like regret?

My heart beats erratically, bouncing against my chest as I struggle to regain control over myself. Every stitch of clothing feels too tight. The cottage feels smaller somehow, as if all the heat of my desire is pouring into the air and stifling me.

Wolfe pushes a door open and has to bend his head to step through. We walk into a dim space, and the Prince hits a switch. Lights fizzle and pop as they turn on, bathing the room in a soft, yellow glow.

We're in a studio.

Blank canvasses lean against the far wall beside a huge shelf full of art supplies. A stack of easels is propped against the side wall, covered in a thick layer of dust.

But my eyes drift to the left, where a blank wall has been covered with dozens of paintings. Big and small, they cover the space. I drift over to them, eyes widening.

"Is this...?" I peer at the first painting, recognizing some of the sketches from the archives, where they'd been reproduced in history books.

"My great-great-grandfather painted that. I might have missed a *great* in there." The Prince grins. "He lived here full-time."

"That's what the palace used to look like?"

"He helped design it. Showed this painting to the architects and builders, and they made it happen."

My jaw hangs open as I stare at him. "This is the original painting?"

Dipping his chin down, he lets his hand sweep across my lower back. His touch feels so good, I find myself leaning into it. We take a step over, staring at the next set of paintings. A view from the castle out to the meadows in full bloom. A brown bear is in the foreground with a cub.

I shake my head. "Gorgeous."

"When it was first built, the palace served as a place to hold court, too. There were offices and community events here. It was the real seat of power in the kingdom."

"And that changed when Stirling became the capital?"

"Sometime in the last hundred years, the Summer Palace

became a vacation home for the royal family. The gates were made taller, and it was closed off from the public, except for approved tours during periods my family isn't here."

"You don't agree with that?"

Wolfe lets out a sigh, pinching his lips together. "I think we have an opportunity to give this place back to the people. Show the people that the royal family remembers where we came from."

I nod, my eyes lingering on the Prince. He stares at the centuries-old paintings, a wistful look in his eyes. I wonder, not for the first time, who this man really is. Is he the cold, rude man I first thought? Or is he a man who's seen trauma, death, grief—and wants to give something back?

"What's your vision for the Summer Palace?" I ask.

The Prince flashes a smile at me. "You're the architect."

"You're the client. You've already shot down my first design. I need direction."

"We can't spend millions making a beautiful palace that will look good on postcards," the Prince says after a pause. "This has to mean something more."

"An homage to Nord's birthplace."

"You've been doing research," he says.

I grin. "You gave me a serious dressing-down when I first got here about not understanding the place." I flush, shaking my head at my choice of words. "I mean a reprimand."

Just a slip of the tongue. It doesn't mean anything.

Right?

The Prince pounces, grinning. "I gave you a dressing-down, too. And I'd do it again."

I shove my shoulder against him, turning my back to him to hide my blush. "I don't believe you were the one to undress me. There was a doctor and a bodyguard there. One of them would have done it."

The Prince leans in so his breath tickles the edge of my ear. "You have a mole just above your belly button."

My eyes widen as I stare straight ahead. "You…"

"Right about here," he says, letting his fingers drift over my stomach. Heat pools beneath his palm as my head spins. Wolfe chuckles, leaning into me. His smell is everywhere. Woodsy and spicy and so deliciously male. I inhale him, not wanting to step away. His chest is so broad against my back.

Why did I refuse him earlier, again? Why wouldn't I tilt my chin up and let him kiss me?

"I'm attracted to you," I say, staring at the wall.

"I know."

Rolling my eyes, I turn my head and glance up at him. "*But,*" I start. "I don't think acting on it is a good idea."

"You said that."

"You disagree?"

"Completely."

I suck my bottom lip between my teeth, watching Wolfe's eyes darken. Amber pools of desire stare at me, tempting. Asking. Promising something good. His hand slides from my stomach down lower, resting just above my mound.

Yes, I want this. I want his hand to move lower still. To touch me. Feel how wet he makes me. Let me come apart in his arms before I have to leave this place again.

Would it really be that bad if I gave in to temptation?

I turn to face the Prince, letting my hands slide up his chest. Every bump of muscle sends shivers tumbling down my veins. His body is insane. My hands wrap around the nape of his neck, twisting into the dark locks of hair that curl at the ends. His hair feels silky as my head spins.

"If we sleep together, it means nothing," I say.

The Prince's lips tug into a wicked grin. "Are you telling me, or yourself?"

"You," I say, sounding more confident than I feel. "If we act on this...whatever this is between us, it has to stay here."

"Anything you want, princess. So long as I get to have you."

"You have to stop calling me princess."

His hand sweeps over my jaw, tilting my face up to stare at his. With a flash of his eyes, he grins at me. "But that's what you are. My princess."

Oh, those words. Treacherous, beautiful words. Silly words that make my heart thump and my panties soak through.

Why do I care if he calls me his? Why does it stoke my fire if he tells me I belong to him?

The only way this works is if I walk away and there are truly no strings attached. One night of fun. One night of Wolfe. One night to feel like a princess in her prince's arms.

As if he reads my mind, Wolfe tilts my head up and crushes his lips to mine. He kisses me breathless. Crashes into me, so I can feel the power coiled within him. His arms wrap around me and hold me to his strong chest, trapping me against him.

Not that I'd want to be anywhere else. My fingers twist in his hair. Tugging. Pulling. Eliciting delicious little groans from him that do nothing but make me burn hotter.

When his tongue slides between my lips, I know I'm done. He tastes like heaven and hell, all wrapped in one. Like good and evil in a tug of war with my heart. He tastes like I might regret this later when I'm nursing my broken heart—but it's too sweet to pull away. When he whispers my name against my lips, I melt. His fingers sink into my flesh, clawing at my clothing and tugging it free so he can feel my skin.

My body is in overdrive. My veins are full of molten fire. I moan into his mouth, kissing him harder as his hands sweep over my back.

I'm in trouble. I'm in too deep. I'm definitely going to regret this later.

15

___

ROWAN

WHAT IS REGRET, really?

Feeling sad or disappointed about something we've done in the past? About something we didn't do? Feeling the tug of *what if?*

So, as the Prince lets out a soft moan, his lips brushing against mine, I have to wonder.

What would I regret more—if I stopped, or kept going?

Wolfe's hands sweep up my sides, his palms leaving goose bumps in their wake. His touch feels too good. My head spins. Every sense is wrapped up in him.

His smell everywhere, urging my heartbeat faster. The sight of his body straining against the fabric of his clothes. The touch of his fingers against my skin. The sound of those little grunts and moans and groans that slips through his lips when he kisses me.

But oh, the taste of him. That's what does me in. My kisses drift down his neck and I let my tongue slide out to touch his skin. Hard and smooth and warm and *mine.*

I want more. I claw at him, tearing at his shirt until he pulls it off and tosses it aside. With a grunt, the Prince picks

114

me up so I wrap my legs around his waist. The heat and hardness of his erection presses against my center, and I wish we weren't wearing so many clothes.

I need him inside me. Need him on top of me. Underneath me. Everywhere.

The Prince starts walking, kicking the studio door open and stepping through. My hands tease through his thick, black hair as my lips find his. His stubble scratches my skin, and I wonder how good it would feel if he brushed it against the inside of my thigh. If he teased the very center of me with that deliciously bad tongue of his. He carries me down a narrow hallway and through another door, finally setting me down.

"You've been driving me wild since the moment I saw you lying in the snow," the Prince says. His eyes are dark, burning with hot fire. He nudges his nose against mine, his hands splayed across my lower back. When he slips the tips of his fingers beneath the waistband of my pants, I let out a low whimper.

More. I want more.

"Wolfe..." I tilt my head back as his lips brush my neck, teasing the sensitive skin all the way up to my jaw.

With a low growl, the Prince pulls away. "I love the way you say my name."

I meet his gaze, my vision hazy with lust. "How do I say it?"

"Like you need me."

"Easy, tiger." I grin. "You're tipping into *arrogant asshole* territory again."

"That's why you're here, isn't it?" With a grin, the Prince pulls me close. He rolls his hips toward me, letting me feel the length of him. I sigh, my eyes fluttering closed.

When he gently pushes me away, I let out a low whimper.

"On the bed," the Prince commands. He spins me around and marches me to the side of the four-poster bed, watching as I climb on top the plush mattress. I lie back while he flicks the lamp on.

"I want to see your face when you come," he says, flashing a grin at me. "See if it looks like what I've imagined."

"You're an ass," I say, biting the tip of my finger. "It's a good thing you've got that body to make up for it."

The Prince grunts, scooping his hand underneath me to flip me over. He lays a smack across my ass as I yelp, laughing.

"You deserve a good spanking for speaking to your liege like that," Wolfe says.

Glancing over my shoulder, I see his eyes darken. I turn around again, biting my lip. "Technically, I'm not from here, so you're not my—"

In one lightning-fast motion, the Prince tugs my pants down to mid-thigh, throws me onto my stomach, and lays another smack across my ass. I squeal, breathless, my face mashing into the pillow as stinging pain flashes across my bare skin.

And...wow. Another sharp crack of his palm against my skin.

I like it.

Again.

"You'll learn the proper way to speak to me," he growls, laying his palm across my ass once more.

Yes. My yelps turn to moans and my back arches as I push my ass toward him. Dirty, dirty, dirty. I don't even care. My pants are locking my thighs together and the Prince is spanking me like I've been bad, and oh, it feels good. Pleasure rips through my core as his hand slides over my stinging skin, softly, softly.

When I glance over my shoulder, Wolfe meets my gaze

with a wicked grin on his lips. Sliding his hands between my legs, he lets out a soft groan. "You're wet."

I mumble something unintelligible in response. His hand is warm as it slides through my slick folds, teasing every sensitive inch of flesh. As I lie on my stomach, arching my back toward him, my cheeks burn.

This isn't what I expected to happen when we came here, but I don't want it to stop. The Prince teases my opening, sliding a finger inside me as I moan.

He feels *good*. His other hand slides over my bare skin, caressing the red imprints left by his hand. Teasing the edges of my lower lips. Spreading me wider and sending more fire racing through my veins.

When he slides his finger out of me, I let out a whine. He chuckles, tugging my pants all the way down my legs.

"Turn around," he commands.

I comply. Lying on my back, I watch him kneel between my legs, his eyes hanging low as I wiggle toward him. I reach for his waistband, but he catches my hand.

"Stay there," he says. Gruff. Commanding. He takes my wrist, pinning it above my head. With his other hand, he skates his palm over my stomach and tugs my shirt up and off. He unclasps my bra and tosses it aside, feasting his eyes on my naked body.

I love the way he looks at me. How he licks his lips and lets out a soft growl. How his fingers leave the barest whisper of a touch over my sensitive skin, teasing the edge of my breast, circling my nipples, drifting all the way down to my heated core.

"You have a beautiful body," the Prince says. He grips my thighs with his hands, pushing them wider. He lets out a soft groan as he stares at me, completely open for him.

"Touch yourself." His voice is low and confident, leaving no room for hesitation.

Am I weak for wanting to listen? Is it wrong that I want to watch his face as I touch myself? I want to do whatever he tells me.

I let my hand drift down my abdomen, pausing just above my mound. The Prince inhales sharply as my fingertips tease my slit, barely brushing the edge of my clit. I tremble.

This feels different with him watching. It's not like touching myself, alone under the covers. It's not like squeezing my eyes shut with a vibrator between my legs.

This is something more.

I bite my lip as my fingers circle my clit, the Prince's palms making slow circles over my thighs. "That's it," he says softly, urging me on. "Show me what you like."

It should feel wrong to be spread wide like this. To be displaying something so personal. To be opened up for him to see everything—but it doesn't feel wrong at all. It feels so right and so fucking hot.

I play with my clit a bit faster as the Prince strokes my thighs. My eyes drift over every muscular plane of his stomach, chest, shoulders, but they linger on his face. The openness. The pure pleasure of seeing me touch myself.

Has a man ever looked at me like that before? Like watching me pleasure myself is the most sacred thing he's ever seen?

As my fingers move faster over my sensitive bud, the Prince slides his hand down my thigh. His thumb brushes my folds ever so softly. I buck toward him, breath trembling. Everything is sensitive. Everything heightened. I can feel the fabric of the duvet against the skin on my ass, still red from my spanking. I can feel his palms. Fingers. His breath. His heartbeat.

"Don't stop touching yourself," he growls, moving his fingers toward my opening. "Do you hear me?" His eyes flick to mine.

I nod. "Yes."

"Don't stop until you come on my hand."

I suck in a breath, holding his gaze. As the Prince sinks his finger inside me, a moan falls from my lips. I grind against his touch, needing more.

And he gives it to me. Another finger. A third. Leaning forward, he works his hand between my legs as I pleasure myself. Heat winds tight around my core, pressure mounting with every thrust of his fingers. Wow, that feels good. I close my eyes when I feel his lips on my breast, sucking and nipping and teasing it as his hand works magic between my legs.

"Come on my hand, Rowan," the Prince says, his lips brushing against my pebbled nipple. He lays a soft kiss on it, driving his fingers deeper. "Give it to me, princess."

The Prince's teeth scrape across my nipple as his fingers drive in and out of me. My own fingers tremble as they dance over my clit, the heat in my core mounting and mounting and mounting and—

Ohmygodyes.

Back arching, sharp inhalation, silent scream. The Prince urges me on, whispering dirty nothings to me as I clench around his fingers. Squeezing my eyes shut as my whole body contracts, I listen to his grunts, and I realize he's enjoying this.

My pleasure—he likes it. Loves it, even.

When he lifts himself off me, dragging his fingers out and bringing them to his lips, I feel flushed. Dizzy. So fucking horny all I want is more, more, more.

And I see the pure, unbridled lust in his expression.

This time, when I reach for his waistband, he doesn't push me away. He watches me unbuckle his belt and lower the zipper, pushing the layers of fabric off his slim hips. Standing up to help me, he drops his pants to his feet.

My breath catches.

I've never thought penises to be beautiful, but I was wrong. He has a gorgeous cock. Long and thick and so incredibly hard.

And right now, it's mine.

The Prince produces a condom from somewhere. I don't see where. I'm too busy staring. I lean back on the bed, watching him position himself between my legs and roll the condom over his shaft.

I'm done thinking about regrets. We've crossed a thousand lines, and I'll cross a thousand more to get what I want.

And what I want is him. Right now. Deep inside me.

But he teases me. He brushes his tip against me, then moves backward and drops his lips between my legs. Closing my eyes, I let my head fall back.

His tongue feels like magic. It sends fire rushing through my veins and steals the breath right from my lungs. It makes my nipples tighten and my legs fall open. As I tangle my fingers in his hair, I find myself grinding against his face.

It's brazen and naughty and not at all what I'm used to doing.

But wow, it feels good. When the Prince moves up to kiss me, I taste my own arousal on his lips. He drives his tongue inside my mouth and kisses me hard, rolling his hips against mine.

Then, with a slight adjustment, he gives me what I've been wanting all day. All week. My whole adult life, maybe.

His cock spears me deep, making my back arch and my lips drop open.

"*Wolfe*," I cry out, running my nails down his broad, muscular back.

He grunts in response, driving inside me again. His body is all raw, commanding power. Every muscle bunches and releases as he thrusts inside me, and all I can do is cling onto him. My hands grip his shoulders, my legs wrap around his waist.

This is better than I expected. I won't regret this. No way. There's nothing I could regret about this. I didn't even know sex could feel this good. I didn't realize that—

I'm coming again.

This time, I scream. I say his name over and over again, crying out as my nails leave long red streaks across his back.

Wolfe, Wolfe, Wolfe.

He whispers in my ear in response, "*Yes, princess. Come for me, Rowan. Come all over that cock.*"

Dirty words that make my core clench and my orgasm ride higher. I forget that he's a prince, because right now, it doesn't matter. He's a man. Beautiful, sexual, powerful man.

My body is on fire. My legs are wrapped around him like a vise, but he manages to push them open and roll me onto my stomach. I'm a rag doll, and I like it. I *love* it.

I love the way his arm scoops under my stomach and pulls me up to all fours. I love the way he lifts me up higher, so my back is against his chest. I love the way he enters me again, like this, clamping my body against his chest and fucking me senseless.

I didn't know it was possible to come so many times in a row. What day is it, again? I'm not sure I even know my name. There's a piece of hair in my mouth, but I barely have the wherewithal to spit it out.

And then I feel it.

Throbbing. Stiffening. The sheer power of his orgasm

emptying into me. I gasp, trembling against him as he holds me close, his hand cupping my breast as my head rests against his chest.

Then, stillness.

We both fall forward, me on my stomach and him on top of me. We stay tangled in each other, until I groan and shift, and the Prince slides out of me and rolls over.

I'm covered in a blanket of bliss and a sheen of sweat. I stare at him through my messy hair, loving the way his cheeks are red and his face looks totally, completely relaxed.

He doesn't look like an arrogant prince right now. He's not a cocky asshole used to getting what he wants. Right now, he's gentle. Soft. Smiling at me.

Then, he groans and glances down. "Shit," he says, frowning.

I follow his gaze to his groin, where his cock glistens with sticky wetness, the remains of a broken condom wrapped around its base.

The Prince glances at me, gritting his teeth. "Tell me you're on the pill."

16

WOLFE

SHIT, shit, shit.

If there's anything that ruins post-coital bliss, it's the knowledge that the condom broke and we're stuck in an isolated cottage in whiteout storm conditions.

Rowan's eyes widen, sapphire blue turning slightly deeper as she stares at the mess between my legs. She shakes her head, eyes still wide with shock. "The pill made me really moody and gave me headaches. I stopped taking it when I broke up with my ex."

"You stopped taking it?" I frown.

"Well, it's not like I was having sex with anyone," Rowan snaps, turning away from me. She glances between her legs, sucking in a long breath. "I don't... What do we do?"

Pulling the broken latex off my cock, I stand up and toss it in the garbage. "Not much we can do. Hopefully by the time the storm clears we can get back to the main castle. Dr. Williams might have a morning after pill or be able to get some in town."

"Okay." Rowan frowns, counting on her fingers and whispering to herself. She glances at me, straightening up. "I just got my period recently. I'm pretty sure I'm not ovulating. I think the chances of..." She doesn't say the words *getting pregnant*, but they hang heavy between us. Rowan takes a deep breath. "I think the chances are low."

"Still."

"I'll still take the morning after pill. Of course. I'm not trying to make my life more complicated than it already is." She huffs out a laugh, putting a hand to her forehead. Clearing her throat, she reaches for her top and clutches it to her chest, as if she doesn't want to be naked with me right now.

It stings and I'm not sure why.

"Bathroom?" she asks. "I'd like to take a shower."

I jerk my head to a door adjoining the bedroom and watch her scuttle toward it, still hiding herself behind her sweater.

I glance down at my cock, letting out a long breath. That was probably a dumb idea. I shouldn't be having sex with anyone right now, and especially not a woman I just met.

Especially not when there's a possibility she could get pregnant.

Fuck.

Flopping onto the bed, I scrub my face with my hands. I let my cock get the better of me. It's been begging me to act on these desires since the first day I met Rowan. Now what?

I shouldn't have done that. I shouldn't have given in. I should have ignored the thumping in my chest and the burning desire to have a taste of her. I came to the Summer Palace exactly to avoid this kind of thing. To spend the month by myself, sorting through the mess in my mind. To weather the storm that October brings for another year.

The bathroom door opens, and Rowan emerges in a cloud of steam. She has a fluffy white towel wrapped around her body. The deer-in-headlights look in her eyes has ceded to a more closed-off expression, and she gives me a quick nod.

"Go ahead."

We don't say another word as I walk by her in the bathroom, and although her cheeks are pink, she doesn't meet my eye.

She regrets this. Wishes we hadn't slept together.

She's probably right. It was a dumb idea.

By the time I'm done showering, Rowan isn't in the room. I find her in the main space, in front of the fire sipping her forgotten drink. She glances back at me, nodding.

"Any food in this place?"

"Mostly non-perishables."

"At least there's alcohol." She gives me a smile, but it's not quite as bright as it was an hour ago.

I sit down opposite her, picking up my own discarded drink. I jerk my chin toward her. "You okay?"

"Fine, why?"

"You regret what we just did?"

"I guess that depends on whether or not I get pregnant." She says it as a joke, forcing out a laugh, but it falls flat. Her lips drop and she turns to the fire, wrapping her arms around herself and taking another sip.

"It'll be fine. By morning we'll be able to get back to the castle, and Dr. Williams will have something for you to take."

Rowan nods. "The odds are super low, anyway."

"Exactly."

I open my mouth to add something, then hesitate. I want to ask her if she'd regret it even if she wasn't pregnant. If she'd ever want to do this again. If she felt something while we were in the bedroom that might have felt like more than just sex.

I sure as hell did—not that I'd ever admit it.

Rowan drains her glass and glances at me. "Well, I have a lot to think about with that new design. I might sketch out some drawings based on those paintings tonight and then turn in. I'm assuming there's more than one bedroom in this place?"

I nod, my face remaining neutral. "You can take the room we were in. It's the master. I'll sleep down the hall."

Rowan gives me a pinched smile, carrying her glass as she walks over to the studio. I hear the door opening and closing.

I'm alone.

I stare at the fire until it dies down, then I go check on the dogs and head to bed. I don't see Rowan again until morning.

WHEN I GET UP, I give the dogs breakfast in the kennel and head back inside to find Rowan making coffee. She turns to face me with a mug of coffee in her hand. Her face looks lined, as if she barely slept last night.

Was she worried about the broken condom? Or something else?

"Weather looks pretty clear," she says quietly.

"We can head back after coffee," I answer.

There's distance between us, and I hate it. I hate that she regrets what happened. Most of all, I hate that I care. So, what, I sleep with a woman and suddenly I'm in love? Why do I care if Rowan regrets this or not? It's not like we're together. She's the architect in charge of the redesign of my palace, for shit's sake. She's not exactly marriage material. We fucked. It was fun. It's over.

End of story.

I drink my coffee in the kennels as I get the dogs ready,

then wait for Rowan to emerge. We ride back to the main palace in silence.

No delicate laughs. No stolen glances. No teasing touches and definitely no kissing.

Whatever happened between me and Rowan is over.

And you know what? Good. It should be over. Keep things casual. She was a good lay. It was fun. That's it. That's all it should be.

But when I watch her walk toward her room on the opposite side of the Summer Palace, something in my chest twinges.

Rubbing my sternum with the base of my palm, I trudge through the castle walls until I get to my chambers. Stripping down, I take a shower and wash the memory of yesterday away. Then, I call for Dr. Williams and hope he'll be able to extinguish any last regrets from my mind.

17

ROWAN

THERE AREN'T any morning after pills in the palace, Dr. Williams informs me with nothing but professionalism and tact. I try to swallow down the shame and wonder how many other staff members know what I did with the Prince.

"By the time the roads open up for us to get supplies, it'll be too late to take it," the doctor says.

I nod. "I understand. I don't think I'm ovulating, so it shouldn't be an issue."

The doctor nods, shifting uncomfortably. He opens his mouth, reconsiders, and bows his head before backing out of my room. I flop down onto the bed, groaning.

I'm a healthy young woman who has sex. I'm not ashamed of that.

But *ugh,* did I really have to give in to those feelings? Throw away every shred of logical thought for a few minutes of passion?

I stand up and wrap a cardigan around my shoulders, then head to the library. At least I feel comfortable there. As I pad through the hallways, I feel like I'm being watched. The staff is whispering about me. They must know by now, right?

I wonder if the Prince does this with every new woman he comes across. Maybe this is his way of dealing with the grief of his fiancée's death.

I shove the library door open with my shoulder, shivering at the chill in the room. It takes me a few minutes to get the fire started, and I sit on the hearth with a throw blanket wrapped around my shoulders. As the fire grows, I stare at the dancing flames and try to make sense of my turbulent thoughts.

Sleeping with the Prince was a mistake. I shouldn't have done it. I'm attracted to him, yes, but he's royalty. I'm not. I'm employed by the royal family to do a job, and I'm not even from Nord to begin with.

It was just one night of fun. That's all.

"I thought I might find you here," a deep voice says from the doorway.

I almost groan at the sight of the Prince in well-tailored slacks and a fitted sweater. I remember what he looked like with nothing on, too. Both versions of him are delicious—and both of them are totally off-limits.

"Your Highness," I say with a nod, choosing not to get up to curtsy.

"We're back to formal titles, are we?" He arches a brow, padding toward me. He stalks across the room, coming to sit down on the sofa beside me.

I wrap the blanket tighter around my shoulders. "The doctor told me they don't have any morning after pills."

The Prince grunts. When he doesn't speak for a few seconds, I turn to glance at him. He's watching me. "What?"

He shrugs. "Trying to figure you out."

"Well, if you do, let me know what you find." I grin, shaking my head. "I'm still working on that myself."

Clearing his throat, the Prince shifts in his seat. "As I said before, I've organized the plane to take you to Stirling as soon as it's safe. Your grandmother has an apartment there, courtesy of the royal family, and I'm sure she'd appreciate the company while she recovers. I've also asked my sister to make an office available to you at the Stirling Castle."

My mouth hangs open. "You...You what?"

The Prince's eyebrows tug together. "You do want to see your grandmother, don't you?"

"Of course. But I didn't think you would..." I trail off. *I didn't think you'd understand. I didn't think you'd be kind. I didn't think you'd care.*

"I don't regret what we did yesterday," the Prince says, his voice sending heat flowing through my veins.

I gulp, turning back to stare at the flames. "No?"

"Not a bit."

"Just another notch on your bedpost, I guess." The logs crackle as the flames climb higher.

The Prince is silent for a beat. "I guess so," he says quietly. He stands up and heads for the door, closing it softly behind him—no minions needed this time.

My heart squeezes.

Maybe the Prince isn't who I thought he was. Maybe he's not the arrogant asshole with an army of servants. Maybe he doesn't sleep with every woman who crosses his path.

Maybe he *cares.*

Letting my eyes close, I turn back to the fire and tuck my legs into my chest. I wrap the blanket tight around me and rest my chin on my knees, trying to still the thumping of my heart. I don't understand what's going on. Why is he being so generous? So kind?

He doesn't regret what we did yesterday.

What does that even mean? My heart beats uncomfortably as I think about the possibility of him and me...

No. It's not possible. He might not regret it, but he's not the one who needs this job in order to progress in his career. I'm the one who needs to be here. I'm the one who's relying on this job to make a name for myself. I'm the one who built my architecture business from the ground up and who can't afford to mess this up.

He might not regret it, but I do.

The door opens again, and my heart jumps. Is he back?

Vikki pokes her head inside, a soft smile tugging at her lips. "Hey you."

"Hi, Vikki," I say with a smile.

"How was the cottage?"

"Beautiful," I say.

She nods, crossing her legs as she sits down beside me. I offer her one side of the blanket, and she shimmies closer to wrap it around her shoulders.

"I heard you're going to be leaving us soon." My new friend sounds sad, and I wonder how lonely it really gets up here, isolated in the wilderness.

"I'll be going to Stirling to spend time with my grand-mother and work on my designs."

Vikki makes a soft noise, glancing at me. "The Prince likes you."

I stiffen. Does she know about last night? Does *everyone* know? Who else did the Prince tell? "Why do you say that?"

"He organized a car for you. I heard him on the phone to the Queen, asking for space for you to work. Really fought for you to get it."

My chest constricts. "Oh. That's not...normal? He doesn't do that for everyone?"

Vikki laughs. "Prince Wolfe is the most loyal, protective person in the world...if he cares about you. Otherwise, he'll tear you to shreds or completely ignore you. I've been in the 'ignore' camp my whole life. Never once has he made time for me to go see my family and actually put effort into making it happen. He doesn't even know my name."

"Maybe he believes in my design for this palace," I say, my voice sounding hollow and empty.

Vikki snorts. "Yeah. That's probably it. He definitely doesn't ask us to make sure you have everything you need three times a day ever since you arrived here."

My eyes widen as I glance at my friend.

She shrugs, grinning. "You have a fan."

I shake my head, standing up. I heap my half of the blanket onto Vikki's lap, stretching my arms out. "I don't think so. I'm going to do a bit of work before I turn in tonight."

Vikki stares at me curiously, tilting her head. "You like him, too."

"I do not."

"Do too."

"Do not."

Vikki laughs, eyes widening. "You *do*. Rowan Reed!"

"I have work to do."

"You have a brand-new office in the Stirling Castle to do it."

"Well, I guess I'll have to settle for the archives until I get there."

Vikki stands up, folding the blanket and setting it on the arm of the sofa. She shakes her head, grinning at me. "You two might have just found the perfect match for each other. Both of you grumpy about it. Both of you in denial. It's perfect."

"Goodbye, Vikki," I say, heading for the door to the archives. "I'll see you tomorrow."

Her giggle follows me through the doorway as she calls

out a goodbye to me. I flop down on the desk chair in the archives and listen to her walk out of the library before dropping my head in my hands.

Groaning, I try to shake the thought away.

The Prince does *not* like me. Not like that. Sure, we slept together, and he's a bit more of a gentleman than I expected.

That's it.

Anything more is just too complicated. Too messy.

Too...real.

18

WOLFE

WHEN ROWAN and I were at the visitor's cottage, I felt a closeness I haven't felt in a long time. A sense of companionship, like there's someone else in the world who understands pain the way I do. She's resigned herself to loneliness, just as I have.

It's been four long years of trudging through life with weights around my ankles. Four years of wishing it had been my heart that stopped, not Abby's. Four years of wondering what the point of it all is without Abby by my side.

But now... I shake my head and stare at the ceiling above my bed. Rowan doesn't want me that way. I'm not so dense that I can't read body language. I might not regret our time together, but she does.

Is it because the condom broke? She doesn't want kids?

Or is it simply because she slept with *me*?

It's hard not to think about the taste of her lips, and the way her skin felt against mine. It's hard not to wonder if she'd ever give herself to me fully. Let go of the inhibitions and walls that she's built up and let me have her. Completely.

For the first time in four years, my blood feels warm and alive and thick in my veins.

It feels *good* to do something for her. To provide a place for her to live and work. I want to make her happy.

So...I'm screwed, basically.

Chief, sensing my unease, jumps up on the bed beside me. He lets out a low rumble and nuzzles in beside me, letting me bury my hand in his fur and fall asleep beside him.

I WAKE up to a bright day with clear blue skies. Rowan will be leaving soon.

I can't let that happen.

Jumping out of bed, I shower quickly, throw my things in a bag, and call for Eyvar. The big, pale-eyed man arrives within minutes.

"I'm going back to Stirling," I say, slipping my laptop into its bag.

"Sir?"

"Stirling," I repeat, glancing at Eyvar. "The capital."

"I know what Stirling is, Your Highness, but what I'm wondering is *why*. The anniversary hasn't happened yet. The memorial..." He trails off, but we both know what he's going to say.

I've been away just over two weeks. The memorial is tomorrow. If I leave today, I'll arrive in the capital just in time for the anniversary of Abby's death. I'll be bombarded with images and memories of the worst day of my life.

Right now, it doesn't seem so daunting. Maybe I have to be there this year. Maybe my grief is ebbing away, and it's time to move forward.

When I don't answer, Eyvar grunts and backs out of the room. I gather a few things, leaving the staff to pack up the rest. I don't need much, anyway. I have clothes and toiletries at every royal household in the kingdom. All I need are my personal things.

When I stride down to the dining room to grab some coffee and breakfast, I'm surprised to see Rowan there, too. She straightens up in her chair, swallowing a bite of food.

"Your Highness."

"We talked about that title," I growl, sitting down at the head of the table and nodding to the staff as they pour my coffee.

"I'd rather keep things professional," Rowan replies, eyeing me from across the room.

My lips twitch. I would very much rather keep things *un*professional, but I like the fight in her. Last night, the distance between us made me ache. I wanted to wrap my arms around her and take her, right there in the library.

Now, though, I feel like a weight has been lifted off my shoulders. I'm not carrying around four years of grief. I'm not running away from difficult emotions.

I'm moving on.

Rowan clears her throat. "I wanted to thank you for organizing a house and office for me. You didn't have to do that."

"I know I didn't," I reply. A waiter places a plate of steaming scrambled eggs and perfectly golden toast on the table. A butter dish is placed down in front of me, the butter soft, but not melted. Perfect. Why does everything seem to taste better today?

"I appreciate it, is what I'm saying."

"I was impressed with the effort you put into your research while you were here. I think you earned a place to work. Plus, this way I'll be able to keep an eye on you." I flick my gaze to Rowan, whose face flushes all over.

She keeps her eyes on her plate. "I thought you were

staying here for a few weeks," she says casually. Maybe too casually.

"I've changed my mind. I'm heading to Stirling with you."

That earns me a glance. Her eyes are wide as they stare at me across the table, her perfect, plump lips dropping open.

"But what about..." she trails off, just as Eyvar had.

How long have I let my memories hold me back? How much did I wear my grief like a badge of honor? Even a woman who's known me mere weeks can tell that my decision to go to the capital is unusual.

I dab the corners of my lips with a thick cloth napkin, meeting Rowan's eye. "I think it might be time for me to face my fears head-on, don't you?"

She pauses, reaching for her coffee cup. "Whatever you think is best, Your Highness."

"That doesn't sound like you, Rowan."

Her eyes flick up to mine when I say her name. Her throat clenches and releases as she swallows, spots of red flushing over her cheeks. "How do you know what I'm like?"

I grin in response, which earns me a huff from Rowan. It feels like a weight has been lifted from my shoulders. I can breathe fully for the first time in years.

I'm going to Stirling. I'm not afraid of the memorial. I'm not afraid of the pictures and videos and reminders of my fiancée's death. I can't run away from it all anymore.

Even if Rowan doesn't realize it yet, having her near makes me feel stronger. Being close to her gives me energy. It gives me life. It makes me feel like there's hope for a brighter future, and like I don't need to run away from the past.

But as she finishes her meal and nods to a waiter as he takes her plate away, I see the tension in her shoulders. She steals a glance my way, and I'm not sure if she feels the same way I do.

. . .

AFTER BRINGING Chief back to the kennels and giving him one last pat on the head, I find Rowan in one of the sitting rooms, ready to go. We make our way to the garages just as the last of Rowan's bags are loaded into the trunk. She slips into the back seat, and I circle around to the other side. When I slide into the seat beside her, I can feel the distance between us like a chasm.

We set off in silence, rolling through the countryside. Finally, when we pass the train station, Rowan lets out a long sigh. I reach over and place my hand over hers, squeezing gently.

"I was so scared when I first arrived," Rowan says quietly. She laughs, shaking her head. "It's embarrassing to think about it now."

"Don't be embarrassed," I answer, my voice low.

"Thank you for stopping. For saving me," she says quietly. When she flicks her eyes toward me, the look on her face makes my blood pump thick and hot in my veins. She gulps, turning her hand over so she can intertwine her fingers in mine.

This feels right. It feels *good*. Being here, beside Rowan, heading back to the capital that I call home—it feels like it's exactly where I'm supposed to be.

Rowan glances at me, letting out a soft sigh. She leans back in her seat, keeping her hand curled around mine, and stares out the window at the passing snow-covered landscape. For once, it feels like she belongs here.

With me.

19

ROWAN

WE DRIVE to a private airfield a short distance away from the train station where I arrived. The Prince slips his hand out of mine when the car stops, and I immediately miss his closeness. My fingers tingle where they touched his skin, and I remember what it felt like to be in his arms.

It felt good. And right. And *real*. As much as I try to deny it, I love having him beside me.

The Prince puts his hand on my lower back as we walk toward a private jet, flight attendants waiting at the bottom and top of the stairs to help us on board. The Prince's huge, pale-eyed bodyguard follows us, carrying my bags toward the plane.

When we get inside, my breath catches. I've never been in a private jet before—obviously.

It's massive. We're greeted with a fully stocked bar and kitchen. Beyond, two huge chairs are set up on one side, with a big L-shaped couch on the other. And farther still, beyond a small partition, a king-sized bed takes up the far end of the cabin.

My heart thumps at the sight of the bed. I know the flight

to Stirling is only about an hour, but the thought of sleeping with the Prince is still fresh in my mind.

I sit down on one of the individual seats. I'm given a glass of champagne and a selection of hors d'oeuvres. Nuts, lox, and even a decadent chocolate truffle.

The Prince watches me from the long sofa, a grin teasing at his lips.

"What?" I ask, glaring.

"You look completely out of your element."

"Can you blame me?"

"Just enjoy it, Rowan."

Ugh, I love the way he says my name. I never want him to stop. I want to hear it whispered, gruff and low in my ear. I want to hear him say it softly as he wraps his arms around me. I want to hear him grunt it as he spills his orgasm inside me.

No. Stop.

I can't think that way. That was a one-time thing. It's not going to happen again.

I'm here for *work*. That's all.

We settle in for take-off. Eyvar disappears into a door near the front of the plane, and I realize there's a whole other, smaller, self-contained apartment up there. The flight attendants serve us more drinks—I opt for water, since I don't trust myself with alcohol around the Prince anymore. The staff then disappears behind a door on the other side of the kitchen.

"Have you made any progress on the design?" he asks after takeoff.

Good. Work—that's a safe topic.

I take a sip of water before answering. "I have. I think you'll like the new iteration. Or at least, I hope so." I smile, watching his eyes flick down to my lips.

Why does that make heat curl around my abdomen? Why do I never want him to stop looking at me like that?

My heart thumps, and I clear my throat. "This plane is incredible. It's nicer than my place in Farcliff."

The Prince makes a soft noise in response, his eyes still tracing the lines of my lips. His gaze runs down the length of my body, sending fire spilling through my veins.

Yes, I like that. I like when he looks at me. When we're alone, with no one else to see us, I think I like it a bit too much. I turn to the window to watch the clouds rush by. It's safer that way.

"Are you afraid of me?" he asks after a few minutes.

I frown, glancing at him. "No. Why?"

"You seem to want to stay as far away from me as possible."

"Do you remember what happened last time I let myself get near you?"

His smile widens. "How could I forget?"

"This isn't the same for me as it is for you, Your Highness," I say, heart thumping uncomfortably. I straighten my shoulders, jutting my chin out at him.

He leans back on the sofa, stretching his legs. "What do you mean?"

"I mean, you're a prince, right? Royalty? You can have whatever you want, whenever you want." I wave a hand at the luxury around us. "Look at this plane. I arrived at the castle on the train, with no privacy and a seat half the size of this one."

"I don't understand what that has to do with us."

"Of course you don't." I snort, shaking my head. "You don't understand that for you, I'm just a bit of fun. I'm just a girl who walked into your life, who's below your station, who has to do whatever you want me to do."

"You don't have to do anything I want." His face hardens, jaw tensing.

I let out a sigh. "I don't mean I was coerced. I'm just a girl who came to the castle. Just like a million others, probably. I mean nothing to you."

"How would you know what you mean to me?" There's an edge to his voice. An intensity to his gaze.

A lump forms in my throat, and I hesitate. Threading my fingers together, I squeeze my hands against each other. I take a deep breath. "You are in a position of power over me, Wolfe."

He frowns. "Is this about the office? About the plane? I'm trying to help you."

"It's about the fact that I've worked my ass off to be a respected architect, and I don't want you—or anyone else—to think that I'm here for other reasons."

"You don't think I respect you?"

Frustration bubbles inside me as I draw in a deep breath. How can I make him understand that my career means everything to me? It's my lifeline. It's the one thing that ensures I have to rely on no one, ever. Sleeping with him was a mistake. It was in direct conflict with my desire to be successful. It blurred the lines between us and confused me on the deepest level.

He still thinks this is a game, and he'll toss me aside when it's over.

But this job? This design?

It means *everything* to me. I left my boyfriend for this contract—not that the loss of that relationship really cut me deep, or anything, but I still gave it up. I gave up my social life to build up my business to what it is now. I put all my time and energy into my work. Everything I've done has been to ensure I can stand on my own two feet.

Getting involved with the Prince puts all of that into question.

"Rowan," he says softly and damn it, my walls weaken. His gaze drills into mine, and I find myself standing up from my armchair and moving to sit next to him on the sofa when he pats the seat.

He reaches over to me, tucking a strand of hair behind my ear. "I haven't slept with anyone since Abby," he says.

I lift my gaze to his, eyes wide. "What?"

"Why is that so surprising?" His lips tug at the corners.

I wave a hand in the general direction of his rock-hard, virile body. "I mean... You know."

"There aren't a million other women in my life. You're not just one of many women on a conveyor belt in and out of my life." He pauses, fingers drifting over my cheek. "I don't know what you are. You're special."

"I'm here for work," I say softly, but the conviction is gone from my voice. My eyes betray me, drifting down to his lips.

The Prince doesn't hesitate. He leans toward me, pressing his lips to mine, and oh, my body gives in. I sigh into his kiss, wrapping my arms around him. I tangle my fingers into his hair and pull him close, moaning into his mouth.

It should be illegal for a kiss to feel this good. It shouldn't be allowed for one man to have so much power and sex and masculinity imbued into every pore.

But damn, it feels good. His kiss tastes dangerous but so sweet. When he groans, it sends shivers rushing over my skin. He wraps his arms around me, pulling me over to straddle him on top of the couch. His hands run down my neck, over my chest, around my waist. Everywhere.

And I want it. I want his hands on my body, on every inch of me. I want to feel his bare skin against mine. His cock buried deep inside me. His lips between my legs. Everything. I want it all.

My hesitations and fears seem so silly when he's tangling his fists into my hair and kissing me hard. Work doesn't seem so important when his hips grind against mine, reminding me of everything I've missed while I've been convincing myself I don't want him.

He pulls away from me, resting his forehead against mine. "I feel alive for the first time in years, Rowan," he says softly. His voice gruff, as if he needs to push the words through his throat.

I let myself believe his words—that I'm special, and different, and I mean something to him. I let myself melt into his embrace and I let him kiss me senseless as my body heats up.

Maybe there's more to life than work. I might have missed the point of all this when I've been so focused on providing for myself and making sure I don't end up a burden to anyone else. Kissing the Prince feels better than work.

What if these feelings are real? What if this could work?

As my head spins, I pull away and stare in the Prince's eyes. They're soft. Warm. Loving. My chest constricts, and I find myself leaning my cheek against his chest.

He wraps his arms around me and lays a soft kiss on top of my head as we sit there in silence until the flight attendant reappears.

I pull away, cheeks burning, which makes Wolfe chuckle. His arm stretches out across the sofa behind me, and the flight attendant doesn't even blink. We're served snacks and refreshments, and I finally let myself enjoy the luxury of the flight.

20

WOLFE

When we land in Stirling, Rowan straightens her shoulders and schools her features. The intimacy we shared on the flight to the capital dissolves away, and her professional mask is back on.

It's hard not to feel sad about it. I liked the way she looked at me when no one was watching.

When the plane door opens, though, there *are* people watching. Lots of them. The media was warned of my arrival, obviously, and have jostled their way onto the tarmac, being held back by an army of palace guards. A black car is waiting for me and Rowan at the bottom of the stairs.

"What's going on?" Rowan whispers as we stand at the top of the steps. Eyvar has already disembarked and is standing by the car, holding the back door open.

"I'm not usually in the capital in October. The press must have gotten wind of it." I lift an arm toward the crowd of photographers, painting a placid smile on my face.

It's only after a second that I realize my other hand is resting on Rowan's lower back. I drop it, heart thumping at the thought of the photos that will be published online within minutes. It'll look like we're together—but do I really mind?

I motion for Rowan to step down first, sensing her every movement. The wind carries a whisper of her scent toward me, and I let out a quiet sigh. We're led to the waiting car, and once inside, Rowan releases a long breath.

"Is your life always like this?"

"More or less." I grin.

"I prefer anonymity."

"I wouldn't know what that's like."

Rowan's eyebrows tug together, and for the first time, I see sadness in her eyes. Except it doesn't bother me the way it usually would. She's not pitying me for my loss—that, she understands. She feels sad for something I've never had. Privacy, anonymity.

My fingers itch to reach over and clasp her hand in mine. I want nothing more than to feel her skin, wrap my hand around hers and show her I want her beside me. Even as we stepped off the airplane, it felt right to be with her.

But we're not together. She works for the palace. She's not here to drag me out of my own doom and gloom or heal the wounds that have festered for four years.

I instruct Eyvar to bring her to her grandmother's place first, and we drive in silence. The distance between us is only a car seat. Just a foot of space, but it feels unsurmountable. In that space, I feel the weight of the royal expectations on my shoulders. I feel the shackles of my previous loss. I feel my failure to keep Abby safe. Why would I deserve to have another chance? Why would a woman like Rowan—who has a career, a business, and a future—want to throw all that away to be with me?

I already know she left her boyfriend to pursue her business. Why would I be any different? She told me plainly that all she wants is independence.

When we stop outside a small brick house a stone's throw away from the Stirling General Hospital, Rowan finally turns to look at me. With a soft smile, she dips her head. "Thanks again for organizing this for my grandmother."

"She's been loyal to the royal family for decades. It's the least I could do."

"Still," Rowan says. "I appreciate it. I..." She bites her lip. "I hope I'll see you around." A faint blush stains her cheeks, and I can't quite hide my grin.

"You will."

I wait until she opens the front door before nodding to Eyvar. We drive to the castle and to Eyvar's credit, he says nothing. He knows me well enough to realize I feel something for Rowan—but he's diplomatic enough to keep quiet about it.

When we drive through the gates to the city castle, I immediately feel claustrophobic. There aren't miles of space between the gates and the castle, like there are at the Summer Palace. There's no majestic mountains and vast expanses of white snow.

Everything is gray.

Gray stone façades. Gray sculptural arches. Gray snow and slush pushed in great big gray snowbanks on either side of the drive. When we stop, a footman rushes to open my door. I step out, nodding to Eyvar as he drives toward the garages. I enter the main foyer of the castle, sighing when I see my sister's lead advisor heading straight for me.

"Your Highness," Frederick says with a bow. "Welcome back. We weren't expecting you for another four weeks."

"I changed my mind."

"Her Majesty the Queen would like to have a word." Frederick sweeps his hand toward the door to the left, and I know I have no choice but to follow. We walk through echoing hallways toward my sister's offices, and I feel the weight of the stone walls pressing down on me.

I miss the Summer Palace. I miss the space.

Or maybe I just miss Rowan.

My sister sits behind a massive, polished desk, her back straight as a rod and her face as icy as ever. Blond hair is twisted into a tight bun at the nape of her neck, and her demure blouse does nothing to soften the harsh angles of her face.

She's always been as broken as me.

"Brother," she says, nodding to a chair, as if I need permission to sit with my own sister. Right now, though, she's not a sister. She's the Queen. Penelope leans back in her seat, watching as I adjust my jacket and lean back in the armchair across from her. She tilts her head, not a single wrinkle marring her skin, the youngest queen in Nord's history. "You're back early."

"I am."

She arches a brow. "Why?"

"Am I not allowed to come back home when I feel like it?"

"It's been four years, Wolfe. You're never here for the anniversary of Abby's death. I'm only asking because it's out of the ordinary."

"I hate calling it an anniversary. It sounds like we're celebrating the fact that she's dead."

Penelope sighs, standing up and turning to the floor-to-ceiling windows that line the wall of her office. She clasps her hands in front of her, staring at the city sprawled at her feet. My sister is a true queen—but one without an heir.

She was Abby's closest friend, which sometimes I forget. Where Abby was celebrated and loved by the media, Penelope hasn't been treated so kindly. The Ice Queen. Black Widow. Cold Monarch. Vile Witch.

They call her every name under the sun except *Her Majesty the Queen of Nord.*

"You slept with the architect," she says, still facing the window.

My body stiffens. "How do you know that?"

"The doctor," my sister responds. She glances over her shoulder, her simple diamond stud glittering in her earlobe. "You didn't use protection."

"I wasn't aware I needed your permission to fuck, Penelope."

"I'm trying to prevent another disaster," she snaps. Her lips pinch together as her pale skin grows even paler. The Ice Queen, indeed.

Reality snaps back to me, and Abby's death feels like it was yesterday. Grief hits me like a wall as I remember the secret that no one but a chosen few ever knew. One I didn't even know until Abby's autopsy was performed.

"I'd hardly call Abby's pregnancy a disaster," I reply, my voice terse.

For a fraction of a second, pain flashes across Penelope's eyes. She, unlike Abby, was never able to get pregnant before her husband died. An heirless, aging queen, tipping just past thirty years old as the kingdom whispers of her failures. Her suffering is written all over her face, but in an instant, the pain is gone, and my sister's icy demeanor is back to normal.

My shoulders drop. "I'm sorry, Penelope. Don't worry. Rowan isn't pregnant."

"Good. I also understand you've been working with her on the redesign of the Summer Palace."

I nod. "I gave her some comments."

"Well, you can take the lead on that project. Silas and

Jonah have expressed zero interest, and we need someone in the family to be the face of the project. You spend the most time at the Summer Palace anyway, so the natural choice is you." My sister places her fingers on the edge of the desk, leveling me with a stare. "That is, as long as you keep your dick out of the help."

I grind my teeth to stop myself from biting back. Instead, I suck in a breath and give my sister a pinched smile. "Of course, Your Majesty."

Penelope arches an eyebrow, knowing I used her title sarcastically. She'll always be my sister, no matter what office she holds in this castle. At the end of the day, I know Penelope has suffered. She lost her husband, just as I lost Abby. Not only that, but she's had to suffer the criticism of the media and hide her health issues from the public. She carries all that on her narrow shoulders, so it's no wonder she's adopted a frosty exterior. Anyone would need a defense mechanism if they'd been through what Penelope has experienced—all while ruling the kingdom.

Still—it wouldn't kill her to be nice to me, especially this time of year. If anyone knows loss, it's her, but that shared suffering seems to be tearing us apart instead of bringing us closer together.

I head to my chambers and find Eyvar waiting for me. He greets me with a quick bow of the head before combing his fingers through his beard.

"What is it, Eyvar?" I push the door to my chambers open, trying to keep the annoyance out of my voice.

"Miss Reed has requested access to the new office tomorrow."

"Already? Doesn't she want to spend time with her grandmother?"

"She seems to value her work, sir."

I grunt. Of course she does. I know this about her. I nod to Eyvar, jerking my head to the door. "The staff should have set aside a room near the lavender sitting room. Confirm that it's ready and tell the garages to be ready to send a car for her whenever she requests it."

Eyvar bows his head and disappears down the hallway. I close the bedroom door, feeling excitement curl in my gut.

Leaving Rowan at her grandmother's house felt like a goodbye—but what if she wants to be near me, too? Maybe she has more than just work pulling her here to the castle.

The kiss we shared on the plane felt like more than just lust. It felt like a deeper connection growing between us. Like two souls intertwining in a way I've never experienced before, even with Abby.

I just don't know if Rowan feels it, too.

21

ROWAN

My grandmother is asleep when I arrive at the small three-bedroom house in the center of town. As I step inside, a nurse greets me. She introduces herself as Alice.

"I've been expecting you," Alice says. Her cheeks are round and rosy when she smiles, and she leads me down the hallway to a tidy, compact bedroom. She sweeps an arm at the small room. "This is you."

I smile, nodding in thanks. Gone is the luxury of the palace. There's no four-posted bed and chrome-plated fixtures. No floor-to-ceiling windows and meadows of snow and ice.

I'm back to reality.

"My grandmother?" I ask.

Alice leads me down the hall. When I poke my head inside my grandmother's room, my heart squeezes.

She looks older than I remembered. Deep wrinkles line her face, and her skin looks pale and clammy. I tiptoe inside and leave a soft kiss on her forehead before retreating back to my laptop. Back to my work, where life is simple. When I'm focused on my business, my emotions make sense.

I TWIST and turn all night before waking up at dawn and fixing myself a cup of coffee. When I poke my head in my grandmother's room, I walk to her bedside and curl my fingers around her icy hand.

Grandma lets out a sigh, opening her eyes to smile at me. "Rowan," she says. "You didn't have to come here."

"Of course I did."

"How is everything at the palace? Did Vikki help you get settled in?"

"It was perfect, Grandma." I smile, sitting on the edge of the bed. "I got all the information I needed. But how are you?"

I try to keep the concern from my face, but my grandmother lets out a soft chuckle.

"I look that bad, do I?" She squeezes my hand, and I'm relieved at the strength in her grip. "You're just like your mother. Worrywart. Always wanting to carry the world on your shoulders."

"I'd hardly say that," I reply.

Grandma snorts. "No? When that bastard left the two of you out in the cold, your mother straightened her shoulders and stayed in Farcliff for a better life, even when I told her to come to the Summer Palace with me. She was determined to do it on her own. Said she could provide for you without having the memory of that man tainting her future."

I frown. "I thought she stayed there because she wanted him to be with her."

Grandma shifts in her bed, sitting up with a grimace. "Hardly," she says, fire shooting from her gaze. "He left your mother high and dry as soon as she told him about you. She got a better job in Farcliff than we could offer her at the palace, so she took the hard road of doing it on her own. She was a fighter, Rowan." My grandmother stares at me, clear blue eyes sparkling. She shakes her head, lifting a crooked finger to stroke my cheek. "And you're just the same. You think you have to do everything on your own."

"I don't," I say weakly.

"No? You just built your architecture business by yourself for fun?"

"I wanted..." I trail off. What have I been doing? What do I want? I'm not even sure anymore. Three months ago, I would have said all I want is to run a successful business. I want to be independent and have the security of a large nest egg. I want to be able to live a good life without worrying about food or electricity bills like my mother did.

But...for what? Who am I providing for? Myself?

As I sit beside my grandmother, realizing just how frail she's become, the world seems to tilt on its axis. I've spent the better part of a decade burying myself in work and ignoring the family I still have. I've prioritized work and business over relationships every time I had to make a choice.

But what if Grandma had a worse accident than a broken hip? What if she wasn't as fit and active as she is, and her fall had more severe consequences? What if I lost her, too, without ever expecting it? Then I'd truly be alone, and being alone doesn't feel quite the same as being independent.

"Mom worked hard, but she wasn't able to get ahead because she had me," I say, my voice choking on my words. "I'm different. I don't have a baby dragging me down."

"Oh, hush," Grandma says, swatting my leg. "Dragging her down? Is that what you think you did?"

"She could have had a better life if she hadn't had me. She had to feed and clothe me and make sure I got a good educa-tion. She never even dated anyone after my father, and I'm pretty sure it was because she didn't want to bring a man into my life." My throat tightens. I stare at the floor, willing myself not to cry. "Then she died, Grandma. She gave me everything, and then it was over. If she'd been on her own, maybe..."

"Look at me, Rowan." My grandmother's voice is stern.

I close my eyes for a moment, then drag my gaze to meet hers.

Grandma takes my face in her hands, holding me still. "You were not a burden, Rowan. You were a *gift*."

"She would have been okay without me. She might have lived—"

"Stop it. You were the light of her life. You don't know what would have happened if she hadn't had you. Every time I called her, all she ever talked about was you. Your achievements. Your grades. Every time you scored a goal when you played soccer."

"You don't think that's a burden?" My voice cracks. "Everything she did was for me. She died when she was just forty, Grandma, and she didn't even know she was sick until it was too late. She was too busy taking care of me. Always me. Never herself."

My grandmother intertwines her fingers around mine. She stares me in the eye, squeezing my hand. "It was not your fault your mother passed away, Rowan. Do you hear me?"

I sigh, looking away. Grandma jerks my hand until I meet her gaze.

"Do you understand?"

"I understand, but I'm just not sure I agree." I push myself to my feet, giving Grandma a pinched smile. "I should let you get some rest. I've got work to do."

"You're more like your mother than you think," my grandmother says, shaking her head. She closes her eyes to let me know the conversation is over, and I let out a deep sigh.

As I walk out of the room, my head spins. There's only one thought that steadies me—the Prince. When I think of the way I felt when I was with him, the whole world seems to come into sharp focus. Nothing felt complicated when I was with him. Nothing felt difficult.

Yes, I'm still fighting my attraction to him. I know we have no future together, but these questions about who I am? About who my mother was? About what I really want out of life?

None of them matter when I'm with Wolfe.

Finding the card with the palace phone number in my purse, I take a deep breath and call. I try to put on my most professional voice as I request access to the office. They instruct me they'll send a car right away, and I feel almost like royalty myself.

I glance down the hallway toward my grandmother's room, and I try to push down the unease in my gut.

What if she's right? What if all my work to be independent is for nothing? What if my mother didn't see me as a burden at all? Her death wasn't my fault, and I shouldn't carry it on my conscience?

What if there's more to life than just independence, and I've spent the last ten years chasing something meaningless?

As my stomach clenches, I make my way to the bathroom to take a shower, get my laptop and work things together, and I wait for the royal car to pick me up.

When we roll through the castle gates, my eyes travel up, and up, and up. This castle is much taller than the Summer Palace. It looks like it's been stretched toward the sky, all towers and stone, with tall, spiked fencing encapsulating it. I glance at the multitude of windows, wondering which one belongs to the Prince.

Has he thought about me since he dropped me off? Has his world shifted as he wonders if his whole life has been a series of unfortunate decisions? Or is that just my sad self?

A footman opens the door for me as I thank the driver, and I'm led through the grand entrance and down a winding path to the back corner of the castle. The hallway is narrow and there aren't quite so many paintings and chandeliers at this end of the castle.

The footman stops at a modest door, pushing it open and giving me a slight bow. "Your office, Miss Reed."

"Thank you." I smile at him before shifting my gaze past his shoulder and into the room.

It's small, but it's unlike any office I've ever had before. The walls are a soft cream color, with a rich red carpet below my feet. I smile, wondering if Wolfe chose this office for the color. My feet carry me to the window at the far end, which overlooks manicured lawns and fountains spraying tall jets of water—even with winter fast approaching. I lean my forehead against the cool glass, letting out a long sigh as I stare out at the richness below me.

I don't belong here, but the least I can do is enjoy it while it lasts.

"Didn't take you long to come back to work," a rich voice says behind me. I turn to see Wolfe in the doorway, his shoulders brushing either side of the opening. He's too big to exist in these spaces, but the sight of him filling the doorway makes a bud of heat unfurl in my stomach. I want those strong arms around me.

I gulp, forcing a smile. "The Summer Palace isn't going to design itself."

He steps inside, closing the door behind him. We're alone.

Again. Somehow, it feels more scandalous to be alone in this castle with him. At the Summer Palace, as the storm raged around us, it felt intimate. Here, in the capital, it feels like I should be on my best behavior.

The Prince walks toward me, not stopping until his hand sweeps over my hip. He wraps his arm around my back and pulls me close, pressing his chest against mine.

"I think you missed me," he whispers, a grin teasing the edge of his lips.

"Of course you would think that." I roll my eyes, but there's no animosity in it.

Yes, I missed him. Yes, I came here hoping, in a hidden corner of my heart, that he'd come find me. Yes, my heart is fluttering at the thought of him doing just that.

But I'm not going to admit it.

As my gaze crawls up to meet his, the Prince's smirk sends fire rushing through my veins. He doesn't need me to say it, because he already knows.

I'm not here to work.

I'm here for him.

22

WOLFE

ROWAN'S BODY belongs next to mine. I can feel it when I hold her close. As I sweep my hand over her cheek and hear a soft moan fall from her lips, I know my heart is in jeopardy.

This is more than lust. It's more than a carnal urge.

I feel whole for the first time in four years. I could have a future—a bright one, full of laughter and love. I could hold a woman in my arms and feel her love soak into every pore.

Ha. Love.

Who said Rowan loves me? Why would I think that?

Is it because her lips fall open when I tangle my fingers into her copper hair? Is it because the thumping of her heart sends shivers rattling through my core? Is it because I feel something dangerously close to love for her?

If she loved me back, would I be able to protect her, or would I fail her just as I did Abby?

When I kiss Rowan, my thoughts are finally silent. There's only Rowan and me. Our kiss. Our hands. The burning passion that makes me claw at her clothing and spin her toward the tiny desk behind me.

I sit her down, cupping her face with my hands and I taste

her once more. Her lips are like candy, and I'd never get sick of kissing them. She clings to my shirt, pulling me close as her legs wrap around my waist.

"We shouldn't do this," Rowan whispers against my lips.

I chuckle. "This again. Why not?"

Her brows draw together, but no words come out. I kiss the tip of her nose, her cheek, her jaw, her lush bottom lip.

I growl, kissing her still. "Why not, Rowan? Tell me."

"Because we can't be together. It's not going anywhere."

"Says who?" My lips brush against her neck, which prickles with goose bumps wherever my kisses land.

"Says...everyone, Wolfe."

I groan. "I love it when you use my name."

"I shouldn't. What if someone heard me calling you anything but Your Highness?"

"They'd know I asked you to." I pull away, running the backs of my fingers over her cheek. I brush my thumb over her mouth, watching her eyelashes flutter at my touch.

She's gorgeous.

"When I saw you lying in the snow outside the palace gates, I thought you looked like an ice goddess," I whisper, brushing my lips over hers. "I thought you were part angel."

"Must have been a rude awakening when you realized I wasn't." She grins, but I don't. Her self-deprecating humor has no place here, when all I want to speak is the truth. I want to tell her everything in my heart. Show her that we can make this work—if she wants it.

Running my fingers down her sides, I pull her shirt up. She lifts her arms, letting me take the garment off and toss it aside. I let my hands brush her pale skin, running over the thousands of freckles dusted across her body.

"I'm still not convinced you're fully human," I whisper,

leaning down to kiss her shoulder. I slip her bra strap down her arm, following it with my lips.

"I'm a flawed human, through and through," Rowan answers, her fingers reaching around to the nape of my neck. With her other hand, she leans back on the desk, arching toward me.

"Show me a flaw, Rowan," I growl. "I've been looking for one."

"They're all hidden under layers of sarcasm and bitterness."

"Nothing about you tastes bitter." I kiss her clavicle, moving slowly across the bone until my lips brush the center of her chest.

Rowan lets out a sigh, leaning farther back to let me kiss her. Her body softens, melting under my touch as I unhook her bra and take her breast in my mouth.

And it's true—nothing tastes bitter. She's sweet, delicious, perfect. Crafted just for me by some higher being who wanted to show me that good things still exist in this world.

Rowan's fingers flick the buttons of my shirt open as her hands crawl hungrily over my chest. She pushes the fabric off my shoulders, then moves to tug at my belt. Her eyelids hang low, lips still glistening with my kiss—and my God, she looks like the sexiest woman in the world.

I let her tear my belt off and tug my pants down. When she wraps her fingers around my cock, I let out a low groan. I reach down her skirt and beneath her underwear to the sweet honey between her legs. When I touch her, Rowan shivers, moaning gently.

I could listen to that moan on repeat and never get sick of it. I could watch her eyelids flutter and her mouth form a soft O. I could kiss every inch of her until the day I die, and I'd be a happy man.

Me. Happy.

I never would've thought it could happen—but with Rowan, it's possible.

As I tease the pleasure out of her, I love the way her face relaxes. How her mouth falls open and a little whimper slips through her lips. She pumps my cock in short jerks before getting lost in her own lust, forgetting about her hand on my shaft for a few seconds. I watch her orgasm build as her nipples harden, her stomach clenching, back arching. I drink in the sight of her like this, just for me.

And I love it. I want more of it. Every day, all the time.

I want Rowan.

Not because she's an angel. Not because I found her in the snow and brought her back to life. Not because I'm looking for someone to save or to protect.

Because she doesn't need me to do that for her. She's strong and brave and beautiful. She comes on my hand, digging her fingernails into my arms as her legs tremble on either side of me. My cock throbs, leaking precum against her stomach as she clings onto me.

And fuck, I want this. *Really* want this. I want everything Rowan's willing to give me. I don't want this to have an expiration date or a long list of conditions.

I want Rowan to be mine. Forever.

"Wolfe…" she whispers, eyes hazy. Her hand finds my cock again, rubbing me as the last thrills of her orgasm make her body buck and grind against me. I pull my hand out of her pants and wrap it around hers, still gripping my shaft. I love the way her eyes widen and her breath shortens as I pump my cock with her fist.

Her other fingers crawl up my chest as her legs wrap around my hips, holding me close. The heat of her core presses up against me as I jerk myself off with her hand.

"I want to see you come, Wolfe," she whispers, glancing at me through thick lashes. She bites her lip, and that's what does me in. I grunt, spurting hot, white seed onto her stomach as she grips my cock and clings onto my body, grinding herself against me as I finish.

My lips find hers as my chest heaves, but I'm not quite ready to back away. There's a glow around us. Inside me, a desire burns to tell her everything I feel.

I want her beside me. She's given me life. Hope. Maybe even love. She's shown me that life isn't over because of a loss —no, maybe it can be even sweeter, because now I know how true pain feels. Now that I've seen the darkness, I can appreciate the light.

But as we fall apart and I stare at her flushed face, words stick to my throat. She giggles, reaching for a tissue to wipe my seed off her stomach, shooting a cheeky grin my way. "That wasn't exactly the royal welcome I was expecting."

"What other welcome would I give you?" I grin, but my words feel empty. What I want to say is, *stay. Be here with me, but not as an architect. Walk out onto a balcony and hold my hand in front of an army of photographers. Let me kiss you on the steps of the palace as the world watches.*

Rowan wipes the last of my orgasm off her stomach, and my heart clenches. A week ago, I was worried about not having access to the morning after pill. Now? I'd love nothing more than to see her belly swollen with my child.

I shake my head to scatter the thought, clearing my throat as I reach for my shirt. Rowan does the same, getting dressed in silence. She glances at me a few times, as if trying to gauge what I'm thinking.

"I should probably let you get to work," I say, buttoning the last ivory button on my chest.

Rowan straightens up, dipping her chin down. "Right. Yes. Of course."

When she meets my gaze, there are walls up between us. Walls which, by all rights, *should* be there. They'll always be there—because, after all, she's from Farcliff, and she's in Nord for work. I'm a prince, and I knew the moment Abby died that I was destined to be alone.

Isn't that the truth?

All those other thoughts—about life and happiness and beauty—they were just lust talking.

"Let me know if you need anything," I say and walk to the door. When my fingers are on the handle, though, I stop.

Why does it have to be this way? Why do I have to turn my back on her? Why not walk into the light and appreciate Rowan's presence for what it is: a gift. Happiness, bottled up and presented to me in the form of a beautiful, copper-haired goddess.

In three strides, I'm back beside Rowan again. I wrap my arms around her and crush my lips to hers, kissing her with all the strength of my emotion.

I want this. Her. Us.

When I pull away, we're both flushed and panting.

I grin. "I couldn't leave without doing that one last time."

"Not the last, I hope," Rowan says. Her smile widens, and there's no distance between us at all. No walls.

"Definitely not," I say, pressing my lips to hers, as if I want to convince myself that it's true. I'll get to kiss her again, and again, and again.

She lets out a happy sigh, casting a tangled web around my heart that I'm not sure I'll ever be able to escape.

23

ROWAN

WHAT AM I doing with my life?

Everything is upside down. Every day, I go to the castle to work, and I end up wrapped up in Wolfe's arms. Even when I go home to Grandma, I'm reminded of him there, too. He's the one who made sure she had a place to stay while she recovered. He's the one who organized a nurse for her. He's the one who set aside an office space for me to stay for as long as I need.

Below the arrogant, princely exterior, he's thoughtful and soft and loving and—

Uh-oh.

I'm in trouble. I know I'm playing with fire, but I can't help myself. As the days pass, my feelings grow stronger. All it takes is a glance from Wolfe. A tug of his lips. A brush of his fingers along my cheek.

The spell he's put on me is strong, but I'm not sure I want to break it. I *like* the feelings invading my heart. I like the comfort of his arms and the heat of his embrace.

One week passes. I work, steal moments with the Prince, take care of Grandma, eat, and sleep. There's a memorial for

165

Wolfe's fiancée, but he still comes to see me in the office. When I ask him if he's okay, he smiles softly and touches his forehead to mine. "Better now that I'm here with you."

His words send warmth spiraling through my core. My heart thumps. These feelings are growing.

Another week passes. Then another.

I'm in a haze. I've been in Nord for just over six weeks. The Prince and I first made love at the visitor's cottage a month ago. How have four weeks gone by already? I barely even remember my life in Farcliff. Business? What business? Now, in my life, there's only the design of the Summer Palace...

...and the Prince.

He features front and center in my brain now—not that I mind. Every time the royal car picks me up and drops me off at the castle, a thrill pierces my belly. Every time the office door opens and the Prince ducks his head to enter, I can't keep the smile off my face.

My life is *good*.

Six weeks ago, I wanted to be independent. Free of any personal relationships and chains that might hold me down. I wanted to be a burden to no one, standing tall on my own. Being independent was my way of honoring my mother's memory. I didn't want anyone else to feel the weight of responsibility for me.

But now...everything feels different. Independence feels a little too lonely. I *like* having the support of the Prince, and knowing he'll take care of Grandma even if I can't.

On a clear, cold afternoon, the royal car drives me away from the castle. I realize I've been here for exactly seven weeks—hardly an eternity—but I feel more at home in Nord than ever before. I *belong* somewhere.

Pushing the front door open, I call out into the house and

find my grandmother in the kitchen. She looks tired, but her face is flushed with happiness.

"You're home early," Grandma says, smiling at me from the kitchen table.

"Doctor's appointment in an hour," I explain. I tilt my head. "Why do you look so pleased?"

"I walked today." She beams.

Dropping a kiss on her soft, white curls, I wrap my arms around her. "Already? That's amazing, Grandma."

"The physical therapist was happy. She said my recovery is going faster than expected, but she doesn't think I should go back to the Summer Palace until spring."

"Of course not. Wolfe said you can stay here as long as you need. I'll stay here with you, too, and head back up to the Summer Palace when construction starts." Why would I go back to Farcliff, anyway?

Grandma's eyes zero in on me. "Wolfe?"

Glancing away, I walk to the sink. "The Prince, I mean. His Highness."

"Rowan…" Her lips purse. That tone of voice—I know it well. She sounds just like my mother.

I fill a glass with water and take a gulp before turning around slowly, lifting my eyes to meet hers. I paint an innocent look on my face, but I know she can see right through it. "Yeah?"

"What's going on with you and the Prince?"

"Nothing," I lie.

"Rowan."

"*Nothing.*"

Yeah, double down. That's the right thing to do. When caught in a lie, just lie again. That always works.

I clear my throat, gulping down the rest of the water. "I have to get ready for my appointment."

I scurry out of the kitchen and rush to the bedroom to avoid my grandmother's stare. The last thing I want to do is explain that I'm going to get a Pap test and checkup for a birth control prescription. The Prince and I have been using condoms, but I want to go back on the pill. Neither of us is sleeping with anyone else, and it feels...right. I want to be intimate with him on another level, and I want to make sure an accident doesn't happen.

I can't tell Grandma that, though.

As I change my clothing and run a brush through my hair, I try to still my beating heart.

She's right. Something's going on between me and the Prince, and we haven't really talked about what it means. All I know is the best part of my day is when I see him. I want to spend more time with him. I want this to be real...

...but how could it be?

He's still royalty, and I'm just a contractor working for the royal family.

Swallowing down my fears, I push my flame-red hair back over my shoulders and call out a goodbye through the house. I grab the puffy red jacket Grandma organized for me at the castle, zipping it up and bracing myself against the cold. When I step outside, the royal car is waiting for me in front of the house. I frown.

Eyvar, the Prince's most trusted bodyguard, leans against the passenger side door. He nods to me. "His Highness wanted me to drive you to the doctor."

"I told him I'd take a taxi."

"He insisted."

My heart flutters. Is that all it takes now? The Prince sending a car for me, and all of a sudden I'm all gooey inside?

I nod to Eyvar and let him open the back door for me. Slipping inside, I put my purse on my lap and wait for him to get in the driver's seat. We travel in silence until I can't take the tension in the car anymore.

"I know you don't like me, Eyvar."

He glances in the rearview mirror. "I have no opinion of you. I work for the Prince."

"Oh, please. Come on."

His jaw tenses. "The Prince is... He's been hurt before."

"You don't think he's ready for a relationship?"

"That's not my place to say." His eyes stay on the road.

I huff. "Eyvar."

"He's not like you and me, Miss Reed."

"What's that supposed to mean? He's human, isn't he?"

"He's royalty." The words come out quietly, but the weight of them makes me still. I glance out the window, watching the kingdom pass us by. It's foreign and familiar, all at once. Like I'll never quite belong, but I'll miss it if I leave.

Eyvar thinks the same thing my grandmother does—that getting involved with the Prince is trouble. And damn it, don't I know that? What's the end game, here? He can't be with me. He'll probably end up married to some princess. Maybe one of the daughters of the Farcliff royals.

He won't marry some lowly architect, no matter how many awards I have on my office wall.

Chewing the inside of my lip, I push the thought aside. We pull up outside a doctor's office, and Eyvar comes around to open the door for me. His eyes stay focused on some distant spot, and I choose not to engage him in conversation. Instead, I head inside for my appointment.

I know I talk to the receptionist and fill out some forms, and I probably sit there for ten or twenty minutes as I wait— but the truth is, I don't notice any of it. My mind is with the Prince. With the inevitable demise of our romance. What other possible outcome could there be? If he'd wanted to make our relationship public, wouldn't he have said something by now? We've been seeing each other for over a month, but it feels like I've known him my whole life. It feels more than casual.

The doctor is a tall, slim woman in her late forties or early fifties. She asks me a few questions, then instructs me to get up on the examination table. It's not until my pants are off and my legs are up on the stirrups that I finally snap back to where I am.

I'm doing this for him. For me, too, obviously. I want to have safe sex. But I want something more with the Prince. I want intimacy. I want to feel his skin on mine.

I want a *relationship*. Not behind closed doors. Not hiding away in my office in the far corner of the castle. I want to *be* with Wolfe.

What if I never get it? What if Eyvar, Grandma, and the whole rest of the world are right, and this romance will end sooner rather than later?

The speculum is cold. I grimace as it cranks.

Then, the doctor makes a soft noise. She pops her head up between my knees, rolling her stool back to meet my eye. "We'll need to do a blood test as well."

"Why?" My voice is small. In this position, no matter how friendly the doctor is, I feel exposed and vulnerable. "Is everything okay?"

"Miss Reed," she says, keeping her face neutral. "Is there any chance you might be pregnant?"

24

ROWAN

Your cervix changes color when you're pregnant, apparently. It gets softer, too, or so the doctor says when I ask why the heck she thinks I'm pregnant.

A blood test confirmed it—I'm carrying the Prince's child.

A torrent of emotions rips through me, burning a wide swath straight through my heart. It's the best and worst news I've ever heard.

Worst, because it changes the entire course of my life. How am I going to tell the Prince? How will I take care of it? Will he even want the baby?

And it's the best news, because after the initial shock wears off, and I stand outside the doctor's office with a handful of pamphlets, I finally feel like my life has a purpose.

It hits me like a sack of rocks to the side of the head. *Meaning.*

I thought *work* was my purpose? I thought building a business and being independent was my calling? Those things mean nothing.

Weak sunlight warms my skin as I tilt my head up toward its rays, feeling like my whole life has changed in an instant.

My heart beats erratically as my emotions wage war with each other. Panic nips at the heels of excitement, and if I look too closely at it, I fear panic will win. Fear and love and uncertainty grab their weapons and face off inside me.

Eyvar clears his throat, nodding to the door he's holding open. "Miss Reed?"

Mechanically, I shuffle toward the car. I slip inside, seeing nothing. Feeling everything. My hand smooths over my stomach as Eyvar closes the door, and I jump at the sound. Everything is too loud. Too sensitive. Too warm and somehow too cold, too.

I'm *pregnant*.

I stare at my past through shards of a broken mirror, realizing that in all the years I've worked myself to the bone, I've achieved nothing. Well, nothing that really matters.

Yes, I have a business. I have money. I have a contract to redesign a royal residence.

For what? For who?

In the weeks that I've been in Nord, I befriended Vikki. I fell in love with Wolfe, and I reconnected with my grandmother. As the car snakes through the snowy streets of Stirling, I think about that little four-letter word. *Love*. For the first time in my life, I've felt it in all its forms, all at once. Family, friendship...and Wolfe. I was a fool to think I could fight these feelings. As soon as he stepped into my life, a tidal wave was crashing into me, and I thought I could fight it off with a crude stick as a weapon. Love swept me out to sea, and I couldn't do a damn thing to stop it.

I'm *in* love with Wolfe. The prince who looked at me like I amused him. The man who opened up to me, day by day, showing me that we aren't really that different from each other at all. He makes me feel less...alone. I feel more fulfilled here than I ever did in Farcliff, no matter how big my corner office is, or how nice the view is from the top.

Eyvar pulls up outside my house, and I let myself out of the car. I call out a breathless thank you and rush through the front door, locking it as soon as I'm inside. I listen for a beat, but the house is silent. Grandma must be resting.

My heart hammers uncomfortably. I'm flushed and terrified and so fucking excited.

Why am I excited? Shouldn't panic be winning?

Somehow, I can't keep the smile off my face. When I catch a glimpse of myself in a hallway mirror, my eyes shine unnaturally and there's a goofy grin on my lips. Sucking in a deep breath, I try to make sense of what's going on. I pad down the hallway and lock myself in my room, sitting on the edge of the bed and staring at the carpet.

Think, Rowan.

I'm keeping the baby. That, I know. I already love it, even though it's probably the size of a seed. A smile drifts over my lips as I think of my own mother. She must have felt this way about me, too. It's the reason she went to look for my father in Farcliff. It's the reason she worked herself to death to provide for me. It's the reason she never complained about it.

She loved me in a way I didn't understand. Like only a mother can.

Squeezing my eyes shut, I take a deep breath. Dark, insidious thoughts creep into my frazzled mind. My past grins at me, reminding me that things don't always turn out the way we hope. My father didn't want me. He already had a family. Will the Prince want this baby? Am I doing exactly what my mother did with me? Subjecting myself to the kind of difficult life I saw her fight—and lose?

I think of the past four weeks, and how the Prince's eyes soften every time he glances at me. How his fingers drift over my skin, sending shivers flowing through my very core. The way he looks at me feels...*real*.

What if he wanted this baby, too? What if royalty wasn't a wedge between us? We could...We could have a family.

Curling up on the bed, I tuck my knees into my chest and let out a long breath. For one night, I allow myself to hope things will work out. I hope the Prince will feel as good as I do. I hope this baby will have a father.

For one night, I ignore my past. I ignore the blaring warning signs that tell me this isn't a normal situation, and things might not work out for me and my child.

WHEN I GET up in the morning, the sound of the doorbell strikes fear in my heart. No one comes to this house, especially not this early in the morning. Is it the Prince? Did he find out about the baby? Did Eyvar say something? Or the doctor?

My grandmother calls out from her bedroom, "Who's that?"

"I'll get it," I shout, shuffling down the creaking wooden floors to the front door.

I open it to an army of reporters shouting my name, cameras and microphones shoved in my face. They assault me, snarling and snapping their teeth at me like bloodthirsty beasts.

Screaming, I slam the door. My hands tremble as I lock it, fumbling with the latch until it finally snicks. I lean against the door, sucking in a deep breath.

What in the...?

Do they know about me and the Prince?

Scrambling for my phone, I type in a random string of

keywords that might bring up what I'm looking for. *Nord news Prince Wolfe.*

My face pops up on the screen, and my stomach falls out of my ass.

Oh, shit. Oh, shit. Oh, no, no, no.

My hands tremble. My grandmother calls out from her room. My ears ring, this high-pitched whine that drowns out everything else. What the hell is going on?

Horror ices my veins as I read article after article about myself. Exposés about my life, my history, my business. A timeline of my trip to Nord, and frighteningly accurate theories about how my romance with the Prince began.

And, most damning of all, a picture of me outside the doctor's office, with a zoomed-in insert of the pamphlet in my hand, the word *pregnancy* emblazoned on it in bold, blackletters.

They know. Everyone knows. The whole world knows that I'm pregnant with the Prince's baby—and I didn't even get a chance to tell the Prince myself.

The doorbell rings again, followed by a knock on the door. Grandma shuffles to her bedroom door, poking her head out. She has a silk scarf over her head and sleep still clouding her eyes. "What's all that about?"

My eyes are wide with terror. I open and close my mouth. "I... I..." I stammer, shuffling toward her. "Reporters."

"What do they want?"

I glance at the entrance, watching as someone's shadow tries to peer through the skinny window beside the door. "They want *me*."

Grandma stares at me, confused. Sighing, she hobbles past me and heads for the kitchen, mumbling something about needing a cup of coffee. I follow her blindly, accepting a mug when she hands it to me. Am I even supposed to be drinking this? I feel so incredibly unprepared for pregnancy. For *motherhood.*

Oh, God. Panic might win this fight, after all.

When Grandma sits down across from me, she stares at me until I meet her gaze. Leaning back, she dips her chin. "Now, Rowan. Are you going to tell me what this is about?"

My dear, sweet, no-nonsense grandmother. She must have had this exact conversation with my mother, except the man who impregnated *her* wasn't literal royalty.

I gulp a mouthful of coffee past a lump in my throat, burning the roof of my mouth in the process. It's bitter and hot and disgusting, but I swallow another sip down anyway. When I finally put my mug down, I glance at my grandmother and let out a sigh. "I'm pregnant with the Prince's baby, and dozens of reporters are outside trying to ask me about it." There. That was easy. Sort of.

Grandma's eyebrows twitch upward ever so slightly, but otherwise, her face doesn't move. That tiny movement of her brow nudges me toward a full-on breakdown, but I resist.

My hands grip the edge of the kitchen counter and I don't trust myself to pick up the coffee cup. Taking a deep breath, I try to sort through the mess in my mind. "I... I want to keep it, but I can't subject the baby to all that." I wave a hand toward the door. "And the Prince... He hasn't talked about making our relationship public. It's always been secret. I'm not sure he wants..." I squeeze my eyes shut, cheeks burning. I'm embarrassed. Ashamed, even. Why would I allow myself to be in this position?

Everything is confusing. Shame tastes bitter at the back of my throat, and there's an oily coating over my skin. I don't even know what I'm ashamed of. Not the baby. Not Wolfe. So...what?

"Have you told him?"

I shake my head. "I only found out last night."

"Will you tell him?"

I nod. "Today."

"Good. Will you keep it?"

"Of course." My voice is strong. I grip the edge of the counter so hard I'm afraid it'll crumble in my palms.

Grandma makes a soft noise. "Okay, honey. You have to tell him."

The heady, euphoric feeling from last night turns black inside me. Reality isn't rose-colored. Reality is dark, and I stare at the hallway leading to the front door. "What then, Grandma? What are my options? If he wants to be with me, it means I have to give up my whole life. My business. My independence. I basically choose this"—I jerk my head to the door—"as my new reality. What kind of way is that to raise a child? I'm not sure I even want that for myself. I saw the headlines—they're all just comparing me to his dead fiancée. I'm the other woman, just like Mom was, except in my case, the first woman isn't even alive."

Grandma tilts her head.

"Say it, Grandma."

"Say what?" Her voice is neutral.

"Something, something, apple, tree..." I turn to the counter and stare at the black coffee in my mug, cheeks burning. "This is exactly what happened to Mom, wasn't it?"

Grandma chuckles, patting my hand. "It's slightly different, Rowan. For one, I think the Prince cares about you, and I know for a fact he doesn't have a secret family hidden away in another kingdom."

I let out a long sigh. "Right. But he's still a prince. If Wolfe doesn't want to be involved, do I raise this kid without ever telling them who their father is?"

"Let's just deal with one problem at a time, Rowan."

"I can't stay here." I meet my grandmother's eyes. "If I stay, I either get wrapped up in this whole media machine and become part of the royal family, or I'm an outcast. My child is a pariah. I can't let that happen. I need to go back to Farcliff. I need to just do this on my own—that's the best chance I have at giving this kid a normal, healthy upbringing."

"You need to tell the Prince."

I chew my lip, tears welling up in my eyes for the first time since I found out about the baby. Nodding, I push myself up to my feet. Then, an even scarier thought. "What if he wants it? What if he wants me to stay? What if I have to give everything up..." My eyes widen. If he doesn't want it, fine. I can leave with my tail between my legs. I can show this baby love and devotion. But if Wolfe *does* want me the way I thought I wanted him...

"Then you either stay and let him be part of the baby's life, or you leave. It's your choice, Rowan. You need to do what's best for the baby."

"And if he doesn't want it?" My voice is small. My heart aches.

"Then the choice is made for you, honey."

I blink a tear down my cheek and wipe it away in an instant. There are no good choices. My mania from yesterday has vanished. I'm staring at a bunch of bleak options for a sad future, that oily film coating everything from my head down to my bare toes.

If I stay, I'm subjecting the baby to media scrutiny—even worse so if the Prince doesn't want to be a part of our lives. What kind of future is that for a child? Everyone would know who the father is, and everyone would judge me and the baby. What if it affected the baby's future? Judging by the crush of reporters outside, they wouldn't just forget about us. The kid would be in the newspapers for his or her whole life.

They could be bullied, or judged, or stopped from getting jobs and opportunities.

Even if Wolfe wants the kid, do I really want to take that chance? Do I want to subject my child to that kind of future?

If I go back to Farcliff, I'm giving up my relationship with the Prince. I'm leaving the only place I've ever felt at home—but I'm giving my child a chance at a normal life. I'm choosing independence and anonymity. Privacy. Normalcy.

My life is crumbling around me and I feel so sad it makes my chest ache, but I feel like I finally understand the choices my mother made for me. I understand the pain she must have felt, and I understand the devotion. My hand slips over my stomach and I let my eyes close, knowing I'll do anything to keep my baby safe.

25

WOLFE

EVERY NIGHT that Rowan isn't in bed beside me is torture. Since we've been in the capital, we've stolen secret moments together in her office, or sneaked up to my chambers, or gone for walks on the palace grounds—but it's not the same as being together. Really *together*.

A knock sounds on my bedroom door. I open it up to see Frederick, my sister's little lapdog. His mustache is particularly thick and luscious today. "Good morning, Your Highness," he says with a small bow that's hardly more than a nod. "Her Majesty requests your presence."

I let out a sigh. It's too early for this, but Frederick just stands there and stares at me. I pull a sweater on over my head, then motion for him to lead the way. We walk across the castle to my sister's private chambers, where I find her sitting at a vanity, putting on her jewelry like she's readying for battle. She glances at me through the mirror.

"Brother," she says, her voice cold as ice.

"Your Majesty," I reply with an insolent bow. I'm not in the mood for this. I don't want her to chastise me for something or tell me I'm not doing a good enough job with the

Summer Palace design. Ever since her husband died, Penelope changed. She's not the bright, happy sister I once knew.

I can't judge her for that—didn't my personality change when Abby died? Didn't I become dark and lonely?

But now...things are different. There's light in my life again.

The Queen turns around, delicately picking up a cell phone from the edge of her vanity. Tapping on the screen a few times, she turns it toward me with an arch of her brow. "Explain."

I glance at the screen and frown. It's a photo of Eyvar and Rowan outside the doctor's office with headlines screaming about my affair with her and proclaiming that she's carrying my child. Skimming through the article, my stomach drops.

The journalists—if you can call them that—have written a brief history of Rowan's life. They point to the photo of us disembarking the royal jet together, coupled with my arrival in Stirling during the month of October when I'm usually away. Apparently, that's evidence of our romance.

Which, I mean, fair point.

Worse, still, they point to 'sources inside the palace'—which is bullshit speak for *we made this up*—saying that her visit to the doctor is as a result of our sexual affair. A secret pregnancy, they say, with a zoomed-in photo of a pamphlet as irrefutable proof.

Right.

And, I mean, we *have* been sleeping together. That's true. But how fucking dare they?

"Well?" My sister's still staring at me, waiting for an explanation.

I sigh, shaking my head. "How could they possibly know any of this?"

"So it's true."

"Is it true that Rowan and I are involved? Yes. Is it true it started at the Summer Palace? Yes. Is it true that she went to the gynecologist because she's pregnant? Absolutely fucking not." My breath shortens as anger clouds my vision. I click through to another article, which is an exposé of my relationship with Abby, and a brilliant think piece about whether or not I might have moved on to a new woman.

Fucking wonderful.

"This is exactly what happened with Abby," I say. "The media made up a bunch of stories and crafted this narrative about our relationship. They became obsessed with her. Why do they care about who I date? Why is this newsworthy?"

"Well, dear brother," Penelope replies with a tilt of her head. "You are *royalty*. Or have you forgotten?"

"It's bullshit."

"It's not," she shoots back. "You just said yourself that you're having an affair with this woman. How are we supposed to let her redesign the palace now?"

"Because she won the contract, Pen. This has nothing to do with me. She's a talented architect. And it's not an...*affair*."

"What is it, then?"

I stand there trembling, but I say nothing. The words don't come. What is going on between Rowan and me, really?

The Queen folds her hands in her lap, but I don't miss the tension in her jaw. "It doesn't look good. It looks like we gave her the job because you're sleeping with her."

"That's not what happened," I snap.

Penelope arches an eyebrow.

I sigh, dropping my shoulders. "I hate the media. They twist our lives into some sorry soap opera. Abby died in my arms, and in all those dozens of photographers that surrounded us, not one called an ambulance. Not. One. They snapped photos of her last moments instead of helping."

They did nothing, just like me. Isn't that why I hate those images? Because it reminds me of my greatest failure? How I froze, holding my dying fiancée, unable to move or help? How *I* failed to call anyone? How *I* failed to perform CPR? How *I* watched her die and did absolutely nothing to stop it?

Penelope lets out a sigh, lowering her eyes to the floor. For the first time in a long, long time, I see the tension rippling through her shoulders. She's usually the strong one. The unshakeable, unbreakable one—but is that weighing on her? Have I been too hard on my sister?

She lifts her eyes to mine. "Is she pregnant, Wolfe?"

"No," I reply emphatically. "No, she's not pregnant."

She nods. "I'll get the media team to do some damage control. They usually advise us to do nothing in cases like these. Feeding the beast only makes it hungrier. We won't respond to rumors." Turning back to her vanity, she sits down and starts dusting her face with powder, signaling that I'm dismissed.

I leave the room, letting out a heavy sigh. My sister is still my sister, but she's the Queen first. She has to bear the weight of the crown and think of what's best for the family. She has to make decisions I wouldn't want to make—all while carrying her own scars.

I know why she has a cold exterior. I know why she seems callous sometimes—but damn, if it doesn't make my blood boil. I feel like a child who's just been scolded. I'm a grown man!

I make my way to the dining room, hoping to find my brothers. When I walk in, Jonah glances up at me. He reaches for a platter full of bacon, heaping a few rashers onto his plate before looking at me again. "Haven't seen much of you around lately." He grins, pushing his cropped black hair back off his forehead.

Silas grunts from the corner of the room. A tumbler of bourbon dangles between his fingertips. "He's been too busy banging the architect."

"Screw you," I grumble. "Isn't it a bit early for a drink?"

"Hair of the dog." Silas grins. "Late night last night. Need to take the edge off."

"How am *I* the one in the tabloids?" I frown, staring at Silas' rumpled clothes and half-drunk, half-hungover face.

Jonah whistles, wiggling his eyebrows. "So it's true."

"You like her." Silas ambles over to me, his blue eyes flashing. His rich, chocolate hair curls around his temples and makes his eyes look even more piercing. He's the one who always has women screaming for him. Not me. He's the one who's slept with every pretty maid who's ever walked the palace halls.

And now he's giving *me* shit?

Silas claps me on the shoulder, laughing. "About time you got laid. Four years is a long time without a nice, warm pussy."

"Shut up, Silas." I pour myself a cup of coffee.

Silas throws his hands up as he backs away, grinning. He sinks into a chair and stretches out, wrinkling his nose when a waiter offers him eggs and bacon. I guess bourbon is the breakfast of champions in Silas' world.

Jonah glances at me from across the room, trying to read my mood. How could he, though? How could he know what thoughts are going through my mind?

I'm here with my brothers, with my sister, in the castle where we spend most of our time. Things, from the outside, are exactly as they were a couple of months ago.

But I *feel* different. Deep in my gut, I know I've changed. My steps aren't as heavy. My spine is straighter. When I wake up, I don't feel the dark sense of dread that kept me down for four years. My grief isn't quite as painful as it was before, and a thin seed of hope has sprouted in my heart.

...but for what? For who? For me to date Rowan, officially? My sister the Queen didn't seem too happy about that, and her word is law around here.

But, but, but... what if?

Who says we can't be together?

As I listen to my brothers, I try to let my thoughts drift away from the red-haired goddess who has occupied them for the better part of the past two months. I won't let the media tear her to shreds the way they did to Abby. I won't let her be exposed and dissected by the public. If she's with me, I'll protect her. I'll do what I couldn't do before, even if it kills me.

AFTER BREAKFAST, I'm already waiting in Rowan's office when she arrives.

"Come here, beautiful," I growl, reaching for her hand.

Rowan stiffens, letting me pull her into my chest but not wrapping her arms around me or tilting her head up for a kiss.

Something's off. A cold jet of ice water shoots down my spine.

I frown. "What's wrong? Was your appointment okay?"

She gulps. "It was..." She shakes her head. "Yeah, it was fine."

Her eyes don't meet mine. I frown.

"Is this about the article? We have the royal media team dealing with it. They'll probably get most of the articles taken down and threaten newspapers with lawsuits for making up those stories, citing slander. It'll all blow over. It's just because the memorials were a couple of weeks ago, and this is the first time I've been seen with anyone."

Rowan lets out a snort, shaking her head. "That's the problem, Wolfe. I'm just a controversy. I'm the sad, desperate woman trying to fill your dead fiancée's shoes. I'm the outsider who doesn't belong. I'm someone you keep secret from your family and friends and the media—"

"The media are animals," I snap. "They tore Abby to shreds even when they pretended to love her. I won't let them do that to you."

"It's not about that, Wolfe," Rowan says. Her shoulders stiffen as she drops her chin. Taking a finger, I tilt her head back up to meet her eye. Her bottom lip trembles.

"What is it, Rowan?" My voice is soft. My heart is breaking. This relationship will end—I just know it. I thought we could make it official? I thought I could protect her? Who was I kidding?

Rowan takes a step back, splaying her hands on my chest as she pushes me away. She drops her arms and takes a breath, lifting her eyes to mine.

"I'm pregnant, Wolfe. It's yours, and I'm keeping it."

26

ROWAN

MY LIFE CHANGED twelve hours ago. As soon as the doctor told me I was with child, it felt like everything I thought I knew just vanished from my mind. The future I saw for myself, gone. The priorities I've upheld for a decade...just, *poof!*

I'm having a baby. I *want* to have a baby. I'm terrified, of course, but there's a deep well of love already flowing inside me.

Ever since I came to Nord, I've been wondering if I missed something from life. I've tried so hard to be independent, to work my way to financial stability, to not be a burden on anyone—I've missed the connections that make life worth living.

I know I can't have that connection with the Prince. He's royalty. Having a child out of wedlock would be frowned upon, to say the least. I'm already plastered over every newspaper with a horde of reporters following me around.

I can't be with the Prince. I know that now. It would be bad for the baby. I can't let my child grow up with its face on newspapers. I need to give it some kind of stability, and I can't do that here.

But I *can* have a connection with my grandmother. I can love this child with every bit of my heart and give it the best possible chance at a good life. For the first time ever, I understand my mother's perspective.

Grandma was right—I wasn't a burden, and my baby isn't one, either.

Those realizations all hit me one after the other between the time the doctor told me I was pregnant and now, when I stand in front of the Prince and tell him the truth. They've only grown stronger as the minutes have ticked by.

I know what I need to do. I know I need to leave—not just for myself, but for the baby. So it has the best chance of a good, stable life.

I need to leave for the Prince, too. To save him from controversy, and to stop old wounds from splitting open. He can tell me that he's moving on, but I know he still aches for his fiancée. Those shoes are too big for me to fill.

Right now, though, he's staring at me like I've sprouted another head. Shock doesn't even begin to cover it. The lips I love to kiss open and close again. His throat clenches and releases as he swallows, and his palm moves to rub the center of his chest.

"You're...You're pregnant?" He frowns, confusion written over every inch of his face.

I nod. "Yeah. About five weeks, apparently. So...The visitor's cottage."

"I thought you said..."

"I was wrong." I inhale slowly, preparing myself to make the speech I've rehearsed all morning. Squaring my shoulders, I face the Prince. "I'm not expecting you to go public about it, and I'm prepared to keep you out of the baby's life, if you prefer. I'll go back to Farcliff to raise the baby. That way, the media attention will die down, and I'll go back to my anonymous life. It'll be better for the baby. No pressure. No controversy. No prejudice."

Wolfe starts to say something, but I hold up my hand.

"I'm not giving this baby up. I'm not going to be ashamed of it, and I'm not going to do anything except love it and provide the best possible life I can for it."

He stares at me, blinking two or three times. His eyes drop to my stomach, then slowly climb back up again. Wolfe nods, a slow breath passing through his lips. He rubs his forehead with his middle finger, gaze drifting off into nothing.

"You don't want me involved?" His voice is small. Faraway. He's hurt.

Ouch. My heart. This is harder than I thought it would be.

I take a deep breath, turning to glance out the window. "When I woke up this morning, there were a dozen reporters waiting outside my house. I had to rush to the car like some criminal hiding my face. That's not the life I want for me or my child."

"I wouldn't want that life for you either," Wolfe says slowly. "Those journalists are animals. Vicious, bloodthirsty jackals who only want to get a headline."

I nod. "I've made arrangements to head back to Farcliff. My grandmother will come with me until she's well enough to go back to the Summer Palace in the spring."

"You're leaving?" Pain cracks through his voice, sending agony spearing through my heart. Why is this so much harder than I thought? Leaving doesn't seem so simple when the Prince looks like I just stabbed him in the chest.

I square my shoulders and nod. "If I stay, the rumors will only get worse."

This morning, as I got ready, I decided I needed to go. Not

just for the baby, but for me, too. I can't stay in Nord, seeing the castle and the newspaper stories about the royal family without feeling my heart break. And I know the Prince and I can't be together, so I have no choice.

But now, as I watch the Prince's face crumple, it doesn't feel right. I thought he'd understand. I thought he'd appreciate me leaving and not dragging him into a messy controversy. I thought he'd *want* me to go. I know how much he hates the media. How much Abby's death hurt him. I thought I was doing him a favor.

Inhaling deeply, Wolfe takes slow steps toward me. He wraps his arms around my waist, pulling me close. His hand climbs up my spine and tangles itself in my copper locks, and the Prince holds me tight.

My resolve weakens. He smells like home. His embrace feels like heaven—and I'm supposed to leave it behind?

The Prince pulls away, cupping his hands on either side of my face. "Is that what you want? You want to leave?"

"It's what's best for me and the baby...and you."

His breath trembles. Brows draw together as his gaze shifts from one eye to the other. "But is it what you want?"

"Wolfe..."

"You can't say my name like that—like it means something to you—and pretend you want to leave."

"What choice do I have? What are you going to do, marry me? Keep me locked up in this castle and call me your princess for the rest of my life? That's not what I want for my life, Wolfe. You know that. I want to be able to stand on my own."

Dropping his hands from my face, the Prince backs away. He nods, turning his face away from me. "You're right. I'm sorry. It's too much to ask of you. You have a business and a life in Farcliff."

"It's better if I leave. It makes things easier for you, too."

"How would you know that?" His eyes cut to mine.

I don't answer. What can I say?

The Prince inhales deeply, rapping his knuckles on the desk. He chews his lip and finally nods. "You're right. It's safer for you in Farcliff. I already lost Abby." His eyes lift to mine. "I can't lose you, too. I'll make sure you have everything you need for the baby."

Why does that hurt to hear? He says it like I'm asking for his money. Like I came here begging for a few coins to rub together.

I shake my head. "I don't want your money, Wolfe."

"That baby is mine, and I'll make sure you're taken care of."

"And what happens when the media finds out? It'll be a lot worse than one article and a few paparazzi outside my house." I shake my head. "This has to be a clean break, Wolfe. I have to leave. You have to let me go."

"So that's it, then? You inform me you're the mother of my child and then tell me it's over?"

"*What's* over, Wolfe? Sneaking around behind closed doors? Pretending we're not together whenever we leave this room?"

Tension ripples between us. I square my shoulders as pain shatters across my chest. This morning, leaving seemed logical. The best, most painless thing to do. Better for me, and the baby, and the Prince.

But right now, with him looking at me like I've just ripped his heart out of his chest, it doesn't seem so good. I turn away, staring at the wall. My eyelids burn, but I refuse to cry. I *will not cry.* I can't. If tears fall from my eyes, my resolve will weaken.

I need to leave. I need to be on my own and have my independence. I need to keep my child's life free from controversy and the pressure of the media.

When my mother died, I vowed I'd take care of myself no matter what. That I wouldn't rely on anyone. I wouldn't be a burden. How can I turn around and stay here? How can I put this problem on Wolfe's shoulders? How can I ask anything from him except to let me go?

And why does it make me want to cry until it hurts to breathe?

I turn to look at him in all his muscled glory. Crisp, white shirt tailored perfectly over his broad frame. Dark, slightly curly hair. Pale amber eyes like warm honey that made me fall in love with him the moment I saw them across from me.

In three steps, I could be in his arms. I could nuzzle against his skin and tear his clothes off, begging him to take me right here. I could ask for his forgiveness and tell him I'll stay. He doesn't have to marry me, or admit to being with me, or claim to be the father of my child. I'll be happy with whatever scraps of attention he's willing to give me if it just means being near him for one more minute. One more second.

But my feet stay glued to the floor, and my pride keeps me from dropping to my knees. I lift my chin up, knowing I can't ask him to take care of me. I can't beg him to love me. I can't let him carry me through life when I know I can walk on my own.

My mother showed me exactly how strong I need to be to do this. I'll take care of my baby, even if it kills me just as it did her.

This child isn't a burden. It's not a controversy, or a scandal, or a royal bastard to be splayed across the kingdom's headlines.

This baby is my gift, and I'll cherish it, even if it means saying goodbye to the Prince.

"Will you let me meet the baby, at least?" Wolfe's voice is low. His brows are drawn together and damn it, my heart just shatters right there in my chest.

I won't cry. I can't cry. I need to be strong, to follow this through to the end and make sure I do what's best for my child.

I should say no. I should tell him it's a bad idea—his every move is tracked and photographed. How could we do it without fresh headlines being penned?

Call me weak, but I just can't make my head shake. Instead, I just dip my chin down. "Maybe."

Wolfe's hands ball into fists as his teeth grind together. Amber eyes pour all their hurt and pain and anger into me, and I accept it all. I drink it up, because on some level, I think I deserve it.

Then he blinks, and the emotion is gone. "Okay. If that's what you want. Goodbye, Rowan."

I watch him walk out of the office, leaving the door open so I can listen to his fading footsteps.

27

WOLFE

I'M SHELL-SHOCKED. I walk through the castle and find myself in the back gardens, staring at the frost-covered branches without feeling the chill in the air.

I'm going to be a father, but Rowan doesn't want me to be involved.

Fate is laughing at me. It's the only explanation.

Abby died in my arms, and I didn't even know she was carrying my child. She probably didn't know either. Her heart just stopped, and I couldn't do a thing to save her.

Rowan's carrying my child, too, but she's taking it away from here to choose a better, more normal life. Twice I've loved. Twice I've let myself open up to a woman. Twice they've carried my child.

And twice, I've lost.

I would fight for Rowan. I'd beg her to stay, but deep down, I think she's making the right decision. What kind of life can I give her?

Luxury, sure. All the finest clothing and food and wine she can imagine. A private tutor for our child and a big, expensive wedding.

Not her own business. Not her independence. She'd have to give up the things she cares about most just to be with me.

I wander through the castle gardens, powerless and alone. Broken-hearted. Resigned.

It was foolish of me to think I could have it all with Rowan. It was naive of me to believe I could have love and happiness. I already know what life is like. It beats you down and kicks you when you hit the ground. It batters you, day after day, until all you can do is blindly put one foot in front of the other.

Rowan was just a reminder of everything I've lost. She was a flash of happiness in my sad, gray life.

Of course she's leaving. Why would she stay?

I walk until my fingertips turn blue, and finally head back inside. Winter will be here soon, and I'll have to stay inside and think about everything I've lost. Everything I failed to protect.

Isn't that what happened with Rowan, too? I was too much of a coward to ask her to be with me officially. I was too afraid, and the rumors got to her first. The media stood outside her door, and she felt unsafe, because I wasn't there beside her. I couldn't even give her the decency of a real relationship.

Now, she's making the only choice she can, for herself and our child. She's leaving.

I find my brothers in the billiards room. Silas looks relatively fresh, considering he was out until all hours last night. Jonah glances up at me from the felt-covered table. He takes a shot, then straightens.

"What happened to you? You look like death."

"Feel like it, too." I slump down onto a chair, dropping my head in my hands. "She's leaving."

I expect Silas to come out with some snarky comment. A

callous jab at my sad little feelings. Instead, I feel a palm on my shoulder and I see my youngest brother looking down at me with nothing but sympathy. "Sorry, brother," Silas says, his voice quiet. "Is it because of the article? All that will blow over. The newspapers just needed a headline—it'll be forgotten by next week."

"She's leaving because the article is true." I look from Silas to Jonah. "She's pregnant with my kid."

Jonah leans his pool cue on the wall, roughing his hand through his hair. "Oh."

"Yeah."

Silas takes a seat beside me, blowing a breath out. "What are you going to do?"

"Let her go," I reply. "What else can I do?"

"Um, *not* do that." Silas frowns. "You care about her, right?"

"What can I offer her, though?"

Jonah scoffs, then spreads his arm around. "All this? A royal title? Riches beyond her wildest dreams?"

I shake my head. "A gilded cage. She's spent her entire adult life building up her architecture business. She's been independent since she was young. She doesn't want to be coddled and taken care of."

"Everyone wants to be coddled and taken care of," Silas says, snorting.

"Not Rowan. The media will eat her up, just like they did to—"

"Don't say Abby," Jonah interjects. "Stop blaming yourself for her death. She had an arrhythmia. Her heart malfunctioned. No one could have predicted it and even if she'd been in a hospital, it's not certain they could have saved her."

I shake my head. "It's not about Abby. It's about *me*. I just don't deserve a woman who has as much spirit and heart as Rowan."

Silas and Jonah exchange a glance. After a long pause, Silas squeezes my shoulder again. "Why don't you go back to the Summer Palace? Clear your head for a while. At least there won't be reporters crawling all over the place. You'll have some privacy."

Swallowing past a jagged lump in my throat, I glance at my brother. "Maybe I should have stayed there to begin with. I only came back to be with Rowan."

"Does she know how you feel?" Jonah asks.

I shake my head. "It doesn't matter. She doesn't want a relationship with me. She was pretty clear about it. She said it was best for her, the baby, and for me if she left. No need to save face. Less controversy. Less mess."

"Just because she thinks that doesn't mean it's true," Silas says quietly.

I glance at my brother, surprised to see he cares. He's typically moving from one woman to the next, not worried about love or relationships. I didn't even think he knew love existed —but he's staring at me with understanding in his eyes.

Do I even really know my siblings? We've all been through our own battles, but I've been so focused on my own failures and pain that I haven't taken the time to see them for who they are. I've been drifting on my own, wrapped up in my own grief. Silas isn't just a party animal. Penelope isn't an ice queen. Jonah isn't the calm, logical person he appears to be—he has scars of his own. Don't we all?

Just goes to show how fucking useless I've been. I couldn't help Abby, and I don't even know my own brothers and sister.

Rowan was right to want to leave. It's the best thing for all of us. I'm better off on my own, away from people I can't help.

Sighing, I nod to Silas. "You're right. I'll head back to the

Summer Palace until spring. At least I'll have some time to clear my head, and Chief will be there to keep me company."

As I stand up, I feel the weight of my past on my shoulders. I've failed so many people, so many times. Even my siblings—haven't I failed them, too? I don't even know them. I don't know their pain.

It's better for me to leave. Nodding to my brothers, I stalk out the door and call for Eyvar to make arrangements for my departure. I'm going back to the Summer Palace, and I'm not coming back until I know I won't hurt anyone else.

28

ROWAN

I STARE at the castle staff member at the door to the office, trying to make sense of what he just told me. Wolfe is gone. He left without saying goodbye.

That's his right, I guess. Just yesterday, I told him I intended to leave Nord this week and go back to Farcliff. Why would he stay here?

But for him to turn around and just leave? Like I'm nothing? Like the past six weeks didn't even happen? He didn't even *tell* me?

That hurts more than I can say, but I put on my best, professional face and thank the man for the information. I glance around the tiny office, thinking only of Wolfe.

There, on the desk, where we made love. How he scraped his teeth across my neck and drank me in with those eyes full of fire. The window where we stared out at falling snowflakes, feeling blissfully in love and unaware of the bombshell that would hit us.

All the while, I was carrying his child.

And he's gone without a word.

It...hurts. Aches down to my marrow.

Slumping down in a chair, I drop my head in my hands. Logically, I know this is the right decision. If I stay, I force the Prince to either deny his connection to me or make it official.

I don't want to enter a relationship with someone under those circumstances. Even if he wanted me to become part of this family, I wouldn't want to feel like it was forced. Isn't that just a recipe for disaster? The perfect place for resentment and bitterness to grow?

By leaving, I remove that choice. I make sure my child is protected from the reporters who just want a headline. I can live life on my terms. I can keep my business.

My little, safe life in Farcliff.

Empty.

Loveless.

Meaningless.

Tears fall down my cheeks as I sit in the office that Wolfe organized for me, and I feel like a complete failure. All I wanted from life was to never be a burden to anyone else. I wanted to stand on my own two feet—but it feels like all I've ever done is make a mess of every relationship I've ever had.

The hinges on the door squeak as someone pushes it open. My eyes widen when I see the Queen standing in the doorway. She's wearing a deep blue boatneck dress, with her hair twisted into a sleek bun. Her eyes are sharp, bright aqua. The Queen steps inside the office, her presence filling the room from wall to wall.

I scramble to my feet, dropping into a curtsy and doing my best to wipe the tears off my cheeks.

"You can sit down," she says softly.

Confused, I glance at her. Every image I've seen of her, she looks hardened and cold. She stands with her spine straight and her lips pinched—but now, in person, she looks soft. She's shorter than I thought she'd be, reaching only to my shoulders, even in heels. I do as she says, sliding back down onto my chair. The Queen takes a seat across the desk from me, crossing her feet at the ankles and folding her hands on her lap.

She tilts her head, studying me. "You're carrying Wolfe's child."

I gulp. "Yes, Your Majesty."

Sighing, the Queen leans back in her chair. Her eyes drift over my shoulder to stare out the window as I fidget in my seat. Even though I've spent the past six weeks with the Prince, I still don't know how to act around other royals. I have a feeling the insolent flirting I did with Wolfe won't exactly go down well with this monarch.

The Queen doesn't seem to notice my squirming. She stares out the window, the light angling through it in a way that makes her pale skin glow like moonlight. With platinum blond hair and pale blue eyes, she looks like a Nordic ice queen. Still as a statue, the sight of her makes my mouth turn dry. Tilting her head, she studies me. "When I was growing up, my best friend was Abby Mansfield."

"Wol—His Highness's fiancée?"

The Queen dips her chin down. "She was kind, and soft, and funny, and her death shocked us all."

"I'm so sorry," I reply quietly, shifting in my seat.

"She was pregnant, too."

My eyes snap to the Queen's. "With his child?"

She nods. "No one knew until they did the autopsy."

"I...I'm so sorry." The world is spinning. Wolfe lost his fiancée and his first child that day? They both died in his arms. Oh, no—he never told me that. So the pain in his eyes when I told him about our baby...

"Wolfe took it hard." Her eyes never leave mine. I try not to fidget as another bombshell is lobbed at my poor, broken soul. The Queen lets out a long breath, pinching her lips into a smile. "He almost seemed like himself these past few weeks. I thought..." The Queen shakes her head, not finishing her thought.

She pushes herself to her feet, and I scramble to stand. The Queen extends a hand to me. "I just wanted to meet you, is all," she says. "I love the new design you've created. We can start the renovations in the spring, once the snow melts."

I frown. "You still want me to finish the design?"

"You're the best person for the job, and you've done most of the work already. Besides, firing you would only feed the gossip. The media team have decided not to address the controversy in the newspapers at all. Any official comment from the palace will only spur them on. I understand you're leaving?"

I nod, a huge lump lodged in my throat. "Yes."

"You'll come back for the construction?"

"That depends..." My hand slides over my stomach.

Her eyes flick down to the movement, pain flashing across her face for the briefest moment.

"I'm keeping it," I blurt out. "If I have to return during the palace construction, I'll be eight or nine months pregnant. The media..."

"Of course. We'll make arrangements for things to be done remotely if necessary." The Queen walks to the door, every step graceful and measured. She turns to look at me, eyes soft. "If you need to visit the site, we'll arrange for you to travel privately. I'm sure you'll want to see your work when construction is finished."

"Thank you, Your Majesty." I drop into a curtsy as my heart hammers. The Queen walks out of the office as my ears ring.

She knows I'm carrying Wolfe's child. Why did she tell me

about Abby's baby? Was it to make me feel bad about leaving?

...Or was it so I'd understand why Wolfe left without saying goodbye?

Sadness crushes me. I sit down because it's too difficult to stand. Everything hurts. I feel like I've taken Wolfe's child away from him after he suffered such an awful loss four years ago, but at the same time, I need to think about what's best for me and my child.

The Queen didn't try to convince me to stay. She didn't tell me to chase after Wolfe and follow him to the Summer Palace. The only reason she didn't want to fire me was because it would look bad in the media.

Telling me about the Prince's loss wasn't some ploy to get me to feel sorry for him. Everything she told me was in order for me to understand the position of the palace, and make sure there was the least amount of controversy possible.

I'm not part of this world. Even though I'm carrying Wolfe's child, I'm just a satellite orbiting around him. I'll never belong here, and the best thing for me to do is leave. I knew that yesterday, and nothing has changed. I need to go— for all of us.

Sliding my hand over my stomach, I squeeze my eyes shut and draw strength from the only thing I know is true. I'm having a baby, and I love it with all my heart.

WOLFE

THE SUMMER PALACE IS COLD, and lonely, and desolate—and it feels like home. Days march on at a slow crawl as the wind howls outside and fires crackle in every hearth.

Chief stays by my side, and he's my only anchor in a world that doesn't make sense.

Twice, I've loved. Twice, a woman has carried my child. Twice, I've lost. Those words ring in my head like church bells every hour, on the hour.

I thought the pain of Abby's death was the deepest cut I'd feel—but somehow, Rowan leaving feels worse. I know she's somewhere south of here, living her life without me. I know our child is growing in her womb, and I might never get to meet it.

I could have her if things were different—but they're not. She doesn't want my life, and she's not here.

It's a painful, slow kind of torture to watch the seconds tick by, knowing I'm alone. I'll *be* alone.

On a clear day in December, I take the dogs out to the visitor's cottage. As soon as I get there, I'm wrapped up in my own sadness. I see Rowan everywhere. On the couch, where I first told her about Abby and she opened up about her mother. In the studio, where her eyes lit up. In the bedroom, where—

I turn away, shaking my head. That's where everything went wrong. In that bed is where I crossed a line and allowed myself to believe I could have a better life. That I deserved happiness. That I might have met someone who meant something to me.

Naive. Stupid. Silly.

I turn around and throw my jacket back on, heading for the kennels. I'm back on the dog sled within minutes, returning to the castle.

Even with the wind whistling past my ears, and the blue bird sky singing above, I feel the weight of my own loneliness. The sled flies over hard-packed snow and the dogs huff in front of me, running fast as they were meant to do, but it feels empty.

It just reminds me of Rowan. How bright her eyes shined when she sat in the sled for the first time. The mischievous little grin on her lips when she threw a snowball at me.

How is it possible to lose so much in such a short period of time? I wish I'd never met her. I wish I hadn't believed I could be happy, because this feels worse than grief.

The staff gives me lots of space. Even Eyvar is quieter than usual—if that's even possible. They let me mope in the palace and spend time with my dogs, and I do my best to forget about the woman who plagues my dreams.

Days turn into weeks, weeks into months, and soon, the mornings are brighter and the evenings are longer. I watch water droplets dripping down from the eaves outside my bedroom window, spying the first of the birds returning for the summer.

This place will be alive again, but I'll remain dead.

IN LATE MARCH, a long procession of royal vehicles drives along the slushy road leading to the palace. My sister, or maybe one of my brothers, has arrived.

I pad through the silent halls to the front entrance, ready to greet them. I can't quite put a smile on my face, so I don't try.

What is there to smile about? Spring will burst into summer, and soon it'll be winter once more. The world will keep turning, and I'll keep standing still.

My sister emerges from the second vehicle in the convoy, a thick jacket wrapped around her slim body. She lifts her eyes to mine, dipping her chin down in greeting.

"Hi, Pen," I say, too exhausted for formalities.

She puts her hands on my arms, squeezing. Her eyes search mine. "You look like shit."

"Thanks." I shrug her off.

"It's that bad, huh?"

"What do you mean?"

"Your broken heart." She throws me one more glance, then brushes past me to walk into the palace.

You could say my sister is callous. Heartless, even, but I know the truth. She's been hurt, too, and the only way she knows how to shield her pain is through a thick layer of frost. Who am I to try to change that? I'd rather hide away in the Summer Palace year-round than deal with my own scars. We're more alike than I want to admit.

My sister's heels click on the floors as she pulls off her gloves, handing them to a footman holding a silver tray out for her. When her jacket is stripped off, Penelope turns to glance at me. "Come to the office. We have construction logistics to discuss."

Following my sister to the office near the palace library, I try not to think of what this will mean—constructing the design that Rowan spent months—years—working on. Erecting the building that came from her mind. Will I really want to live in a building she drew? Every aspect of this renovation will have Rowan's essence soaked into it. I won't be able to escape it. It's stifling and exhilarating all at once.

When I sit down across from my sister, she nods to one of her personal staff members, who pulls out a laptop and a stack of large, rolled-up construction drawings. I listen as they outline the project's timeline, various stages of construction, and expected disruption to the current palace staff and myself.

It's beautiful. Rowan changed her design from a modern mansion to a full-scale restoration. The three-dimensional images she's created make my heart swell.

Rowan *gets* it. She understands this palace—this land. In her design, I see how much she belongs here. When I first met her, I thought Rowan was an outsider. I thought she'd never feel at home here—but her design shows otherwise. She's restored this palace to what it was a century ago, while still maintaining all the eco features and modern touches her original design boasted.

It's fucking perfect, and it makes me want to cry.

Big, bad Wolfe indeed.

When the presentation is over, Penelope glances at me. "Any questions?"

"Rowan," I croak. Even saying her name is painful. I haven't spoken it since I left Stirling, and I try to ignore the burning pain that slices across my chest when I say it aloud. I blink, trying to regain control over my aching body. "Will she be here?"

Penelope interlaces her fingers and rests them on the desk. She takes a deep breath and finally shrugs. "I told her it was her choice. We'll break ground before she comes up here, but we'll need her approval for some of the later stages of construction. That can be done through photos and email, but..."

"You've been talking to her?" Am I jealous of my sister for that? This ache in my chest feels like betrayal.

Penelope arches an eyebrow. "I had to take over the project, Wolfe. You left."

Shame burns all the way down my throat. I left, when I should have stayed. I should have fought. I should have told Rowan how I felt, but I lost my chance.

She might not even come up here for the project that was meant to be the defining moment of her career.

I took that away from her.

"I'll leave," I say to my sister. "Rowan should be here. She deserves to see this project in person."

My sister's face softens ever so slightly. She dips her chin in agreement, then the stone mask returns to her features. I stand up, take my leave, and walk out of the office.

My feet take me next door to the library, where once again, I'm assaulted with memories of Rowan. She spent so many hours in here, drinking up scraps of information that she poured into the design.

I stare at the ashes in the fireplace before letting my gaze drift to the window, where the sun shines bright and snow melts all around.

This is as much her palace as it is mine, but I'll never get to share that with her.

30

ROWAN

MY SECOND TRIP up to the Summer Palace of Nord is very different than my first. Grandma and I are flown on a private jet directly from Farcliff to the airstrip a short drive from the palace. No cramped train ride with too-small seats. A private car is there to pick us up when we land, complete with a driver in a crisp black uniform who opens the back door of the car for us. He gives Grandma a warm smile as she greets him by name.

It's the beginning of May, and there's no howling gale outside. The sky is blue and although it's still fresh outside, the snow is mostly melted and the whole landscape is green and lush. Only the tops of the mountains and particularly shady spots have remnants of snow still clinging to the earth. A bird sings in a nearby tree, and the air tastes sweet.

Settled in the back seat, Grandma threads her fingers through mine and I lean my head against her shoulder. She spent the winter in Farcliff with me, helping me prepare for the arrival of the baby. I'm thirty weeks pregnant now. I'll be a mother in ten short weeks. Less than three months. Panic and excitement are still waging war within me, as they have every day since I found out about my pregnancy.

If all goes to plan, I'll see the visitor's cottage completed this week, and do some final approvals on details of the main palace design. I've been communicating with the site team via email and phone, but I've come up here to help with the millions of little architectural decisions that need to be made to complete the project. In a few months, both my babies will come to life.

I'm not sure I'll get to see the full palace restoration. Maybe one day. By the time it's finished, in September, I'll have a new baby. My life will be different. Coming up to the Arctic Circle won't be a priority. The Queen promised pictures, so that's what I'll have.

"There will be flowers everywhere in a week or two," Grandma says, sighing happily. Her eyes shine as she squeezes my hand, shifting her gaze to the tinted windows of the royal vehicle.

The Prince was right. It's very different here in springtime, and I can only imagine how beautiful the height of summer will be. I let out a soft sigh, ignoring the clenching of my heart.

I know I made the right decision. There were no paparazzi following me in Farcliff. After the first flurry of articles about my affair with the Prince, the gossip died down. Once I left, there was nothing to feed the rumor mill. My life went back to normal, but I felt far from the same.

Everything is different. I've gone to work every day, in the same office I left behind, but it's like I'm seeing the world through someone else's eyes. I see the awards I've won and the degrees hanging on my wall, but they don't mean anything.

My baby means something. Everything. I spent every

evening trawling through books and online forums about what to expect, preparing myself for every possible eventuality—yet still feeling completely unprepared.

But I've had Grandma with me, and she's reminded me about the importance of family. Her presence, along with the baby growing in my womb, have shown me everything I've been missing.

Work doesn't seem quite so important. Apart from the Summer Palace, I haven't taken on any more projects. I'm planning on taking some time off once the baby gets here.

I still care about the business, of course. I still love architecture. It just doesn't hold the same weight as it did before.

Plus, in a way, it feels wrong to think about another project while the Summer Palace design is still ongoing, like a strange, misplaced kind of infidelity. This palace deserves my full attention—or maybe I just don't have the energy or desire to think of anything else. I cling onto the last thing that reminds me of...of *him*.

As the car drives up to the tall, wrought iron gates, I glance at the spot on the ground where I first collapsed. That's where the Prince first saw me. Where he first held me in his arms and brought me back to life.

Have I ever been the same?

That moment, everything changed. I've been staring at my life through a kaleidoscope, wondering how I could have ignored all the beauty and color of the world around me. How did I exist with only work and business on my mind? How did I miss all the other things that make life worth living?

We drive through the gates, and my heart clenches. I slide a hand over my abdomen, smiling as my baby moves. I grunt, feeling a foot kick me in the ribs. My stomach bulges to the left as the baby shifts, and I rub my hand over it.

We're home. Even after spending all winter in Farcliff, coming back to this palace feels like the homecoming I've always wanted. I belong here. This landscape took a piece of me, the Prince grabbed another, and my baby took the rest. There's a chunk of my heart kept captive here, and I'm not sure I'll ever get it back.

All I can do is just enjoy being here while it lasts.

Grandma must feel me tense up as we get closer to the palace, because she squeezes my hand. "I called Vikki, and she told me the Prince left last week," she whispers. "In case you were nervous about seeing him."

I force a smile, but a spear of sadness pierces my heart. He left—again. Didn't even want to see me.

But it's for the best, right? Keeps up the appearance of nothing ever happening between us. Why would the Prince stay here during a large construction project? That in itself would be suspicious.

It hurts more than I'd like to admit. Call it weakness, but somewhere deep in my heart, I hoped I would see him at least once.

We arrive at the castle but instead of stopping at the front entrance, we're driven to the side door reserved for the staff. My throat tightens, and I know that I don't have special status here. I'm not the Prince's lover or someone who will be given free rein in the building.

I'm an architect. A contractor. A pregnant nobody.

Isn't that what I asked for when I left? This is the choice I made.

Vikki's just inside the door, waiting to greet us. She wraps her arms around me and coos over my growing belly, beaming at me.

"Have you picked a name yet?"

I shake my head, smiling. "Decided to wait to find out the

sex of the baby, so I want to hold the baby in my arms before I decide on a name."

"Smart," Vikki replies, wrapping me up in a tight hug. I let out a sigh as she holds me close, realizing how much I missed her. My time in Farcliff was full of work and not much else—not that I've made many friends over the past ten years, anyway. I've been too focused on the business.

But Vikki is a friend. She kept in touch with me while I was away. She made me feel at home here—still does.

Vikki gives my grandmother an equally big hug, then leads us both to the kitchens, where a meal has been laid out for us. I let out a happy sigh, easing myself into a chair and smiling as I accept a plate full of steaming-hot food.

I'm home, finally. I try not to think of the fact that this is temporary, and as soon as my work is finished, I'll be on my way back to Farcliff. I might never come back.

Right now, though, I just stab a piece of broccoli and smile at Vikki as she tells me everything I've missed over the winter.

"Did the Prince spend the winter here?" I find myself asking.

Grandma and Vikki exchange a glance, and Vikki forces a smile. "He did. He mostly kept to himself."

"Oh," I answer, sadness wrapping itself around my aching heart. I don't know why that makes me sad. Every time I think about the Prince, a wave of sorrow threatens to wash me away. He's the one who got away—the one I never had a right to love in the first place.

The baby kicks, then punches me right in the bladder, as if to remind me that the Prince gave me a child. I grin, glancing down. I'll always have a piece of him, even if our lives can never be joined. It's cold comfort, though.

When I finish my meal, I ask to be taken out to the

construction site. After lacing my steel-toed boots up—well, if I'm honest, I have to ask Grandma to lace them up for me—I'm led through the hallways and out to the back of the palace, where a demountable site office has been set up. A tall, weathered man hands me a hard hat, welcoming me with a grunt.

"You're the brilliant architect who decided we needed to build this complicated glass atrium in the middle of the arctic, are you?"

I grin. "You should be happy. My original design had two glass turrets on either side of the castle. A courtyard atrium is child's play compared to that."

The site manager snorts, gives me a safety briefing, and begins the tour of the site. For the first time since I arrived in Nord, the sadness inside me fades. I'm not thinking of the Prince, or of everything I gave up by leaving. Here, touching the edge of the Arctic Circle, my most ambitious architecture project is coming to life.

By the time the tour of the palace is over, I can't stop smiling. The crew has been working in split shifts through the days and nights for the past four weeks to construct this thing in record time. We need to finish it before the weather turns cold again—and they're ahead of schedule. I won't get to see the full palace done, but the visitor's cottage might actually be complete if I stretch my visit here by a few weeks—and where else would I want to be for the next month?

The site manager drives me out to the visitor's cottage. Works have been commissioned by local artisans, and the whole place looks like a restored ancient tribal palace. I've never been prouder.

There are murals depicting the first meeting of the communities that formed Nord, and carvings of each stage of the kingdom. I meet a historian, who leads me through the visitor's cottage-cum-museum and shows me everything they've done.

It's not a retreat for royals anymore. Soon, there will be a public road leading straight here and full-time staff in the summertime to give tours of the place. It's a living museum that the royal family has restored and given back to Nord. It's...perfect.

When we get back to the main palace, I make my way through the halls. My smile slowly fades as memories flood my brain, and I let out a long sigh.

I was in love with Wolfe. Maybe I still am. I can taste those sweet memories on the tip of my tongue as I wander through the Summer Palace, wondering if I'll ever feel that way about anyone else—and knowing somewhere deep down I never will. I know it was the right decision to leave for Farcliff and tell him I didn't want to be with him. My life has been silent, with no paparazzi and no controversy. He's been able to have a quiet winter. My baby will be born without fanfare.

It's for the best.

But as I pass by the library doors, my ribs constrict and my lungs feel like they're going to collapse. The fireplace is cold, the room empty.

And I feel so, so alone.

31

WOLFE

SUMMER MONTHS ARE USUALLY special in Nord. The sun shines until late in the evening, and the weather is warm and pleasant. In the capital, shops will spill out onto the sidewalk, with many main roads closed off for days at a time to accommodate street festivals and markets. It's like the whole kingdom explodes with life after a long winter of hibernation.

The Summer Palace is magical. Fields of wildflowers and herds of caribou. More birds than you can imagine. The whole place is so, so alive.

Usually, I'm there to enjoy it.

This year, though, I wish winter had lasted longer. Spending summer in Stirling is torture, especially when I know Rowan is only a short flight away at the Summer Palace. The days seem to drag on and on and on, with only a few short hours of darkness when I can sleep and be alone.

My brothers try to take me out hunting and fishing and riding. They try to bring me to sporting events and local festivals.

I go with them, at first, thinking it'll distract me from the black hole in my chest. When, day after day, I realize it's not helping, I keep to myself instead.

A month lasts an eternity. Truthfully, the past seven months since Rowan left have been the longest of my life. It feels exactly like the year after Abby died, when I just drifted through life, waiting for it to pass me by.

Jonah finds me in my study one afternoon, knocking on the doorframe before he saunters in.

"You're still pining over that girl, huh?"

I glance up from the computer screen, where the latest progress report from the Summer Palace project is displayed. Leaning back in my chair, I arch an eyebrow. "Excuse me?"

"You haven't left the castle in two weeks, Wolfe."

"Are you keeping track?"

"Clearly."

"Well, don't bother," I grumble, turning back to the screen. "I'll be heading back to the Summer Palace soon. They're doing the unveiling ceremony for the visitor's cottage next week."

"They're done already?"

I spin the computer toward him. "Three weeks ahead of schedule. Penelope told me we were all expected to head up there for the ceremony. Wants to show a united front and open the cottage up to tourism. She's announcing it at the unveiling."

Jonah kicks his feet up onto the coffee table, leaning back in his seat. His eyes stay trained on me.

I arch an eyebrow, meeting my brother's gaze. "What?"

"Will she be there?"

"Who?"

"Come on, Wolfe." Jonah snorts. "Rowan Reed."

I stiffen at the sound of her name. No one has said it out loud since she left. No one's said anything to me about the

Summer Palace project, except to tell me to leave during construction and ask me to be there for the re-opening.

It doesn't mean I haven't thought of her, but hearing Jonah say her name stirs something deep inside me. I've been lying to myself if I think I'm over it. Her leaving Nord last autumn cut me deep, and I'm not sure how I'll recover.

I could deal with Abby's death, in a way. It was sudden and senseless and rocked my whole existence—but there was a finality to it. Her heart malfunctioned, and she died. A sad, tragic end to a beautiful life.

But it was an end. It was over.

With Rowan, though? There's no end, only an old reel of memories playing on repeat in my mind. Seven beautiful weeks where I thought life was sweet again. Seven weeks where I felt hope for something more.

Then, it was over—but it doesn't feel final. She wasn't ripped away from me in some tragic accident. Rowan left of her own free will. She looked at her options, and she chose to walk away.

How am I supposed to deal with that when my heart is still cupped in the palm of her hand? For the past four weeks, she's been tantalizingly close, but I've stayed put in Stirling. Am I supposed to just go back to the Summer Palace and ask her for my heart back? Bow my head and beg her to release me?

Jonah punches my arm, arching his brows. "Well?"

"Sorry, what?"

"Will Rowan be at the ceremony?"

I shrug, trying to look more nonchalant than I feel. "No idea."

Jonah stands with a sigh, dropping a hand on my shoulder. "How long are you going to live like this, Wolfe?"

I meet my brother's gaze, frowning. I don't know how to answer that.

He pinches his lips together, shakes his head, and walks away. My head spins as my brother leaves.

What am I supposed to do? Knock down the Summer Palace and plead with Rowan to come back to me? She made her choice, and her choice was to walk away. I'm not going to get down on my knees and beg like some pathetic little dog, and I'm not going to treat her like she doesn't know what she wants.

Rowan left because she thought it was best for her and the baby. She *chose* this.

Sighing, I shut down my computer and scrub my face with my hands. Next week, I'm going to the unveiling ceremony of the visitor's cottage, and I'll do my best to ignore Rowan.

I mean nothing to her, so she can't mean anything to me.

MY SIBLINGS and I arrive at the Summer Palace in a convoy of black vehicles. Inside the palace gates, there are already throngs of security-approved reporters and media representatives, cameras poised and ready. There's a new road leading across the flat meadow toward the former visitor's cottage—now an official museum. My chest clenches, a kernel of tension weighing heavy in my stomach.

I've spent the winter and spring successfully avoiding the public eye. I'd forgotten how much anxiety churns in my gut when I see those hundreds of lenses pointed toward me—but it's impossible to ignore now. My heart hammers as we drive toward the palace. Eyvar is in the driver's seat, his hands clenching over the steering wheel. He can feel the tension radiating off me.

I gulp, squeezing my eyes shut for a moment to compose myself. Every time I see a big pack of reporters, it takes me back to that moment nearly five years ago, when Abby died in my arms—except now, it's not her death that really hurts. I feel like my grief has dulled, but there's still an ache in my chest. A sense of deep loss—loneliness, maybe.

Plastering a sorry excuse for a smile on my face, I exit the vehicle and join my siblings on the landing of the palace stairs. Security personnel surround us, but reporters still shout and snap pictures. I raise an arm, waving, knowing this picture will be online within minutes.

My stomach is tied up in knots, but I swallow down bile and try to keep my face steady. Jonah puts a hand on my forearm, giving me the tiniest nod of encouragement.

Maybe he understands my pain, even if he hasn't lost anyone.

Jonah, Silas, Penelope, and I enter the Summer Palace. It feels different in here. I can hear the distant whine of angle grinders and saws, along with the low hum of generators and machinery. The renovation of the main palace won't be done for weeks, and the place feels...foreign.

Palace staff usher us to another room and prep us for the grand unveiling ceremony that is set to start in less than an hour.

My heart squeezes.

Is Rowan here? Will she be at the visitor's cottage?

I know she's thirty-five weeks pregnant. I've been counting every week on my calendar, because I'm that pathetic and hung up on her. She's about to give birth to my child, and I might get to see her before that happens.

Dropping my head in my hands, I try to suck in a breath. I'm not sure I can do it. I'm not sure I can see her like that, knowing she doesn't want me in her life. It hurts so damn much. It makes my whole body ache, pain racing through my veins.

I can't do it. I can't do it. I can't do it.

When I look up, Penelope's staring at me. She's the regal, frigid Queen of Nord now, not my sister. Her face is a mask of regal propriety and her spine straight as she sits on the edge of a chair. But her eyes flash, and I know she's able to read every thought and emotion racing through my mind.

She stands, motioning for the staff to bring the cars around. "It's time," the Queen says, allowing her lady-in-waiting to fluff her hair and dust another bit of powder across her forehead.

This is a joyous ceremony. A proud moment where we give back a monument to the people, giving access to the visitor's cottage to anyone who would like to see it. We're unveiling all the artwork and sculptures that have been restored in honor of the people of Nord.

It's a celebration—but it only fills me with dread.

We all pile into two cars—my sister riding in the last one, and my brothers and me in the first—and we make our way across the grassy plains toward the visitor's cottage. When I close my eyes, I see the snow-covered landscape and the bright red flush on Rowan's cheeks. I hear the clinking of the dogs' harnesses and I taste the fresh, cold air.

This is where I fell in love with her, but it'll never be the same. The visitor's cottage where our baby was conceived is gone—and whatever love existed between us has disappeared with it.

Maybe it's a blessing. I won't be able to see where my relationship with Rowan began and ended, right there on that bed.

Bracing myself against my emotions, I grit my teeth and

watch the beauty of the landscape pass me by, seeing nothing.

When we step out, another hundred cameras are pointed at me. A small stage with a microphone has been set up, along with a row of chairs behind it. Beyond, the new museum gleams, the lawns around it well-manicured and the façade given a new lease of life. It looks beautiful— old and new all at once. I can see different placards set up along the pathway leading to the front door, and a huge banner with each of Nord's six provinces' coat of arms proudly displayed. Through the open doorway, I glimpse art on the walls and glass cases full of artifacts from Nord's history.

A staff member opens the car door for me, leading me to a chair near the microphone. I stand in front of it, waiting for my brothers to take their places, and watch as my sister walks up the steps and turns, waving to the assembled crowd.

Penelope makes her way to the microphone, motioning for my brothers and me to sit. There are still empty chairs beside us, but all I can do is stare at the mountain peaks that surround us. They ground me, reminding me I'm home. This is my kingdom. My land. The place where I feel most comfortable.

My sister starts talking, welcoming the assembled crowd and reading a prepared statement from the podium. She speaks clearly and eloquently, pausing for applause at all the right moments.

"We are honored to welcome the lead architect who made this project come to life. The award-winning, much acclaimed Rowan Reed."

Penelope turns to the side of the stage, and all eyes follow.

Including mine.

My heart doesn't stand a damn chance. Rowan is still the

goddess of my dreams. An angel sent down from heaven. My princess.

Using the handrail to help her up the steps, Rowan places a hand on the bottom of her pregnant stomach as she toddles onto the stage. It's the sexiest, most beautiful waddle I've ever seen. My heart feels like it's growing and shrinking all at once.

I fucking love this woman. The months have done nothing to erase that. I love her with every fiber of my being, and she's here. She's *here*.

Red-haired beauty, with a simple burgundy wrap dress on, showing off her advancing pregnancy. She makes it to the top of the stairs, pausing to regain her balance—and that's when she sees me.

Her eyes widen. Those perfect, pink lips drop open. My heart does a backflip, because her chest flushes and her shoulders soften ever so slightly.

She wasn't expecting me. Didn't think I'd come. How could I not? How could I turn down the possibility of seeing her again, even in front of cameras?

A murmur ripples through the crowd, and Rowan's face rearranges itself. She gulps, glancing at the assembled media. Cameras *click-click-click* like a beast's clacking teeth, and Rowan sucks in a sharp breath.

Then, her face twists. She puts a hand to her stomach, frowning—then cries out.

My heart stills, and blood turns to ice in my veins. That noise pierces my flesh like an arrow. I feel her pain in every nerve ending in my body. In an instant, I'm out of my seat and across the stage. She falls to her knees, arms clutching her middle.

Rowan screams again, pain and panic flashing across her face. Another arrow pierces my heart, and my body screams with her. Her eyes are wide as a bead of sweat sprouts on her temple. Her breath comes in short gasps as her face crumples. A trickle of blood seeps down the inside of her leg as my panic rears higher.

I fall to my knees. When I wrap my arms around her and pull her to me, Rowan whimpers. Her breath skates across my skin as her body tenses in pain.

"Wolfe." Rowan pants, eyes wide with fear. Her fingers cling to my shirt. "The baby." A grunt escapes her, followed by another cry. She stumbles away from me, falling to her hands and knees, and my whole world collapses to a pinpoint of light.

There's only Rowan. She's the only thing that exists right now, and she's in pain. Suffering.

Panic laces my blood, pumping hard and fast through my veins. I'm re-living the worst moment of my life. It's happening again. The love of my life fading in my arms. The mother of my child, collapsing as I watch.

Cameras click, immortalizing this moment. Again.

I hear the noise, and the present moment rushes back to me. *No.* I won't let it happen. It's not going to happen. *No, no, no.* Inhaling sharply, I come back to myself. Scooping Rowan in my arms, I carry her off the stage. I'm so pumped full of adrenaline that I hardly even feel her weight in my arms. It's just like the first moment I carried her, nearly a year ago. She needs me. I need to be here for her.

Cameras flash. Reporters shout. Staff members and security agents rush around me, but none of it matters. I don't care that this moment is being filmed. I don't care that our relationship is on full display.

Let them watch. Let them see this moment and draw whatever conclusions they want from it.

The media doesn't matter. Controversy doesn't matter.

All that matters is getting Rowan to a hospital. *Now*. Right now. Right fucking now.

My breath is shallow as I fly toward a vehicle. Eyvar's already there, holding a door open for me. I put Rowan in the back seat, cradling her head in my lap just like I did last winter.

"Drive, Eyvar," I say and this time, he doesn't protest. The engine revs, and we're gone, skidding toward the main palace.

Vaguely, I hear Eyvar radioing ahead for Dr. Williams. I hear arrangements being made for a helicopter to take Rowan to the nearest rural hospital. I hear it all, but the only thing that exists is Rowan.

Her cries of pain physically hurt me. I try to shush her, smoothing my palm over her forehead.

"It's going to be okay," I say gently. "You're with me. You're fine." I'm not sure I believe it, but I say it anyway.

Rowan gasps, clutching her belly. "Wolfe, the baby—"

"It'll be okay. I'm here, Rowan. I'm here."

Her clear, blue eyes stare into mine, and she reaches up to cling onto my shirt. Her forehead creases in pain as her lips part, and I hang onto my breath as I wait to hear what she has to say.

"I'm so sorry, Wolfe." Tears fall from her eyes as her grip on my shirt loosens, and she loses consciousness.

My heart collapses as my tears mix with hers. I press my lips to her forehead, her nose, her lips. I grip her hand in mine and put it on top of her stomach, praying to everything I can think of to keep her safe. Keep our baby safe. Keep her with me.

Please, don't let me go through this again.

32

ROWAN

I WAKE up in a hospital bed with a numb sort of haze clouding my brain. Blinking my eyes open, I listen to the steady beeping of a machine behind me. There's a large shape in a chair beside me, and I furrow my brow to try to focus on it.

Wolfe.

A sharp intake of breath from me is enough to wake him up. He falls out of his chair and kneels next to the bed, clutching my hand and pressing his lips to my fingers. "You're awake." He's breathless, eyes shining.

I nod. "Yeah." My voice is nothing more than a croak, and I frown. So dry. My brain is fuzzy. What's going on? Why am I here?

Wolfe reads my mind, scrambling for a little plastic container full of water—like the ones you get on an airplane. He peels the top off the container for me and helps me lift it to my mouth, wiping away a drop of water as it dribbles down my chin. Sighing, I nod. "Thank you."

"How do you feel?"

My eyes snap open then, hands reaching down to my stomach. Fear spikes my blood, making my blood pump hard and triggering an alarm from the machine behind me.

A nurse rushes in, checking the machines hooked up to me and saying a few calming words.

"Where's the baby? Where's my baby?" I'm screeching. My nails are digging into her arm.

"You had to have an emergency cesarian section," she explains, pushing me back down on the bed. "Your baby is in the NICU and doing fine. He's currently on oxygen support, so we'll have to keep him there until he can breathe on his own."

It's hard to explain the kind of gut-twisting anxiety that grips me. Everything I've lived for over the past eight months is gone. My birth plan is out the window. Worst of all, my baby isn't even here. I didn't get to hold him when he was born. I don't even *remember* giving birth. That moment was taken from me. He can't breathe on his own.

He's a *he*! I have a son! I didn't even know it until now, and this is how I find out?

I blink, trying to make sense of the thousands of thoughts invading my mind. I stare at the nurse, shaking my head. "My baby..."

"He's doing well. He's already passed some of the early tests we've done, and he's responding well to treatment. All signs point to your baby being fine, Miss Reed."

"It's too early," I say. "There's still five weeks."

"He was premature," Wolfe says, finding my hand again. He interlaces his fingers in mine, squeezing. "I guess he was just too excited to meet me."

My heart is still beating erratically, but I manage to force a scoff. "Arrogant as always, Your Highness."

"The doctor told me he's doing well. They need to keep him in the neonatal ward for now, but I've gone to see him every hour since he was born." Wolfe smiles softly. "He's beautiful, Rowan. Looks just like me."

That makes me laugh, which sends pain spearing through my stomach. I groan, feeling a thick gauze bandage across my abdomen. Wolfe smooths my hair off my forehead and kisses my clammy skin.

"I want to see him," I croak, glancing from Wolfe to the nurse.

She purses her lips and checks my vitals on the machine next to my bed. "You shouldn't really be moving right now—"

"I need to see him," I plead, eyebrows drawing together. "Please."

The Prince makes a soft grunt, which draws the nurse's gaze. She lets out a sigh, nodding, and disappears for a minute before coming back with a wheelchair. It takes a minute of painful movement as Wolfe picks me up and sets me down in front of the wheelchair. By the time I'm settled, I'm flushed and sweaty and aching all over.

But I'm in the chair, and I'm going to see my son.

A part of me feels robbed. This isn't what I'd imagined for the birth of my child. It's not what I wanted. I wanted to bring this child into the world surrounded by happiness and family and feel his tiny heartbeat against mine. I wanted my grand-mother beside me. I wanted to kiss my baby's forehead and let him wrap his tiny little fingers around my finger. I wanted to be the first to hear his cries. The first to touch his skin. I wanted so much, and this is all wrong.

But I'm alive, and the nurse assures me my baby is doing well, so I guess I have to be grateful for that. Wolfe tucks a blanket over my legs, placing my feet on the wheelchair footrests, then places his hands on my thighs and gives me a soft smile. "You haven't told me to leave yet."

I stare at his deep, golden-brown eyes, seeing softness there. I place my palm over his. "I don't want you to."

He curls his fingers around mine, bringing my fingers to his lips. "I was afraid you wouldn't want me to stay."

My chest constricts. I feel woozy and anxious and weak from the drugs they must have given me for the operation, and the fact that I haven't seen my son since he was born.

I feel almost like I've lost something. I got so used to feeling my child's movements inside me and now...it's all over. A part of me is just *gone*.

But there's another feeling, too—a deep sense of rightness. Being here, with Wolfe, it feels like exactly where I'm meant to be. The softness in his face, and the tenderness of his touch—they make me feel like pushing him away was the wrong thing to do. I already feel like the Summer Palace is home. How could I ever tell Wolfe I didn't want him? The only thing missing from my life for the past few months has been his presence.

He lays a soft kiss on my fingers, then my palm, and stands up to push my wheelchair out of the room. I lean back, exhausted yet wired, watching the hospital hallway roll past. Wolfe's steps are sure, and any staff we cross steps out of the way and bows in deference. He must like that. They're much better at deference than I am.

One more turn down a hallway marked 'Neonatal Intensive Care Unit', and I see a room full of tiny bassinets. My heart squeezes so hard there must be no blood left in it at all. So many tiny little babies in need of help—and one of them is mine.

Wolfe wheels me past the ward to a small adjacent room.

"They put him in a private room," he says. "So I could visit him often."

Stopping in front of an incubator, the Prince engages the brakes on my wheelchair and drops a hand to my shoulder. My bottom lip trembles. I press my nose to the clear plastic dome, feeling my heart shatter right there in my chest.

He's so tiny. So fragile and precious. Hooked up to oxygen and tiny tubes, sleeping gently. There's a tiny little hat on his head, and a diaper covering his lower half. It's way too big for him.

Tears spill over my cheeks, and Wolfe wraps his arms around me. "He's going to be okay," he whispers in my ear. "They said he's getting better at breathing on his own."

Is that supposed to make me feel better? I cry on Wolfe's shoulder as my whole world twists before my eyes. I've spent the past eight months feeling like I finally have a purpose— like I can see clearly for the first time—and it was almost taken away from me.

With the pads of his thumbs, Wolfe wipes the tears from my eyes. He holds my face until I meet his gaze and kisses each of my cheeks.

"I'm here, Rowan," he says gently. "I'm not going to leave unless you tell me to. We'll do this together."

An ugly sob rakes through my body. God, I must look like a mess. How can he look at me with soft eyes like that? How can there be any sort of love in his face?

But it's there. The love I've been missing. The affection I've been craving. It's written all over Wolfe's face, and soaked into every one of his movements. A strand of hair is plastered to my forehead and cheek, and Wolfe gently pushes it back.

"This isn't how I wanted you to see me." I feel slightly pathetic right now, but all I can do is lean into his touch and close my eyes, one hand still resting on the plastic dome over our baby's incubator.

Our baby.

For the first time since I found out I was pregnant, it feels like I'm not alone. Opening my eyes, I look at Wolfe. At his smooth forehead with black hair curling at the temples. His beautiful eyes and fine, straight nose. At those lips I've missed kissing, tugged in a soft smile.

"You're the most beautiful woman I've ever seen, Rowan. Now more than ever." He rests his forehead against mine, letting out a long sigh. "You're the mother of my son and the love of my life."

I back away, eyes wide.

Wolfe laughs. "Don't act so surprised. You must know I'm in love with you."

"Why would I know that?"

"Because my whole life has revolved around doing whatever you want ever since I met you. Because I've been locked away on my own since you left. Because seeing our son for the first time was the happiest and most terrifying moment of my life." He sucks in a breath, smoothing his thumb over my cheek. "Because I can't imagine going another day without you. Don't make me walk through life alone, Rowan. I...I need you. I love you so much it hurts."

Tears are streaming down my face now. I can't help it. My walls just crumble right there, turning to dust at my feet. I'm done fighting this. I don't want to push him away. I don't want to think about all the complications of being with a Prince, when I know that the alternative feels like hell.

He's here, with me, in my darkest hour. Wolfe is supporting me as I heal from this traumatic birth. He loves me and the baby.

As he wipes another tear off my cheek, I realize how

wrong I was. It was never better for me to leave. Being independent means nothing if there's no one to share it with. Giving my child a better life is impossible if I take him away from a loving father.

And Wolfe? He doesn't care about controversy. I wasn't doing him a favor by leaving. I would never be a burden by staying.

He *wants* me.

He wanted me when I was healthy and full of snark. He wanted me when I was desperate for him, clawing to tear his clothes off. He wanted me when I left. And he still wants me now, when I'm weak, ailing, sweaty, and full of stitches.

"I love you, Rowan," he says softly. "With everything I have."

Emotion wells up inside me, and I feel like I'm seeing a future I never imagined. I could be happy with someone—with Wolfe. I could have love and laughter and children. I could have the support of a strong partner, while still feeling like myself.

"I...I think I love you too," I whisper, lip trembling.

Wolfe's face looks like the sun. His smile brightens the dim room, his eyes shining bright. He kisses me then, trembling against my lips as I cling onto his shoulders like he's the last life raft in a stormy ocean.

When we pull apart, I sniffle, glancing at our son. "I don't want to stop designing buildings, though. I don't want to sit in a castle doing nothing. I want our son to grow up knowing where he came from."

"I'll never stop you from doing what you love, Rowan." Wolfe presses his lips to mine, holding me as if he's afraid I'll slip through his fingers. "So long as you tell me you're mine."

I smile softly, leaning my head against his shoulder. Wolfe wraps one arm around me, then interlaces the fingers of his other hand in mine and places our joined hands on the incubator. I inhale his scent, letting his love soak into every pore. Then I nod. "I'm yours, Wolfe. I always have been."

He lets out a long sigh, then drags a chair beside me, puts his arm around my shoulders, and we both turn to stare at the tiny creation that brought us back together.

Three, together, forever.

EPILOGUE
ROWAN

ACCEPTING Wolfe's love is a kind of release I've never experienced before. Throughout my pregnancy, I thought I understood my mother's decisions. I understood that I wasn't a burden to her, but I still held onto my need for independence.

What I realize with Wolfe is that independence doesn't have to mean being alone. I can be with him—and accept all the support that comes with being associated with the royal family—without feeling like I'm leeching off him.

Because I'm giving him something, too—*love*. Companionship. Partnership.

It's just like my relationship with my mother. I didn't realize that she was getting love and fulfillment from me, even though she had to work hard to provide for me. Relationships aren't about carrying another person—they're about leaning on each other and being stronger together than you ever could be alone, no matter how independent you think you are.

Wolfe's strength is something I desperately need as we stay in the hospital and wait for our son to recover. The first time I hold him in my arms, Wolfe is beside me. His eyes shine as he watches me and the baby, and I know this moment is even more special with him beside me.

I run my fingers over the baby's soft, black hair, laying a kiss on his forehead. He's so small. So incredibly beautiful.

"What do you want to name him?" Wolfe asks, putting a palm on the baby's back. His hand is so big it covers our son's entire body, and I'm reminded just how tiny he really is.

I shake my head, sighing. "I don't know. I thought I'd have a name when I saw him, but nothing happened the way I planned." Glancing at Wolfe, I arch my brows. "I think we should choose a name together."

Wolfe rewards me with a brilliant smile. It reaches from ear to ear and warms my heart. He leans over and kisses my lips, letting out a long sigh.

"Together sounds good," he says, brushing his lips over my temple. "Always together."

Wolfe climbs into the hospital bed beside me, wrapping the baby and me in a strong arm. In his embrace, I feel safe and protected—and happy.

We name our baby boy Wren, after seeing a bird flit from tree to tree outside the hospital window. I lean my head against Wolfe's shoulder, smiling. "That's a beautiful bird," I say, looking at the bird tilt its head as it looks through the window.

"It's very far north for a wren, even this time of year," Wolfe says, watching the bird.

We exchange a glance, smile, and understand each other.

"You know male wrens build a number of nests, waiting for a female to choose one?" Wolfe says, hooking his arm around my shoulder.

I run my fingers through Wren's thin, newborn hair, smiling. "Do they?"

"Uh-huh." Wolfe nods. "Kind of feels like what I've been doing. Waiting for you."

"Except I'm the one who designed our nest." I grin.

"You want to stay at the Summer Palace?" Wolfe's eyebrows jump. "I assumed you'd want to be in the city."

"The Summer Palace is the first place that's felt like home," I say, laying a soft kiss on Wren's head. I can't stop kissing him and running my hands over his soft newborn skin.

Wolfe lets out a low growl, pulling me into his chest. I know what that growl means—it means I've just made him very happy. I've chosen a nest—the Summer Palace, with Wolfe by my side.

WE MARRY in a quiet ceremony a month later, only releasing a few pictures to the media. I'm exhausted, but happy, still sore from the birth and running on too little sleep. Tucked away at the Summer Palace, we insulate ourselves from any gossip and articles, caring only about each other and our son.

It's not a problem. The few snippets of news I see are mostly positive, congratulating us and praising the Prince for overcoming his grief. The opening of the visitor's cottage museum helps the public image, and I see it as my first offering to Nord. Hopefully, in my life, I'll be able to offer much, much more to the land that made me feel complete.

Grandma stays with us, cooing over Wren and smiling at me every chance she gets. Vikki falls in love with the baby, too, volunteering to babysit any chance she gets. She sings to Wren and puts him to sleep faster than I ever can, and I'm grateful for her help.

On one cool autumn day, when the sky is clear and the air is crisp, Wolfe asks Vikki to take care of the baby. He takes me by the hand and brings me to the garages, a grin teasing his lips. My heart flips, and I know I'll never tire of seeing him smile. My husband—*husband!*—hops into a truck, clicking his fingers for Chief to jump in the back.

"Where are you taking me?" I ask, smiling.

"Shh," Wolfe says. "Just enjoy it."

I use his help to get in the passenger seat—my body still feels weak, even months after my operation. I let the drive lull me to a shallow sleep, only opening my eyes when Wolfe stops the car.

We're in front of the new museum, which is dark apart from a single light above the front door. Wolfe grins at me, then takes me by the hand and leads me inside. Chief's nails clack on the hard tile as we walk through the silent building, past the new reception desk, and through the back to the old studio.

Candles are lit everywhere, bathing the room in a soft glow. The painting that inspired the palace design hangs in a place of honor at the end of the room, and a small round table is set up in the center. A waiter bows to the two of us, pulling out a chair for me and laying a cloth napkin across my lap.

My heart grows. Wolfe holds my hand across the table, tells me he loves me, then asks me to enjoy the meal he's organized here, where our romance first began. "One year ago today," he finally says, clinking a wine glass against mine.

My eyes widen. I do some mental math and realize he's right—a year ago today, we kissed in this room and sealed our fate.

Wolfe laughs. "I remember you telling me you'd regret kissing me."

"The only thing I regret is leaving you when I did." I smile sadly at him, but Wolfe's eyes soften. He's already forgiven me for that, and I know our time apart gave me time to heal and realize what mattered. *Love.* Love is what matters. Love is what makes life worth living. Love is what makes independence feel sweet and safe and warm.

"You did a fantastic job on this design, Rowan," Wolfe says, nodding to a waiter in the corner. The waiter approaches with a black binder, bowing and handing it to the Prince.

Wolfe pushes it across the table toward me, smiling softly.

"What's this?"

"I remember you saying that you wanted to leave a legacy. You wanted to do something important."

When Wolfe nods to the folder, I flip it open. My eyes widen when I see the words at the top of the page: *Rowan Reed Architectural Scholarship.*

"I've started talking to universities in Nord about funding scholarships for students of architecture. If you agree, you could serve as director of the board and make sure that the money goes to the most deserving students."

I blink, freeing tears from my eyes. "You did this for me?"

Wolfe shakes his head. "You did it. It was the universities who approached the royal family about it, once they saw what you did with the Summer Palace."

I can't stay on the other side of the table anymore. I get up, walking over to wrap my arms around Wolfe's neck. He pulls me down onto his lap as I yelp, kissing me tenderly. As he cups my face in both hands, we smile at each other and bask in the beauty of the moment.

Together, in the place where it all started.

I don't have to give up my love of architecture—quite the opposite. I can pay it forward to the next young architect who wants to make something of him or herself. Wolfe is giving that to me, too. A child and a marriage and a lifetime of love wasn't enough, he had to give me a legacy, too.

Leaning my head against Wolfe's shoulder, I let out a sigh. "What if we did awards, too? We could do a yearly architecture competition with people from all across the kingdom. They could be asked to design new libraries, or community centers, or daycares—and the Crown could fund the construction!"

Wolfe chuckles, pulling away to look in my eyes. "I knew you'd have a bucketful of ideas. Whatever you like, Rowan. We'll do it all."

Happiness bursts inside me and I laugh, kissing Wolfe's lips, his cheeks, his temples. I'm giving up my business, but by doing so, I can turn my attention to something more worthwhile. Being part of the royal family doesn't stop me from accomplishing everything I want—it allows me to do more.

I'm done holding myself back. I'm done limiting the way I think, because I have misplaced beliefs about being better off on my own.

I'll lean on Wolfe when I need to, support him when he needs me back, and I'll love him with all my heart until the day I die.

That evening, we have a beautiful meal in the place where we fell in love, then return to the palace and find our baby boy sleeping peacefully. Thank goodness for Vikki.

The love in Wolfe's eyes when he holds Wren makes my whole soul sing, and I know there's no better place for me than right here, where I belong.

At home in Nord, with the man I love.

~

EXTENDED EPILOGUE

ROWAN

A WICKED SMILE pulls the corners of Wolfe's lips as his hands slide over my hips. His fingers are hungry as they sink into my body, tugging me against his broad frame. "We're alone," he growls, the sounds reverberating through my chest.

"You're unbelievable," I huff, glancing over my shoulder. I'll never get used to state dinners, not in huge, ornate manors like this one. And definitely not when Wolfe pulls me into empty rooms with sin dancing in his eyes.

"Tell me something I don't know."

"Glad to see your ego is still nice and healthy."

"Rowan," he whispers, brushing his lips over my ear. "Tell me to stop, and I will."

I mash my lips together to stop from smiling. He knows me too well. He knows I want this—him. He knows every time he threads his fingers through mine and ducks behind a closed door, he'll have me undone and panting within minutes.

"That's what I thought." His hands slip lower, gripping my ass as he pulls me close. "We should be quick, but you know I want to take my time. That dress of yours is doing something to me."

"What, this old thing?" My smile widens as I shimmy my shoulders, glancing down at the beautiful, deep purple chiffon gown. I never thought I'd get used to the gowns, the clothing, the jewels—and three years after our wedding, I can't say I'm completely comfortable in them, although I do enjoy the way Wolfe's eyes darken when he sees me.

Grasping my wrists, he backs me against the wall and pins them above my head. "You love this as much as I do." It's not a question. He knows I do. Wolfe's lips trail down my neck, his teeth brushing the sensitive flesh between my throat and my shoulder. A shiver of desire tumbles down my spine and my hips buck despite myself.

"They'll be wondering where we are."

"Let them wonder. Let them imagine all the dirty things I'm doing to you."

"Wolfe..." I meant for his name to sound like a warning, but it came out more like a plea. With my hands above my head, my husband lets his lips drift over my shoulder, my neck, my jaw. Heat knots in my stomach as he lets out a feral, low growl. My eyelids flutter closed, heart thumping in my chest.

Shifting, Wolfe presses his body against me and holds both wrists in one of his large hands. His other hand drifts down my cheek, thumb running over my lip.

"You'll smudge my lipstick." I'm breathless, body winding tighter.

Wolfe's eyes darken. "Good."

That one word sends lava spilling through my veins. His hand drifts down my chin and over my chest, teasing my breast so gently I barely feel the brush of his fingertips. My body trembles, pulse hammering. Back arching, a moan slips through my lips.

"I love you like this," Wolfe says slowly, letting his hand drop down between my legs. The chiffon bunches as he cups his hand between my legs. "Moaning. Trembling. *Wanting.*"

The heat of his hand does something to me. My stomach clenches hard, heat unfurling in tight pulses low in my stomach. I grind against his hand as Wolfe's breath coasts over my shoulder. He drops his lips to my neck, scraping his teeth gently, so gently. His hand presses harder and I can't help myself. With layers of chiffon and underwear between us, I buck my hips against his touch.

"Are you wet for me, princess?"

My head is spinning. Beyond that closed door, just across the hall, a long table is set with fine dinnerware. A visiting emissary from Farcliff is here, along with a dozen other guests. They're having the first course, probably. Our two empty chairs must be a blaring signal of everything we're doing.

But Wolfe doesn't care. He tugs at my dress, still pinning me against the wall. Finding its hem, he slides his hand between my thighs and groans when he feels the heat gathered there. His palm presses against my sensitive bud as a gasp slips through my lips. I'll never tire of his touch. The tips of his fingers brush the crook between my leg and my center. Gently. Torturously. Everything is far, far too sensitive.

I can feel every inch of him against me. His hand on my wrists. His chest against mine. Powerful legs caging me against the wall as I quiver with need. Lips finding mine, Wolfe groans against my kiss. His palm rubs me through my underwear and I'm almost embarrassed at how tight he winds me. I haven't even felt him against my skin. Haven't even had him inside me, and I'm ready to come apart.

We should be sitting at a dinner table having polite conversation. We should be doing our best to welcome the visiting nobles, knowing they could agree to expand the architecture scholarships to universities in Farcliff. We should be doing our duty, but Wolfe pulled me into this room before I could protest.

And why would I protest? Before Wolfe, there was nothing but work. Nothing but architecture. And it wasn't enough.

My life before Wolfe wasn't enough to make me feel sated and happy. Not enough to have a smile on my lips when I wake up in the morning. Not enough to make me feel whole.

Somehow, still, Wolfe knows what I need. While his kiss is gentle, his hand is rough. He tugs my panties to the side and groans when he feels my wetness. "I knew you wanted this."

"Of course I want this," I snap. I glance at the door. We really should get back. We're hosting these visitors. We should be there. It's *my* scholarship they want to expand to new countries. "But—"

His fingers sink deep inside me and it takes all my self-control to stifle a cry. Sensing how close I am to losing control, Wolfe drops his hand from my wrist and covers my mouth with it, wicked light gleaming in his eyes. Mouth parted, he watches my eyes as his hand works magic between my legs. His hand muffles my moans, which start to sound a lot like grunts. Feral, animalistic noises that come from some primal place inside me.

My hips buck, back arching, body moving of its own will. His fingers are deep inside me, palm pressing just hard enough against that bundle of nerves to make me see stars. All the while knowing that not ten feet away, the dinner party awaits.

It's enough to drive me mad.

"You love this, Rowan. You can't lie to me." Wolfe's teeth gleam in the low light of the room as he smirks.

I can't answer. His hand still covers my mouth, and all my strength is occupied holding myself upright. I cling onto his broad shoulders, nails sinking into his freshly pressed shirt. I'll wrinkle it. Everyone will know.

And... And I don't care.

Release hits me hard, his hand doing nothing to silence my cry. I cling onto my husband, hips bucking, giving him the orgasm he demanded from me. But when I lift my eyes to meet his, I know he's not done. He drops the hand from my mouth and tugs me close, his other fingers still deep inside me.

His lips taste like danger, and I'll never get enough of them. I writhe in his arms as he gently skates his thumb over my bud, once, twice—and another orgasm crashes into me without warning.

Wolfe lets out a low growl, the sound sending tremors rushing through my veins. Everything is hot, flushed. My mind is reeling with the pleasure of it all. The wrongness of doing it here. The rightness of his touch.

I hear the jingling of his belt as my eyes clear, a smile tugging at my lips. "You're so bad, Wolfe."

"Why else did you marry me?" Lifting a leg over his hip, he pins me against the wall and in one, swift, strong movement—enters me. My head knocks against the plaster behind it as Wolfe thrusts himself inside me. Deep. Filled.

I'd answer his question if my tongue worked. I'd tell him I married him for a thousand different reasons. I married him because my love for him is endless. Because he makes me feel whole. Because he showed me another way to live, and he gave me two beautiful sons, the second arriving eighteen months after Wren. Because he kisses my C-section scar every chance he gets and worships the stretch marks on my stomach.

But this—yes, I married him for this, too. To be fucked against a wall and made to feel alive. To have him inside me, against me, on top of me. To feel so completely *his*.

Rough hands slide to my breasts and tug my dress down. The cool air is so sensitive against my heated skin. Wolfe's thumb teases my pebbled nipple as his lips leave trails of kisses down my neck. He pistons in and out of me, grunting, neither of us caring about the noises we're making.

Tangling my fingers into his silky strands, I pull his head back up to mine. My kiss is hungry. Needy. I scrape my teeth across his bottom lip as he fills me up, rumpling my dress and my hair and my makeup.

"I love you so fucking much," Wolfe says against my lips, his fiery golden eyes flashing.

"Language," I say instinctively, and he answers me with a hard thrust. "*Fuck*," I pant.

A low chuckle is the only response I get as his movements grow frantic. His hands are everywhere. My lips kiss everything they find. Hair, earlobe, neck, lips.

Then—release. Heat flooding through my stomach, exploding through my body. His strained grunts, body tense against mine. The tightening of...everything...inside me. My core, my breasts, my throat, my back. I arch against him, taking him just a bit deeper as my orgasm splits my world in two then stitches it back together again.

Then we collapse. My leg falls from his hip as he slips out of me, hands clawing at the wall behind me for some semblance of stability. My chest heaves, breasts still exposed, pushed up by the bunched fabric beneath them.

Wolfe grins at me, big, bad Wolfe. His hand slides up my

side and tugs my dress in place again, covering my breasts as he struggles to catch his breath. "You're incredible."

I blush, then marvel at the fact that those words, out of everything, are what brought blood to my cheeks.

My husband leans in, kissing my lips, then reaches between my legs to slip my panties back in place. "I like knowing I'm inside you, leaking out of you, while you go out there at sit at the table like the proper lady you are."

"You have a dirty, dirty mind, Wolfe."

His smile widens, and a jolt of heat passes through my heart.

"I can't help that the sight of you in a pretty dress makes me want to put another baby inside you."

"Is that what this is about?" I laugh, shaking my head. "There are better ways of bringing up the fact that you want a third."

Wolfe catches my arms, curling them over his own shoulders before wrapping his arms around my waist. He nuzzles my neck, chest rumbling. "What if I did want a third?"

My heart does a backflip as I rest my cheek against his chest. "Two sons aren't enough for you?"

"I want a daughter. A baby Rowan with bright, coppery hair like her mother."

"I can't promise that." I smile, resting against his strong chest, swaying softly in the silent room.

Wolfe holds me tight, all the naughtiness gone from his touch. He's tender now. Gentle. His fingers sweep up my spine, drifting over my shoulders and back down my arm. Goose bumps prickle, and I smile against his chest.

After a while, he speaks in a low voice. "We can try," he says softly. "Try for a third and see what happens."

"We really should go to dinner." I pull away, looking at Wolfe's unique eyes, smile widening on my face. "I'll talk to the doctor about removing my IUD. I...I've been thinking about another baby, too."

Wolfe rests his forehead against mine, a smile gracing those full lips. He cups my cheeks and a delicious warmth wraps itself around my chest. When Wolfe speaks, his voice is nothing but a low rasp. "I am so in love with you, Rowan. With or without a third child. You make my life worth living."

"And boring state dinners a bit more fun."

"A lot more fun," he corrects, grinning. Then, with a soft brush of his lips against mine, we straighten ourselves up and head across the hall to dinner.

~

LILIAN MONROE
ICE QUEEN
ROYALLY UNEXPECTED: BOOK EIGHT

ICE QUEEN

AN ACCIDENTAL PREGNANCY ROMANCE

PROLOGUE

A QUEEN DOESN'T MOURN the same way a woman does.

Wife.

Widow.

She doesn't curl up and soak her pillowcase in tears. She doesn't stare at the wall and lose long stretches of time, even when her grief is so heavy it becomes hard to think or breathe or move.

No, a queen must be a queen before anything else. She wears black and looks mournful—but not so much that the kingdom worries for her mental state. She dabs her eyes with a monogrammed handkerchief, but she doesn't wail. Her tears are restrained. Her voice doesn't tremble when she gives a speech to the kingdom, telling its citizens that the man she meant to grow old with is dead.

A queen's back remains straight, her shoulders always thrown back. Her hair is perfectly styled. She knows her clothing will be the subject of scrutiny, so it must remain flawless. She accepts condolences with grace, but doesn't share her own suffering. There's no one to share it with.

She takes her own broken, malfunctioning body—one

that refused to give her an heir—and she accepts that pain with the rest of the agony in her spirit. Gulps it down like a bitter potion, wondering if her failures somehow caused this tragedy to happen. If in some twisted version of reality, she might deserve to walk through life alone.

A queen doesn't buckle or bend or break.

She takes her suffering and buries it under a thousand miles of ice. As she stares out at the cold, snowy kingdom over which she rules, she sees the next decades of her life laid out at her feet.

She'll walk through the snow and embrace the numb coldness in her heart. She'll leave behind the wife she used to be. The mother she never was. The girl who smiled and laughed.

She'll give her kingdom what it needs.

A monarch.

A leader.

A queen.

PENELOPE

A BEAD of sweat starts a long journey at the nape of my neck and travels down my spine. Another adventurous droplet gets a head start from right between my boobs. They both trickle in unison down my body, and I wonder which will reach my panties first. Surprisingly, the sweat race currently taking place on my overheated skin is not the worst thing about today. At least if I focus on how uncomfortable I feel physically, I don't need to think about the emotional riot currently taking place inside my chest.

It's been nearly seven years since my husband died in a skiing accident, but going to weddings still makes my gut twist. Time, it seems, doesn't heal this wound.

Seeing other people's happiness—remembering how full of love and hope I used to be—makes me realize just how frigid I've become.

I guess the names I'm called in the kingdom's newspapers are accurate.

Ice Queen. Heartless Witch. Cold. Bitter. The Worst Thing to Happen to the Arctic Since Climate Change.

Okay, okay. I made that last one up, but I wouldn't be surprised if I saw it splashed across the front page of a tabloid.

A waiter hands me a flute of champagne. He bows his head with trembling reverence, making sure to never make eye contact. I take the glass without a word and relish the cool feeling of the glass beneath my fingertips. The waiter lifts his eyes up to stare at my face and immediately reddens and drops his head.

I know people call me a bitch. I suppose I probably am one. How else am I supposed to act? I have a kingdom to run, and pleasantries aren't high on my list of priorities.

The waiter scurries away as I sip my drink, my lipstick leaving a dusty pink mark on the rim. It tastes terrible—but maybe that's just my own discomfort at having to be here. The champagne is probably lovely and expensive. Fit for royalty.

A warm breeze ruffles my hair. My armpits are soaked. Who the heck decided an outdoor wedding is ever a good idea? And an outdoor *royal* wedding? Somewhere as warm as this?

Please.

That's just asking for soggy paparazzi photos.

Sure, the series of tents they've set up beside the rose garden at Westhill Palace are immaculately decorated. The sun is shining and a string quartet plays delicate melodies that accompany the birds in the trees. It's...gorgeous. I guess.

Farcliff Kingdom is beautiful. It's located between the United States and Canada, to the east of the Great Lakes. The summertime is warm and sunny. Picture-perfect. In the countryside, where we are, the air tastes sweet and flowers are in full bloom.

I just...prefer the cold. I like being wrapped up in a warm

jacket, staring out at a vast, white expanse of tundra. I like sitting on the edge of the Arctic, feeling alone in the wilderness with my people. I like staring into a fire, watching the flames dance and knowing my frail, human body is no match for the elements. My kingdom is called Nord, and I love every jagged coastline, every frozen lake, every explosion of life that happens during the short summer months.

Muggy heat? Happiness? Birds singing in trees and flowers bursting to life all around me while I feel altogether too *damp*?

Stifling.

My brother Silas nudges me with his elbow. "Lighten up, Pen. You're supposed to be happy for Prince Gabriel and his bride."

"It's too warm in Farcliff," I grumble.

"For your cold, dead heart?"

"Don't you have some poor woman to swindle into sleeping with you?" I arch a brow at him.

"I've never swindled anyone." Silas grins, mirth dancing in his deep blue eyes. A curl of rich, chocolate-brown hair falls over his forehead. Somehow, Silas' brow isn't damp with sweat like mine. He looks roguish and happy, not a bit bothered by the sticky heat.

I turn away from him, casting an eye over the wedding guests and all their finery. "No, you just leave a trail of heartbreak wherever you go."

"I leave a trail of something." Silas laughs, gulping down champagne as he scans the room—presumably for a woman who will serve as his next conquest.

I wrinkle my nose. "You're disgusting."

"Come on, Penelope. You haven't left Nord in months, and you haven't seen Prince Gabriel in, what, ten years?"

I nod. "Since my own wedding."

"At least try to pretend to be happy for him."

"I am happy for him. He's marrying the love of his life, which means he'll forever be exposed to having his heart wrenched out of his chest if anything goes wrong. Hooray for him."

Silas lets out a sigh, wrapping an arm around my shoulder in an awkward half-hug. "I know this is hard for you," he says quietly. "I'm proud of you for being here."

Shaking my brother off, I pinch my lips together. "It's fine. It's no harder than the dozens of state dinners I need to attend every month."

"It's a bit different." Brown eyebrows arch as he stares at me, waiting for an answer I won't give.

He's right, of course. This isn't just a state dinner. This is the wedding of an old friend—and seven years after the death of my own husband, it's the first wedding I've had the guts to attend.

Gabriel and I went to the same boarding school. I've known him since I was a child, but we've had vastly different lives. His wife-to-be, Jolie, came to work at the castle as a gardener. She and Gabriel fell desperately in love, and the whole kingdom of Farcliff has embraced their beautiful romance.

How wonderful for them.

Oh—and she's heavily pregnant, which feels like another dagger in my heart. That's one thing I never got to experience before the love of *my* life was taken away from me. Xavier and I didn't have a whirlwind romance. We didn't meet in dark rooms and steal kisses from each other. It was all arranged, approved by the people who needed to approve—but it was far from loveless. Our marriage blossomed into something that felt deep and real and everlasting.

'Til death.

Being here, on what must be the happiest day of Prince Gabriel's life, makes me feel hot and uncomfortable. I readjust the neckline of my dress, bringing my glass of champagne to my lips with a shaky hand. "Where are these mining moguls I'm supposed to scope out?" I ask my brother, scanning the room just like he is.

"Donovan Enterprise's CEO is supposed to be here. Reginald Donovan. He has two large mines in Farcliff, and there have been mentions of his desire to expand into Nord." My brother grunts, jerking his head across the tent. "There."

An old, graying man gives a big belly laugh, looking a young waitress up and down with lecherous eyes. I pinch my lips together. "He wants to mine land in Nord?"

"Hundreds of acres in the north of the kingdom, near Roston. They've found vast diamond fields. He has a bad track record with environmental breaches, and they say his company is in financial trouble." My brother's gaze shifts from the old mining tycoon to the group of ladies again, and I know I don't have much time before he leaves my side.

"Tell me again why it's a bad idea for him to expand to Nord?"

"He's notorious for having little or no regard for the environment, for one," my brother says, shifting his gaze back to Donovan. "And there are rumors he's shorted the Farcliff government out of millions of unpaid royalties. He's bad news, Pen."

"And the Nord Resources Group is in enough debt that they need the Crown to bail them out every year. We can't develop those mines as a public project without external investment." I sigh, shaking my head.

"NRG would be the first option, but the CEO says until

they've finished restructuring, they can't take on any more work. If unemployment weren't so bad in Nord, Donovan would be laughed out of the country, but things are getting dire. We might actually need to entertain his offer."

"I've seen the protests." Thousands of people in the streets, demanding employment. Telling me I've failed them as their Queen.

Silas grunts. "We need to provide jobs for people, and soon. We can't wait for NRG to get their act together."

I let out a sigh. Just another day as Queen, really. There have been dozens of prospectors trying to exploit my country's natural resources. Politics are a delicate tightrope, and I'm growing weary of walking it every day.

Maybe I should just try to enjoy Prince Gabriel's wedding and worry about Mr. Donovan tomorrow.

Weddings are tougher than politics, though. I had what Gabriel has. I had a loving spouse and a bright future. I didn't have a child, but I hoped for one. A decade ago, when I married Xavier, I thought it would be less than a year before I was a mother.

I suppose, in a way, it was a small mercy that I didn't know of my infertility on my wedding day. There was nothing to dampen my spirits that day. Nothing to make me feel the icy chill of my own barrenness.

I have polycystic ovary syndrome. PCOS. It went undiagnosed for years because I was largely asymptomatic. Sure, I had irregular periods, sometimes not menstruating for months at a time—but the doctors said it was normal. I was young. I was a healthy weight, and I didn't have excessive unwanted hair growth. I had a bit of acne, but nothing that caused huge concern. My periods would even out as I got older, the medical team assured me. It wouldn't be a problem for childbearing.

They were wrong.

Nothing became normal. Even when I was twenty-three and getting married, way past the end of puberty. Even as I tried and tried and tried to get pregnant, the doctors assured me it was still possible. My body would cooperate. I just had to keep trying.

And try I did. Every method. Fertility treatments. IVF. Every invasive, heartbreaking procedure that wore me down, month after month after month.

My body betrayed me.

No baby grew in my womb, and I became desperate. I wasn't thinking of the kingdom, of my duty, of my people. I wasn't thinking of politics, or the hundreds of tightropes that were being snipped while I was distracted.

I was only thinking of my own failures as a woman and a wife.

That's when the doctors finally diagnosed me with infertility and PCOS. Three months later, Xavier went skiing, crashed into a tree, and I lost him, too.

I'm a barren, childless, husbandless queen. I've been drifting through life on my own, wondering what I did to deserve this. Was I a naughty child and somehow brought this on myself? Is it because I didn't exercise enough? Because I snuck too much alcohol at parties in my teens? Is it because of the stress of becoming a monarch when I was ten years old? I skipped class too many times at boarding school?

What did I *do*? Why me?

Putting my champagne flute down on a table, I clasp my hands together to stop them from trembling.

Stop thinking of the past, Penelope.

What use is it dwelling on my own failures? I'm still a queen. The reigning monarch of the arctic kingdom of Nord. I successfully led my kingdom out of one recession and made sure my people were happy and safe; now I'm staring down the barrel of another economic downturn. After Xavier died, politics became my sole priority. The wealth and happiness of my people became my only duty.

I've done truly good things for the people of Nord, even though I was the youngest female monarch in the kingdom's history, and I had plenty of detractors. I've silenced most of the criticism, except the ones that call me nasty names.

Straightening my shoulders, I lift my chin.

Silas makes an approving noise. "There she is." He smirks.

"What are you talking about?"

"The Ice Queen."

Turning my head, I give my brother the iciest Ice Queen glare I can manage. Bitter satisfaction gurgles in my heart when his smile slips.

Silas throws his hands up, dipping his chin. "Fine. Be miserable. I'm going to go over there." My brother waves an arm at a group of young women on the other side of the tent. One of them glances at him, hiding her coy smile behind a hand.

I roll my eyes. "You're going to get yourself in trouble one day, Silas."

Flashing an impish grin at me, my brother pushes his silky, perfectly tousled hair off his forehead and sets off in the direction of the women.

My heart pangs, but I shut down the feeling as soon as it appears.

The only thing that's kept me sane for the past seven years has been my strength. My frigid demeanor. My ability to lock up all my feelings into a tiny metal chest and bury it at the bottom of the Arctic Sea.

Even if I pretend to hate the title, I *am* the Ice Queen, who rules over a land of snow and wind. The Queen who listens to the howling of the storm outside and lets a smile tug at the corners of her lips.

Cold loneliness is my home, and I can't wait to go back.

ALSO BY LILIAN MONROE

For all books, visit:

www.lilianmonroe.com

Brother's Best Friend Romance

Shouldn't Want You

Can't Have You

Don't Need You

Won't Miss You

Military Romance

His Vow

His Oath

His Word

The Complete Protector Series

Enemies to Lovers Romance

Hate at First Sight

Loathe at First Sight

Despise at First Sight

The Complete Love/Hate Series

Secret Baby/Accidental Pregnancy Romance:

Knocked Up by the CEO

Knocked Up by the Single Dad

Knocked Up...Again!

Knocked Up by the Billionaire's Son

The Complete Unexpected Series

Yours for Christmas

Bad Prince

Heartless Prince

Cruel Prince

Broken Prince

Wicked Prince

Wrong Prince

Lone Prince

Ice Queen

<u>Fake Engagement/ Fake Marriage Romance:</u>

Engaged to Mr. Right

Engaged to Mr. Wrong

Engaged to Mr. Perfect

Mr Right: The Complete Fake Engagement Series

<u>Mountain Man Romance:</u>

Lie to Me

Swear to Me

Run to Me

The Complete Clarke Brothers Series

<u>Extra-Steamy Rock Star Romance:</u>

Garrett

Maddox

Carter

The Complete Rock Hard Series

<u>Sexy Doctors:</u>

Doctor O

Doctor D

Doctor L

The Complete Doctor's Orders Series

<u>Time Travel Romance:</u>

The Cause

<u>A little something different:</u>

Second Chance: A Rockstar Romance in North Korea